Praise fo
The Cue Ball Mysteries

"The Cue Ball Mysteries are lighthearted cozies that will put a smile on your face."
Escape With Dollycas Into A Good Book

"Ms. Blackburn's clever, tongue-in-cheek voice is evident from the first page."
Ellis Vidler, author of *Cold Comfort*

"Cindy Blackburn's great author voice shines through."
Morgan Mandel, author of *Her Handyman*

"Just plain funny."
ValleyGal

"I love, love, love the witty sense of humor the author Cindy Blackburn delivers."
Terri Berg, audiobook reviewer

"I just love Jessie Hewitt. She is the bomb."
Melina's Book Blog

"Jessie is a fantastic character."
Melissa's Mochas, Mysteries and More

"Jessie is a a sleuth you will want to follow again and again."
Tonya Kappes, author of *The Magical Cures* series

"Jessie Hewitt seems prepared to handle anything life throws her way."
Joyce Lavene, author of *The Missing Pieces Mysteries*

"The antics this quirky cast of characters get into are hilarious. A terrifically amusing series."
Dru's Book Musings

Books by Cindy Blackburn

The Cue Ball Mysteries
Playing With Poison
Double Shot
Three Odd Balls
Four Play

The Cassie Baxter Mysteries
Unbelievable

Unbelievable

by
Cindy Blackburn

A Cassie Baxter Mystery
Book One

In memory of my parents.

They took the girl out of Vermont,
but they didn't take Vermont out of the girl.

Acknowledgements

So many people. So much help! Here are a few of the terrific people whose support, advice, and encouragement made Unbelievable possible: Megan Beardsley, Peter Lacey, Kathy Powell, Linda Lovely, Polly Iyer, Ellis Vidler, Betsy Blackburn, Joanna Innes, Jane Bishop, Bob Spearman, Penny Travis, Kathy Miller, Louise Sobin, Joy Kamani, Teddy Stockwell, Howard Lewis, Traylor Rucker, Beverly Boudreau, Cindy Boudreau, Karen Phillips, and Caroline Miller. Thanks, you guys! And extra special hugs, kisses, thanks, and gratitude to John Blackburn, my husband, my techno-geek expert, my partner in crime, my hero.

Prologue

Do yourself a favor. Never agree to move in with your father. Even if he retires and moves to Vermont to be closer to his only child. And even if he invites you to live with him rent-free. And even if the lease on your apartment runs out, and the owner decides to convert the building into condos, which you couldn't afford, even if your teaching salary were doubled. And even if your father moves into a rambling old house with plenty of room, and offers you the entire third floor with a turret on top. And even if you adore turrets. And even if this old house is in a lovely lakeside town only twenty miles from where you work. And even if you've always dreamed of living on a lake. And even if your father promises to respect your privacy because he knows you're an adult woman capable of conducting her own life.

Don't do it. Even then. Because this is what will happen if you move in with your father. He will: Drive. You. Nuts.

2

Chapter 1

I poked my right foot out from under the sheets and kicked at the rocking chair next to my bed. "Go away."

"But I can't sleep, Cassie."

I kept kicking.

"Would you stop doing that?"

"When you stop waking me up at the crack of dawn." I sat up and tore back the covers. "Move!"

My father rocked the chair backwards, and I skirted past his feet.

I pulled open the curtains and took a look outside.

"The sun's almost up," he informed me. "It's a beautiful day."

"It's 4:42 a.m., old man. There's nothing beautiful about it."

"Let's have breakfast, shall we? How about waffles?"

I turned from the window. "How about you letting me sleep past five at least one day this summer? Move!"

Dad stood up, which put him even more in my way. But at least Charlie got the hint. The big black lab scooted his front half under the bed and out of my way as I stomped past and headed for the stairs.

"We Baxters are early birds," Dad called after me.

"I haven't been an early bird since I was twelve."

"We can put berries on our waffles." My father was, of course, following me.

I stopped at the second floor landing. "No berries. No waffles. I'm going kayaking." I bounced down the remaining flight of stairs, and pulled my binoculars from their hook at the door.

"We can eat when you get back." Dad pointed to the binoculars. "You're going bird watching?"

I grabbed a lifejacket out of the wicker chest on the porch and kept going.

"If we took the canoe, I could join you."

"I'm taking the kayak." I started dragging my kayak over to the dock.

"And if we took the rowboat, Charlie could come."

I looked down at the dog, who had followed me onto the dock, and he wagged his tail.

"Sorry, Charlie," I said gently and climbed into the boat. "It's a one-seater. Single-occupancy. A phrase I am really, really, starting to appreciate."

"Cassie, wait," Dad said.

"For what?"

"You're in your pajamas, girl."

"Who's going to see me at this hour? The geese?"

I paddled away from the dock, and Charlie jumped in to escort me out. "Even the geese will be asleep," I told him.

He turned around and swam back to shore.

***

Turns out the geese weren't asleep. So I guess they did see me. But the woman in the canoe definitely did not see me, even though her eyes were wide open. Because the woman in the canoe was dead.

"This is not happening," I said.

She didn't answer.

"Move!"

She didn't move.

"Move, move, move, move, move!"

Nothing.

Well, if she wasn't moving, I was. But I was a little flustered and ended up banging into her canoe a few thousand times before I finally managed to steer my kayak out of the cattails and into open water.

I left her there unattended. Because, as she had so clearly demonstrated, dead people don't move.

***

"Please don't be dead," I said as I crawled out of my kayak and onto the dock of the Lake Store. I staggered barefoot up the side stairwell and pounded on Oliver Earle's door.

Nothing.

I tried to estimate the time and decided it had to be at least 5:30. And the store opens at 6:00.

"Don't be dead," I said as I retraced my steps downward. I pounded on the back door of the store, and Oliver answered.

"Thank God you're not dead."

"What?" he asked. "Why would I be dead?"

"Why would anyone be dead?" I pushed past him and made my way through the stock room.

"Cassie, wait." He hurried to catch up. "Has something happened to Bobby?"

"My father's fine." I barged through the swinging doors leading onto the main floor. "He's making waffles."

"What?"

I stopped at the deli counter. "With berries."

Oliver skipped a beat. "Do you need eggs? Is that why you're here so early?" He pointed. "In your pajamas."

I looked down at my outfit—pajamas and a lifejacket—and muttered a colorful word. "We need the sheriff," I said and rushed along the bread aisle toward the front counter.

"Sheriff Gabe? Why?"

"Because that's who you call in an emergency, right?" I pointed at the phone. "So please call the sheriff."

"But why?"

"Because!" I said. "There's a dead woman in the lake!"

"Dead!" Oliver grabbed the phone. "Why didn't you say so?"

***

I took a few deep breaths while he punched in the number. I knew Oliver Earle was the man to see. His general store is the heart of Lake Elizabeth, Vermont, and Oliver does most everything around here. He's our postmaster, fire warden, realtor, and Avon lady. Definitely the guy to see in a crisis.

I listened to Oliver listen to the sheriff.

"Mm-hmm," he kept saying. "Mm-hmm," he kept repeating. He glanced at me. "Got it," he said and hung up.

"The sheriff's on his way?" I asked.

5

He held up an index finger and made about five other phone calls before answering my question. "Okay," he said as he finally put down the phone. "Everyone's coming."

I asked who everyone was, and Oliver spouted off the list—Sheriff Gabe Cleghorn, of course, but also the Hilleville Police Department and the Hilleville Rescue Squad. And a little closer to home, the Lake Elizabeth Volunteer Fire Department, and the forest rangers from Lake Elizabeth State Park.

Oliver grimaced. "All nine of them."

"Lake Bess has nine forest rangers?"

"No, but there are nine camp counselors."

Nine college kids. I looked up at the moth-eaten moose head gazing down at me from above the cash register. "It's going to be a very long day," I told him.

Oliver waved the phone at me. "You should call Bobby."

"Good idea." I took the phone. "Dad can make himself useful and bring me some clothes."

My father informed me I'd been gone a long time. "Where are you?"

"At the Lake Store."

"Excellent, girl. Pick up some eggs."

***

Oliver got the store ready to open. I paced.

He made coffee and restocked the dairy case. I counted can openers. He carried in the daily newspapers from the front porch. I got bored in housewares and paced over to frozen foods.

I had counted all the frozen pizzas and was browsing the greeting card rack when my father arrived. I pointed to his empty hands. "Where are my clothes?"

He pointed to the dog. "I brought Charlie."

"My clothes," I said again.

"I forgot."

"Da-aad! I can't face the sheriff dressed like this!"

"I got over here as fast as I could, Cassie. You need my moral support."

"But I also need my clothes!"

"Okay, okay. I'll go get your clothes." He turned to leave, but I yanked him back.

"Stay!" I said, and Charlie promptly sat down. I rolled my eyes and headed to the clothing rack. "I'll make do."

Or maybe not. The clothing rack, usually overflowing with Lake Elizabeth or Lake Bess tee-shirts and sweatshirts, was nearly empty.

"Where are all the tee-shirts?" I called to Oliver.

"All gone." He emerged from the storeroom with a full round of bologna hoisted over his shoulder. "A new shipment's due in later this week," he said and headed to the deli counter. "You want I should save you something?"

I mumbled a no thanks and took a look at my options—a meager selection of children's sweatshirts. But luckily I'm small. If any adult could fit into one of those sweatshirts, it was me.

I found the one remaining children's size large and held it up. Lime green. Fluorescent lime green. But at least it had a picture of a loon on the chest. I reminded Charlie loons are my favorite waterfowl, shed my lifejacket, and tugged the sweatshirt over my pajamas.

Then I tried to convince myself it fit. The neck was too tight, and the wristbands hit exactly at my elbows. But other than that it worked.

I didn't bother looking at the back before putting the thing on, but maybe I should have. When I finally took it off later that day, I discovered the slogan emblazoned thereon. 'I'm looney for Lake Bess,' it read. Hindsight is everything.

My father, Oliver, and Charlie were standing at the coffee pot when I walked over. Everyone stared at me, aghast.

"Put it on my tab," I told Oliver and walked out.

Chapter 2

Chester Stewart and Hollis Klotz stopped short as I emerged onto the porch. "Are those your pajamas?" they asked.

"Bobby needed eggs," I answered and kept on walking.

Trust me, I didn't need to worry about Chester and Hollis. They practically live at the Lake Store and would learn soon enough what was happening. But meanwhile I needed to get down to the dock, since I could already hear the sirens headed our way.

I dropped my lifejacket into the kayak and was fetching my binoculars when Bobby and Charlie joined me. Dad traded me a cup of coffee for the binoculars.

"You know," he said as he lifted them to his eyes. "None of this would have happened if you stayed home and had waffles."

"So she wouldn't be dead, if only I'd eaten waffles?"

Dad and I were frowning at each other when the troops Oliver had promised began to arrive. Trust me, no one did so quietly. Philip Hart and Dustin Adams pulled up in a boat from the Lake Elizabeth Fire Department, sirens blaring. And a second later two forest rangers from the state park arrived in their boat, with their sirens. We got the sirens turned off in time to greet the pontoon boat overflowing with camp counselors. No sirens there, but plenty of shouting, shoving, and jostling as everyone found their footing on the dock.

About then, the rescue squad from Hilleville rounded the bend from Route 19 onto Elizabeth Circle. The ambulance drove into the dirt lot between the Lake Store and Town Hall, and those sirens stopped only after the vehicle was parked. A woman in an EMT uniform popped out.

"Ginger Graham," Philip told me.

Ginger trotted over, toting a stretcher, and Chester and Hollis emerged from the back door of the Lake Store and followed.

"Oliver's busy in the store," Hollis announced. "He put us in charge until Sheriff Gabe gets here."

That seemed about as likely as my father's waffles reviving the dead woman, but no one argued, and Chester asked Ginger if he could hold her stretcher. They were wrestling for control, and I was suggesting someone should use the thing to go get the dead woman, when two patrol cars from the Hilleville Police Department drove into the parking lot.

"Oh, no!" Ginger let go of the stretcher. "Everyone hold your breath."

We held our breath and crossed our fingers, and watched the two police cars park. That accomplished, we emitted a communal sigh of relief. Was it possible that not one, but two, Hilleville cops had managed the drive—all six miles from Hilleville to Lake Elizabeth—without incident? I'm new in town, but even I knew this qualified as a minor miracle. Let's just say the Hilleville police have a habit of getting into accidents, usually with each other, whenever duty calls.

"Keep holding your breath," Ginger ordered. She reclaimed the stretcher from Chester and stood at the ready as the two cops emerged from their patrol cars. They bumped into each other, and one tripped on their way down to the dock.

"We're here to help," the cop who was still standing told us.

***

"Excellent!" I said. I elbowed Hollis aside and stepped forward. "Because there's a dead woman down in Mallard Cove. We need to go get her."

The cop stared at me. "Are those your pajamas?"

"The dead woman doesn't care what I'm wearing."

No, but everyone else sure did. My father tried explaining, but the cop ignored him.

"Who are you?" he asked me, and several other people seemed interested in that, too.

I gave my name.

"Cassie's my daughter," Dad added. "She moved in with me last month."

That might have helped. But Dad was also a relative newcomer to Lake Bess, so some people didn't know him either.

"The Baxters bought the old Tumbleton place," Dustin Adams added. He pointed to the big green house across the lake, and a few people nodded recognition.

Meanwhile the cop who had fallen stood up. "Are those your pajamas?" he asked me.

"Dead woman!" I shouted. "Mallard Cove!" I pointed. "Canoe!" I flapped my arms.

Both cops shook their heads, and Cop A informed me they were out of their jurisdiction.

"Sheriff Gabe has to call the shots," Cop B said.

"We're just here to help," Cop A added.

"And doing a fine job of it!" I snapped.

"You don't have to get all testy about it," Cop A told me.

Bobby reached out a hand to stop me from killing them and appealed to the firemen. But Philip and Dustin also refused to budge.

"Sheriff Gabe called before I left the house and told me to wait for him," Philip explained. "He doesn't want us messing around with things if there's anything fishy going on."

"We have to be patient," Dustin said.

"Cassie's not very good at that," Dad mumbled.

***

Maybe not. But everyone else was an expert at it.

Ginger tossed her stretcher to Chester so she could more fully engage in a conversation with Philip Hart. Evidently, she needed some advice about her tractor, and Philip was the guy to see.

"Tractor?" I asked, and Ginger explained she's a farmer when not driving the Hilleville ambulance.

"It keeps stalling out," she complained.

Philip blamed it on all the rain we'd been getting that summer and began reminiscing about a tractor he had known on his grandparents' farm in Craftsbury.

I lost track of Philip's childhood memories and tuned in to the camp counselors, who were debating the intimate details of Amber Jensen and Derek Moody's breakup.

I didn't know Amber and Derek personally, but I could have predicted that. I'm a college professor and trust me, anything even remotely out of the ordinary gets twenty-somethings all atwitter. Let's face it, that morning wasn't exactly ordinary.

Speaking of all atwitter. My father and the forest rangers were thoroughly absorbed in Dustin Adams' description of the bass he had caught the previous weekend.

"We should try fly-fishing," Dad told me. "We can take the rowboat and Charlie, and go out first thing every morning. It would build your appetite for breakfast." Bobby spoke to the crowd. "Cassie doesn't eat enough breakfast," he announced. "This morning she refused—"

"To get dressed?" Hollis asked.

Oh, yeah. Everyone got a real kick out of that. I myself wasn't so amused. My outfit was from hell, which was about the temperature of things under that stupid, stupid, sweatshirt.

I yanked at the collar and tried to ignore everything and everyone. Everyone except Charlie, that is. The dog sat quietly—Charlie is always quiet—and gazed off toward Mallard Cove.

I patted his head. "Don't worry," I told him. "I'm sure the sheriff is on his way."

"Of course he is!" a familiar but unwelcome voice called out.

I spun around, and Maxine Tibbitts snapped my picture. "Are those your pajamas?" she asked.

***

Maxine Tibbitts. Where to begin?

Maxine's a reporter for the *Hanahan Herald*, Hanahan County's weekly newspaper. Considering her "beat" is Lake Elizabeth, population about 600 on a good day, you'd think she wouldn't find all that much to report. But you don't know Maxine Tibbitts.

She was probably enough of a menace back when she armed herself with only a yellow legal pad. But she got herself a photograph-capable i-Tablet about the same time I moved in next door to her. Oh yeah. Maxine's my next door neighbor. Lucky me.

"Don't you have to go to work?" I asked while she snapped a few thousand more shots.

"You look cute as a button!" she said. Snap, snap.

I glanced at my father, and he reminded Maxine of her other job—she's the librarian down in Hilleville. "Cassie's right," he said. "It must be getting close to opening time."

"Silly! It's not even seven o'clock." Snap, snap. "And it's Tuesday. The library's closed on Monday and Tuesday during the summer. Isn't that lucky?"

Oh yeah.

Maxine stopped snapping to reach for my hand. "I just heard what happened," she whispered. "Let's have ourselves a nice little chat before Sheriff Gabe gets here. What do you say, Cassie?"

I yanked my hand away. "I say, there's a dead woman in Mallard Cove, and we're standing here pussy-footing around while you take pictures!" I waved my arms, and she backed off.

"My goodness," she said. "You don't need to get all testy about it."

Maybe not. Because about then, the sheriff finally, finally, made his entrance.

My father reminded me patience is a virtue as everyone watched the Hanahan County sheriff park his car and strut over. Although I had never met him personally, Gabe Cleghorn's reputation preceded him. Kind of like his beer belly. But let's face it, my sweatshirt really was making me testy. By all accounts the guy was a terrific sheriff with an impressive record of putting the bad guys behind bars.

"Sorry for the delay," he said as he got closer. "Our youngest was up all night with that summertime bug that's going around. Daddy's moving kind of slow this morning."

No. Kidding.

"Now then, what's this about a body?" he asked, and the crowd parted to point at me.

"Sheriff Gabe Cleghorn." He held out his hand. "But everyone calls me Gabe." His smile turned to a scowl. "Are those your pajamas?"

Chapter 3

"There's a dead woman in Mallard Cove," I said as calmly as humanly possible.

"Okay, but why are you in your pajamas?" Sheriff Cleghorn asked.

"Because that's how I found her."

"In her pajamas?"

I rolled my eyes. "Let me show you." I gestured to Dustin and Philip, and they maneuvered their boat around the dock. But when Philip held out his hand to help me aboard, the sheriff pulled me back.

"Better leave this to the experts," he said.

I started to argue, but my father stopped me. "Do you really want to see the dead woman again?" he whispered.

Maybe not. I backed away, and the sheriff lowered himself into the boat. Dustin turned on the sirens and took off, and Gabe Cleghorn fell into his seat.

The forest rangers invited the Hilleville cops to join them, and they took off, sirens blaring. Ginger Graham tossed her stretcher in the pontoon boat, and once she and the swarm of camp counselors had climbed aboard, that boat set out also.

"Exactly how do those college kids qualify as experts?" I asked the crowd left behind with me.

"They give swimming lessons at the beach," Chester suggested.

"That explains it," I said. I'm guessing even Charlie caught the sarcasm.

***

What a shocker, things actually went well for a few minutes. Dad convinced Maxine not to put any pictures of me in my pajamas in the newspaper, Hollis and Chester fetched some folding chairs from Town Hall and offered me a seat, and Oliver took a break from running the store to deliver more coffee.

The mayhem resumed soon enough, however, as a new wave of people gathered around.

"Round two," I told my father, but I shouldn't have been surprised. Virtually every Elizabethan visits the Lake Store virtually every morning. For coffee, for the newspaper, for lunch to go, for conversation, for whatever. I was simply witnessing the typical weekday morning rush hour at Oliver's.

Well, maybe not so typical. Everyone forgot their rush to get to work when they saw the hubbub at the dock. And the hubbubbier things got, the hubbubbier things got. Maxine resumed the picture-snapping thing, and Chester and Hollis resumed their roles as emcees.

"This is even better than last summer when Natalie Pope got attacked by turkeys," Hollis told the crowd. "Remember that?"

"Who could forget?" Chester agreed, and with the help of his co-host, he explained Natalie's trouble with the turkeys for Dad and me.

She had been riding her motor scooter on one of the trails not too far up Elizabeth Mountain when she disturbed a wild turkey roost. The birds went for blood and chased her down the hill and straight into the lake. It happened on a Sunday afternoon when everyone was out on the water, so lots of people had ringside seats as Natalie's scooter careened down the hill.

"Even people who didn't see her, heard her," Chester said.

"She screamed for dear life as she flew through the air." Hollis flapped his arms to demonstrate Natalie flying and added a loud "Whoosh!" to mimic the sound she and her scooter made when they hit the water.

"And the turkeys!" Chester added. "Who knew they could gobble that loud?"

"Not I," Dad answered.

"I wish I had my i-Tablet back then," Maxine said. "I could have captured it on video."

Oh, but that reminded her. She stopped snapping photographs and started shooting a video.

I stood up and grabbed the binoculars from my father. Nothing. The boats were still in Mallard Cove and out of sight.

"Put those things down before you get even more worked up," Dad insisted, so of course I kept looking. Which is when I discovered that every Elizabethan who hadn't joined our party on Oliver's dock was standing on his or her own dock, watching us from a distance.

I braced myself and directed the binoculars toward our little neighborhood across the water. Obviously our dock was empty, as was Maxine's. But our other next door neighbor, Josiah Wylie, was most definitely out on his dock, binoculars in hand, staring back at me.

Insert colorful words . . . Here.

Oden Poquette's arrival on the scene actually did improve my mood. Here was one person completely unfazed by my pajamas. Oden was too busy looking for his goats.

FYI, Oden is almost always looking for his goats, since Rose and Ruby are almost always lost. They roam the Lake Bess community, eating anything in their path.

Oden poked his head into Town Hall. Finding no goats there, he jogged toward us. "Has anyone seen my goats?" he asked, and the gang groaned in unison.

I jumped up from my chair. "They were there!" I blinked at my father. "Rose and Ruby were in Mallard Cove."

"Were they swimming?" Hollis asked.

***

"Here they come!" Dad jumped up and pointed.

I told Oden where I had seen Rose and Ruby, he trotted off down Elizabeth Circle, and I turned to welcome the returning regatta.

"Where is she?" I called out as the first boat drew closer.

Chester elbowed his way through the crowd and stood next to me. "And who is she?"

"We didn't find anyone," one of the Hilleville cops shouted.

"But that's impossible," I shouted back.

Dad held onto me and tilted his head toward the pontoon boat.

"No canoe!" several of the camp-counselors shouted from about halfway across the lake. "There's nothing there!" a tall blond kid screamed. "No body!"

In case anyone on Planet Earth had failed to hear, Maxine shouted back, "What's that you say, Richard? Nothing? No body whatsoever?"

"No body whatsoever!" Richard shouted back.

***

Keeping his record of being the last to the party, Sheriff Gabe Cleghorn was in the last boat to make it back to the dock. He stood at the bow and addressed his audience. "You can all go home now," he said. "Ms. Baxter was mistaken. There is no body, dead or alive."

I glanced at Philip and Dustin, and they gave me the thumbs down.

"Poof, she's gone?" Dad asked. "That's impossible."

"Dead people don't move," I said.

Gabe wasn't the most graceful guy to ever exit a boat, but at least he did better than the Hilleville cops, one of whom ended up in the water.

But the cop-clown act wasn't enough to distract the crowd from what the sheriff said next. "I need to ask you a few questions," he told me, loud and clear. "You do know it's against the law to issue a false alarm?"

"What? What do you mean false alar—" I stopped myself. I plopped down into my folding chair and closed my eyes, but I could still sense movement in front of me. I opened my eyes to see Maxine Tibbitts' i-Tablet about an inch from my nose.

"Would you stop doing that?" I held my hand up to block my face, and several people told me there was no need to get all testy.

About then, I heard the first whispers of "Miss Looney Tunes." Somehow I knew they weren't discussing Maxine.

Chapter 4

I might have been Miss Looney Tunes, but the sheriff still wanted to hear my story.

"Not until you get rid of this circus," I told him, and Dad, Charlie, and I watched in awe as he set about dispersing the crowd. He even managed to shoo away Chester, Hollis, and Maxine.

"Thank you," I said sincerely as Maxine finally left.

"Just doing my job." Sheriff Gabe gestured to the folding chairs, and we sat down.

Dad and I waited while he took a small notepad from his back pocket and drew a diagram of Lake Elizabeth. "For the record," he said.

For the record, the hand-drawn map looked like an upside-down Mickey Mouse head, with the main body of water being Mickey's head, and Mallard Cove and Fox Cove at the south end being his ears. Downtown Lake Bess, where we were currently located, was at the north end of the lake, at Mickey's chin.

But don't let the word downtown fool you. Gabe only had to draw four buildings to depict town center. The Lake Store and Town Hall sit adjacent to each other in front of the lake. And across Elizabeth Circle are the Congregational Church and the Lake School. He didn't bother drawing in the eighty or so houses that dot the perimeter of the lake, but he did put three squares on the edge of Mallard Cove to represent the houses down there.

He handed me the pen. "Put an 'X' where you claim you saw the dead woman."

I marked the spot, and with a warning that our interview was "official," Gabe got started. "First question. Why were you out there at that ungodly hour?"

"It was either that or eat waffles."

"Excuse me?" he asked, and I gave my father a withering glance.

"Cassie was mad at me," Bobby said. "I woke her up too early."

"It was the middle of the night," I clarified. "4:30."

Dad shrugged at Gabe. "She told me she was going bird watching and stormed out of the house."

"I paddled over to Mallard Cove to watch the geese," I said.

"As in Canada Geese?" Gabe wrinkled his nose, and I admitted the geese aren't everyone's favorite bird.

"I know they're messy," I said. "But the goslings are so cute. They were tipped upside-down eating something near the shore. While I had my binoculars focused there, my kayak drifted toward the cattails." I tapped the 'X' on the map. "And that's when I saw her."

Gabe studied me for a long time. "You haven't lived here long, have you, Ms. Baxter?"

"It's Cassie," I said. "I've been here two months."

"That's what Phillip told me. You moved from New Jersey, correct?"

"No." I tilted my head. "Dad moved here from Jersey, but I've lived in Vermont for decades." I told the sheriff I teach history at Crabtree College in Montpelier, but have summers off.

"And this summer you up and moved to Lake Elizabeth?" he asked. "All of the sudden?"

"Not so sudden," Dad said. "It took me months to get her here."

Gabe frowned at my father. "I want Ms. Baxter to answer the questions."

"Cassie," I reminded him.

"And you live across the way?" He pointed to our house, and I frowned, too. Even from a distance, the house stood out. It was bright green. Lime green. The stupid house matched my sweatshirt.

"We haven't had a chance to paint yet," I mumbled. I wasn't using the binoculars but noticed that someone was still out on Joe Wylie's dock. Two people, actually.

"We love our house," Bobby said. "Don't we, girl?"

"Mr. Baxter," Gabe scolded.

"Bobby," Bobby said.

Gabe sat forward. "Listen, Bobby," he said. "I'm trying to understand your daughter's actions this morning. So please stop trying to protect her."

I looked up. "Do I need protection?"

"No. But it's against the law to issue a false alarm. You needed to be more cautious."

"Of course!" I said. "How silly of me to report a dead body."

The sheriff raised an eyebrow. "Maybe she wasn't dead. Maybe the fog was playing tricks on you."

"There was no fog."

"Maybe she was just resting."

"She was dead."

"Did you take pictures?"

"Oh, for Pete's sake! Do I look like Maxine Tibbitts?" I stood up to pace, and Charlie scooted his front half under my chair.

"Pictures would have been helpful," Gabe said.

"Great!" I stepped around Charlie's tail. "Next time I run across a dead body, I'll be sure to snap a few shots."

Dad winced, but I kept pacing as the sheriff tried to convince me the woman was asleep, woke up after I left Mallard Cove, and was right then back home, all safe and sound.

He waved at the houses dotting the eastern shore. "And now she's probably too embarrassed to come forward and admit she was the person you saw."

"Half the town was out here this morning, Sheriff. Why didn't anyone else see this sleeping-beauty woman canoeing around?"

"Because they were too busy watching you." He made a point of staring at my outfit.

I sat down and sighed. "Why are you so sure she was alive?" I asked.

"Why are you so sure she was dead?"

"Her eyes were open, and she was staring straight into the sun."

"What color?"

"The sun's yellow, her eyes were green, and she had red hair. She was young, and tall. And in case you haven't quite caught on—she was dead."

"Did you recognize her?"

I held my face in my hands, and Bobby answered for me. "I think Cassie's made that clear also," he said. "My daughter's new in town."

"Maybe this woman's a visitor," Gabe suggested. "She's probably staying at the Fox Cove Inn down that way. Or maybe she's a camper." He pointed toward the state park. "You'll probably see her at the Lake Store before the day's through."

"So dead people make a habit of shopping at the Lake Store?" I asked. "I didn't see a ghost, Sheriff."

"Please call me Gabe."

"I don't believe in ghosts, Gabe."

***

"Let's look at the map again." Gabe tapped at the houses he had drawn around Mickey Mouse's left ear. "There's three houses in Mallard Cove," he said. "Right where you saw this supposed body."

"Actual body."

He drew a large square beside Mickey's other ear. "Not to mention the Fox Cove Inn across the way." He pointed to the new square. "Anyone would have heard you."

"Heard me what?"

"Scream for help. I can tell you have a voice. A very loud voice, considering your size."

"What's that supposed to mean?"

"You know how to scream," my father informed me.

Gabe asked again why I hadn't screamed. "Sound carries across water. Anyone would have helped you, Ms. Baxter."

"Would you please call me Cassie?"

"All you needed to do was yell for help, Cassie."

I took a deep breath and apologized for not yelling. "I didn't think of it." I looked at my father. "I get kind of flustered around death."

"An understatement," Dad mumbled.

Gabe looked back and forth between us. "You folks want to tell me what you're talking about?"

"No," we said in unison.

The sheriff shook his head. "Okay, so why'd you come all the way down here to report it? Why not go home?" He pointed to our house across the lake, about halfway down the western shore.

I stared at the house. "It never occurred to me," I said honestly. "When I'm flustered I tend to move very quickly."

"An understatement," Dad said again.

I shrugged at the sheriff. "I paddled down here to get to Oliver, okay? I knew he's the person to see in an emergency."

"Why's that?"

"Because he does everything around here. He practically runs this town." I counted off Oliver's various jobs on my fingers. "Grocer, postmaster, fire warden, Avon lady—"

"You were interested in some cosmetics right then?"

I dropped my hands and gave the sheriff my most withering look.

Dad cleared his throat. "Oliver's the high bailiff," he said.

"Say wha—"

Dad elbowed me, and I shut up.

"Cassie knows," he continued, "that Oliver Earle was elected our high bailiff last year. And Cassie knows." Dad glared at me. "What the high bailiff does. Which I'm sure you do too, sheriff."

Gabe scowled. "He takes over for me in case of emergency."

"Exactly!" I smiled at my father. "And this was an emergency."

"Are you single, Ms. Baxter?" Gabe asked.

"What does that have to do with anything?"

"Your marital status, please."

"I'm single."

"Oliver's single, too."

"Okay," I said. "But what does that have to do with anything?"

"How did Oliver react when you visited him in the middle of the night?" Gabe pointed to my pajamas. "Dressed like that."

"It wasn't the middle of the night. It was bright and sunny. You know how early the sun rises up here in the summer."

"You just told me it was the middle of the night when your father woke you up."

"Maybe I exaggerated," I said.

"Figures." Gabe clicked his pen on and off a few times. "What did you say to Oliver? When you showed up. In your pajamas."

I closed my eyes. "I said I was glad he wasn't dead."

Gabe clicked the pen again. "That was an odd thing to say."

"Yes, it was." I opened my eyes. "And the situation was odd. And I was flustered. And maybe I'm crazy. Just ask Chester Stewart."

"Oh, don't worry about that. I'll be talking to lots of people." The sheriff looked at his watch and stood up. "Believe it or not, it's only 8:30. Plenty of time to figure this out before the day's through." He offered me a hand as Dad and I stood up.

"Will you call me when you know more?" I asked.

"Absolutely, but one last question."

I braced myself.

"Was there anyone else who might have seen you, Cassie? Anyone who might have seen this woman?"

"Not unless you count the geese."

"And the goats," Dad reminded me, and Gabe groaned out loud.

"Don't tell me."

"Oden Poquette's goats were on Evert Osgood's lawn," I told him.

"I told you not to tell me."

"Do you have something against Rose and Ruby?" my father asked.

"Only that Faith Chaffee calls me every other day complaining," Gabe answered. "Those goats destroyed her lilac bushes this spring. And now they're working on her lupines. Faith thinks I should arrest them."

"The goats?" Dad and I asked, and Gabe groaned again.

He looked at me. "So you're sure no one—no human being—saw you in Mallard Cove?"

I shook my head. "No one in their right mind was up that early."

"Yep," he said and closed his notepad.

Chapter 5

Here's a bitter irony. I ended up eating waffles that morning.

Dad drove home, and I kayaked. Which means he beat me by twenty minutes, and by the time I got home he'd already fired up the waffle iron. My father, in case you haven't quite caught on, drives me nuts.

"Sit down and eat," he said as I walked in the kitchen.

"Da-aad." I remained standing while I struggled to free myself from my sweatshirt. "You realize waffles are what got me into this mess."

"Don't blame the waffles. Blame me. None of this would have happened if I hadn't gotten you all worked up."

"She'd still be dead," I said from underneath the sweatshirt, which now clung to my face.

Bobby was pointing me to the table when I finally freed myself. But my green torture chamber still had my full attention. I held it at arm's length and read the "I'm looney for Lake Bess" slogan on the back.

I dropped the stupid thing where I stood, and Charlie wandered over to sniff at it. Even he frowned.

I washed my hands, grabbed our plates, and sat down. Meanwhile my father hovered over me like he had when I was ten.

"Sit!" I said, and both he and Charlie sat.

I started eating, but Dad continued staring at me.

"What?" I said and passed him the maple syrup.

"You're exhausted, Cassie. You should have let me drive you home."

"But I needed to kayak. You know I can't sit still when I'm upset."

"An understatement."

I got up for coffee. "You believe me, Dad?" I asked. "About the dead woman?"

"Girl," he scolded. "That goes without saying."

"One down," I told Charlie. I poured coffee into two cups and added a ridiculous amount of milk to both. "Now to convince the other 599 Elizabethans."

"They'll catch on."

"Yeah, right. You heard everyone—I'm Miss Looney Tunes." I sat back down. "With my luck, Maxine will use that phrase in her newspaper article."

"She'll do no such thing." Bobby sipped his coffee and thought about it. "She came over the second I pulled in to find out how things went with Gabe."

"What a shocker."

"She means well."

"No, Dad. You mean well. Maxine's a menace."

"Joe Wylie stopped by also."

I shook my head. "Speaking of menace."

"Joe's a good neighbor, Cassie. He cares about us. He cares about you in particular."

"He was spying on us, you realize." I pointed my fork Wylie-ward. "He was out there all morning with his binoculars."

My father reminded me lots of people had been watching with their binoculars.

"Okay, so why didn't Joe come join us?" I asked. "Maxine did."

My father insisted Joe's more considerate than Maxine. "He saw that crowd, and he didn't want to upset you any further."

"He's upsetting, alright."

"He didn't want to spook you—his exact words."

"He's spooky, alright."

"He's coming for dinner tonight. He wants to help us figure this out. "

I put my fork down. "No, Dad. Joe wants dinner. The man eats here every other night."

"I'm thinking spaghetti with Bolognese sauce. You'd like that?"

Yes actually, I would. I thanked Bobby for thinking of my favorite meal.

"It was Charlie's idea. He thinks you deserve spaghetti after your ordeal."

I was thanking Charlie for his thoughtfulness when the odd machine our odd neighbor works with started beeping, burping, and chirping.

Dad tilted his head. "Sounds like the FN451z is having a rough day, too."

If you're confused here, don't worry, so am I. Josiah Wylie is some sort of mad scientist. He works out of his home with a very bizarre and very loud invention he calls—don't ask me why—the FN451z. Supposedly the FN will someday improve internet and cell phone access in mountainous areas such as Vermont. But so far all it does is make noise. A lot of noise.

The FN continued belching and gurgling as I got up to load the dishwasher. "Are we even sure that thing is legal?" I asked.

***

"Help me," I said the moment Bambi answered her phone.

"Oh, no. What's Bobby done this time?"

"He woke me up at 4:30."

"Nothing new there."

I finished toweling my hair. "Then he threatened to feed me waffles."

"Nothing new there."

"So I ran away." I tossed the towel aside and finger-fluffed my curls. "And straight into a dead woman."

"What!?" Bambi shouted. "You hit someone? Are you okay, Cassie?"

I realized what she thought, and quickly clarified that the redhead was already dead when I got to her. "And I wasn't driving," I said. "I hit her with my kayak."

Bambi hesitated. "Can we start back at the waffles?"

I told her I was hoping she'd say that, climbed the winding staircase to my turret, and found a rocking chair.

"So?" I asked after I summarized the saga. "What do you think?"

"You should have stayed home and eaten waffles."

"Hindsight is everything. Which brings us to the Miss Looney Tunes portion of the story."

"Excuse me?"

I explained the sweatshirt from hell. "Now everyone thinks I'm Miss Looney Tunes."

"Whereas some of us known for sure."

"Very funny. But it gets less funny since the sheriff thinks I'm crazy. He doesn't believe me."

"The Cassandra Syndrome strikes again," Bambi said.

In case you don't have a degree in ancient history, let me explain. Cassandra was a Trojan princess, daughter of Priam, and sister to Paris and Hector. According to Greek mythology, she refused to sleep with Apollo, the god of prophecy. Apollo got ticked off and cursed her with the gift of prophecy.

Not a curse, you say? Well, Apollo added one small caveat. Cassandra could foretell the future, but no one ever believed her. For instance, she predicted the fall of Troy. But did anyone listen?

Ever hear of the Trojan Horse?

Which brings us to me. I don't claim to foretell the future, and no god has ever tried to seduce me. But my name is Cassandra, and people seldom believe me.

"Why don't they believe me?" I asked Bambi, and she reminded me the pajamas probably didn't help.

"But you already know the real reason, Cassie. You're too darn cute."

I groaned, but she was right. I'm teeny-tiny, with curly blond hair, big brown eyes, and a baby face. "I should have outgrown my cute phase by now," I said. "I'm forty-four."

"Take heart. Maybe by age fifty you'll be a wizened old hag."

"One can dream."

"Nope." Bambi changed her mind. "You'll still be too cute even when you're eighty. It's a curse."

"And you'll still be cursed with your name," I told her.

My friend, Dr. Bambi Lovely-Vixen, faces challenges of her own in the being-taken-seriously department.

***

"Speaking of cute," Bambi said. "Is the sheriff right, Cassie? Do you have a thing for Oliver Earle?"

"Spare me."

"He's a hunky-boo."

"Spare me."

"Speaking of hunky-boos—"

"We weren't speaking of hunky-boos," I said. "And can we please stop using that stupid phrase? We're middle-aged, educated women, and you're married, for Pete's sake."

"And I tell Pete he's a hunky-boo each and every day. He'd sink into a complete funk if I didn't."

I rolled my eyes at Charlie, who had come upstairs to check on me, and told Bambi to say hi to Pete.

"Speaking of hunky-boos." She remained on topic. "Did you get Kyle's mass e-mail?"

I stood up, and Charlie and I gazed at the lake while Bambi reminded me my ex-boyfriend Kyle Caprio was in Greece, "pining away" after me.

"Kyle isn't pining away," I argued. "He's with all those students."

"He looked so sad and forlorn in that picture he attached," Bambi continued. "And he was at the Parthenon and everything."

"I have news for you, Dr. Vixen. Kyle looked sad because he's single-handedly herding fifteen undergraduates around Greece this summer."

"Because you bailed out on him. If you'd gone with him, he would have proposed, right at the Parthenon. Right now you'd be sipping ouzo and gazing lovingly into each other's eyes."

"And you wonder why I bailed out?"

"Kyle's company would be better than the dead redhead's."

"Barely." I got up and glanced down the stairwell. "Trust me, breaking up with Kyle was the right choice." I lowered my voice. "But maybe moving here wasn't."

"Your father is a sweetheart, Cassie. And he cooks."

I agreed that the practical arrangements between Dad and me were fine. Bobby cooks and charges me zero rent. In return, I do the cleaning, and pay the taxes, insurance, and utilities. We share the first floor, the second floor is his, and the third floor and turret are mine.

"So what's the problem?" Bambi asked.

"How about a complete lack of privacy?" I whispered. "Between my father and the neighbors I'm surrounded by nosiness."

"The reporter-woman knows about the dead redhead?"

I glanced down at Maxine's place. "Yep." I glanced down in the opposite direction. "My other neighbor knows the whole story, too."

"Josiah Wylie." Bambi sighed. "Now there's a hunky-boo."

Chapter 6

"Girl!" Dad stood at the foot of the extension ladder. "What are you doing?"

"Scraping the house."

"What!? Why?"

"Because that's the procedure." I kept scraping. "Scrape and sand, then prime and paint."

"You're painting the house?" Bobby was incredulous. "Do you have any idea what you're doing?"

I looked down, registered the very long distance to Earth, and silently hoped that I did. "I know how to paint," I said as I climbed down. "I paint old furniture all the time."

"This isn't one of your rocking chairs." Dad waved at the house, a three-story Victorian sort of thing with lots of Victorian-type trim. "Don't you think you should have consulted me on this?"

"Nooo. Not two hours ago you told me to find a use for my nervous energy. You know, while we wait to hear from Gabe."

"Girl! Gabe's going to find the dead redhead long before you finish this project!"

"I have lots of nervous energy."

Dad gave me a withering look.

I shrugged and a few flakes of paint fell off me. "This is part of our arrangement, remember? You told me tó do whatever I want with the place."

"But that was interior decorating. In-terior. Why don't you paint a few more rocking chairs?"

"First things first," I said, and my father whimpered.

"This is almost as kooky as your behavior when your mother died."

"I was ten," I said in my defense.

"Yes, and now you're forty-four. You'll hurt yourself."

"I'll be fine."

"Oh, really?" He pointed to the ladder, and then to the third floor, and then to the turret above that. "How are you planning to get up there? Our ladder doesn't extend that far."

I studied the ladder, which was definitely as big as it could be, if I were the one who'd be hoisting it around. I gazed up at the third floor with my turret on top.

"I'll use a littler ladder," I said eventually. "I'll put it on the roof of some of your second story porches. That will work."

Dad stared at me, aghast. "Are you nuts?"

"Wacko and Looney Tunes." I waved at all the lime green looming before us and at some lemon yellow trim. "And the color of this house is one of the many things that makes me wacko."

"We like this color."

"It's lime green!"

"Kelly green," Dad said. "And we Baxters like bright colors—your rocking chairs, your mother's paintings."

My mother's paintings. Let's get that sad story out of the way, shall we?

Like everyone else in my family, my mother had been a teacher. She taught high school math, but when she got sick and had to give up teaching, Mom started painting. In that last year of her life she painted over a hundred pictures of flowers. What she lacked in talent, she made up for in bright and cheerful colors. "To keep us Baxters smiling," she used to tell me.

"Our house is cheerful." Dad nodded at the expanse of green. "It's jolly."

"It's an eyesore," I said. "It's like living in the Jolly Green Giant."

"What's wrong with jolly?" Dad said. "Jolly's good," he added, and Charlie wagged his tail.

"Gray with white trim," I argued, and the tail stopped still.

My father reminded me we Baxters don't like drab as I stepped away to move the ladder. This took a while, but I ignored the disapproving frowns from him and his dog and finally slid the stupid ladder three feet over.

I caught my breath and started climbing.

"How's Bambi?"

I stopped about six feet overhead. "How do you know I talked to Bambi, old man? You were listening."

Dad pleaded innocence and insisted he hadn't heard anything specific. "But who else would you call about all this? Who else do you call to complain about me?"

Good point. I gave up arguing and reached for the scraper I had left on the windowsill—almost, almost, out of reach.

"Be! Careful!"

I rolled my eyes. "Why don't you go bother Chance Dooley?" I said, and I could hear my father's sigh even from my position two stories above.

"Chance has gotten himself into a real pickle this time, girl."

I smiled at the lime green paint in front of me. "What's happened now?"

FYI, other than driving me nuts, putting Chance into pickles is my father's favorite pastime. When he retired from being an English teacher, he took up writing science fiction, and Chance Dooley is the hero of Dad's yet-to-be-published stories. Chance owns and operates Dooley's Delivery Service: We Deliver Where No Delivery Service Has Ever Delivered Before.

As you can imagine, or at least as Bobby Baxter can imagine, Chance and his Spaceship Destiny—the delivery service's delivery device—get themselves into pickle after pickle, each pickle being a little more absurd than the pickle before.

"Chance needs to get his hands on two new Turbo Thrust Propulsion Pistons," Dad told me. I switched the scraper to my left hand to get at a hard to reach crevice, while he explained the critical importance of the Spaceship Destiny's Turbo Thrust Propulsion System.

"The turbo thrust is what makes deliveries beyond the Crystal Void even possible," Dad said. "Without it Chance and the Spaceship Destiny are stranded on the planet Whoozit—the most remote corner of the Hollow Galaxy—until further notice."

I glanced down. "I take it there are no propulsion pistons on Whoozit?"

"Nope. They have to be delivered. And guess who would normally make that delivery?"

"Chance Dooley." I tackled a particularly stubborn strip of the peeling lime green near my left elbow. "Can't someone from Planet Peacock beam it up?" I asked. If you're still actually following this, Planet Peacock is Chance Dooley's home base.

Dad was shaking his bald head down there. "Think," he said. "If this so-called beaming up business were even remotely possible in the year 5035, there'd be no need for Dooley's Delivery Service."

He sighed again. "Bark if she falls," he told Charlie and went inside to help Chance.

***

I didn't fall, and Charlie didn't bark. Charlie never barks. He doesn't growl, whine, or whimper, either. The vet says there's nothing wrong with him, but Charlie is profoundly mute.

The FN451z suffers from no such affliction.

"It must have propulsion pistons to spare," I mumbled as it went into beeping-burping-chirping mode for the umpteenth time that day.

"What's a propulsion piston," an unwelcome voice called up.

I glanced down to see Maxine Tibbitts' i-Tablet aimed at my backside.

"Go away," I yelled down.

Maxine asked what I was doing, but it seemed perfectly clear to me. "Go away," I repeated.

"I was hoping we could have a nice chat, Cassie. It won't take but a minute, and the *Herald* is most interested in what you have to say."

"Go. Away."

"Did your redhead sound familiar to Sheriff Gabe? Has he found her yet? Has he called?"

I tried to ignore her, but even from ten feet above, I knew she was still snapping pictures.

"Would you stop doing that?" I said. "The *Hanahan Herald* does not want pictures of my backside."

"You don't need to get all testy about it." Snap, snap. "These aren't for my column, anyway. They're for the *Herald*'s new digital archives. For the official record."

"Since when does painting a house deserve recording?"

"But the old Tumbleton place is one of the architectural marvels of Lake Elizabeth, Cassie."

I had news for Maxine—Lake Bess has no "architectural marvels." The town does have some charm, but people have been building their cabins, cottages, and houses along the shores of the lake for about two centuries. The architecture is a hodgepodge of mismatched sizes and styles.

"And isn't this color a marvel?" Maxine continued. "Mr. Tumbleton had such an eye for aesthetics. Have you talked to the folks at Hilleville Hardware, Cassie? Will they be able to match the green?"

"I'm going gray," I said.

"Silly! No you're not. Just look at those blond curls of yours."

I rolled my eyes. "The house, Maxine. I'm painting the house gray."

"Oh, but the Kelly green is so jolly."

Luckily the phone rang. And luckily Dad called out that it was for me.

Maxine held the ladder as I descended. "I hope it's Sheriff Gabe," she told me.

Chapter 7

"Is it Gabe?" I asked as I reached for the phone.

"It's Arlene Pearson." Dad cringed, and I dropped my hand. "She's in a foul mood."

Arlene and her sister Pru own the Fox Cove Inn. And Arlene Pearson is always in a foul mood.

"Worse than ever," he added.

I braced myself and took the phone. "Gabe must have been there," I whispered.

"Of course Gabe was here!" Arlene snapped.

"Was she one of your guests, Arlene?" I found a seat at the kitchen table. "I'm sorry."

"Who? What?"

"The dead woman," I said. "Was she staying at the B and B?"

"Of course not! How dare you accuse me."

"I'm not accu—"

"The first sunny day we've had in months, so what do you do? Send in the sheriff to harass my guests!"

"Gabe doesn't take orders from m—"

"He barged in here and demanded to know what we were doing at five a.m. Five!" she screamed. "What did he think we were doing? Eating waffles?"

I bit my lip.

"What do you think you're doing?"

"I'm painting the house."

"Good! That place is an eyesore. It's bad for my business."

I took a deep breath. "Sooo," I said as calmly as humanly possible. "What did you tell Gabe?"

"I told him we were asleep! Like normal human beings! In our own little beds like good little boys and girls."

"That's too bad."

"What!?"

"None of your guests could tell Gabe anything?"

"What?" she snapped. "You think I actually let him talk to my guests? Gabe Cleghorn can get himself a search warrant before showing his sorry face around here again."

"But surely he doesn't need a warrant just to talk to—"

"What the hell were you doing out there at the crack of dawn? A dead woman in Mallard Cove? Yeah, right! My sister is furious!"

Yeah, right. I don't know the Pearson sisters well, but I do know Arlene's the angry one, and Pru's the meek, timid, tired one. I doubt Pru has ever mustered up the energy to be angry.

But in case you haven't quite caught on, I have no problem with my anger-energy. I told Arlene that whether or not it hurt her business, I know what I saw. "Someone is dead, Arlene. Dead."

"Someone is lying, Miss Looney Tunes. Lying."

***

"Careful, Charlie," I called down. I'd been up on that stupid extension ladder for hours, and I didn't need the dog to start helping.

He bumped into it again.

"Charlie!" I looked down and almost did fall. Yes, Charlie had heard his name and stood at attention. But he wasn't alone. Rose and Ruby were down there also, one goat on either side of the ladder, trying to—

I squinted. "Trying to what?" I asked them.

They looked up, and Ruby, the one with floppier ears, baahed at me.

I considered climbing down to call Oden, but the girls found a patch of fiddlehead ferns at the edge of the driveway to occupy themselves, and I decided they couldn't bother me much more than all my other distractions.

The FN451z was still at it, of course. And I was constantly interrupted by all the boaters who "just happened to be floating by." It was a Tuesday afternoon, so most people were at work, but enough folks still managed to find me.

Everyone asked about the dead redhead, and everyone asked how Gabe's investigation was coming along. They were more polite than Arlene, and no one actually called me Miss Looney Tunes to my face, but still.

When they got tired of harping on about the missing woman, and whether or not she really was dead, they'd point to the extension ladder and ask what I was doing.

Oden Poquette was the only person who couldn't care less what I was doing. I heard him calling for Rose and Ruby while he was still out on Elizabeth Circle. And then again as he ran down Leftside Lane, the dirt driveway leading to our house, Joe's, and Maxine's.

"Last I saw them, they were headed to the Gallipeaus' yard," I told him as he rounded the last bend.

He thanked me and would have jogged on, but I called him back.

"Have they been missing all day?" I reminded him I had seen Rose and Ruby at Evert Osgood's early that morning.

"The gals almost always wander off after their four a.m. milking," Oden said.

"Bobby should have been a farmer," I mumbled.

"What's that?"

"I said," I spoke up. "Where did the gals end up this morning?"

"At the Fox Cove. Thankfully Pru found them."

"Let me guess. Arlene doesn't like Rose and Ruby?"

"She says they're bad for business." Oden finally took a good look at me. "You're on a ladder, Cassie."

About then, we heard the baahing of a lost goat, and he took off. "Please don't change the color," he called over his shoulder.

***

"Want some help?" Joe called down from an open window next door.

"No thanks." I tried sounding way more breezy than I felt. "I can manage."

"I know. But would you like some help?"

I stopped struggling with the extension ladder that had gotten heavier and heavier as the day progressed, caught my breath, and looked up. But Joe was no longer at the window.

"Have you heard from Gabe?"

I jumped and turned, and my neighbor was now at the edge of our adjoining yards greeting Charlie. He stood up and smiled, and I gave him a withering look. Or at least I tried to. I was feeling a little weak in the knees from all the climbing up the stupid ladder, and down the stupid ladder, and moving the stupid ladder.

I leaned against the stupid ladder. "You've been spying on me all day," I said, but Joe claimed innocence. Supposedly he had only poked his head out the window to see how I was doing every once in a while.

"I didn't say anything because I didn't want to spook you." He glanced up at where I'd been balancing on the top rungs. "It's a long way down."

"You were spying on me this morning also." I pointed to his dock, and he shrugged.

"Guilty as charged. Has Gabe called?"

"No."

"You haven't heard from anyone?"

"Oh, I've heard from all kinds of people." I tilted my head toward the looky-loo boaters on the lake. "And Arlene Pearson called. Lucky me, she was even nastier than usual. It sounds like she was pretty nasty to Gabe, too."

"Probably because she knows something."

I held onto the ladder. "Say what?"

"Your father described this redhead to me." Joe bent down and found a stick for Charlie. He tossed it into the lake, and the dog took off. "I've lived here my whole life and she doesn't sound familiar—"

"She exists," I interrupted, and he held up his hands.

"I know that, okay? I'm only saying this woman wasn't an Elizabethan."

I squinted. "You think she was staying at the Fox Cove?"

"It seems logical."

Charlie brought the stick to me, and I tossed it for him. A very wimpy toss.

"Maybe a dead guest would be bad for Arlene's business," I said. "But covering it up seems pretty extreme."

I watched Charlie return the stick to Joe. "Would Arlene actually do something like that?"

"I wouldn't put much past Arlene."

Charlie nudged Joe, and he bent down to give the stick a great big toss. Then he turned and pointed to the ladder. "Want some help?"

Chapter 8

I may be nuts, but I'm not crazy. I accepted help to move the ladder for one more round of scraping, but called it quits by late afternoon. The boats floating by hadn't exactly thinned out, and my knees were getting shakier by the minute.

I took a second shower for the day, and put on a coat of mascara, my nicest pair of shorts, and my brightest Hawaiian shirt to revive myself.

Dad looked up from the stove as I walked into the kitchen. "Your knees are shaking."

I held onto the counter and pointed to the pot he was stirring. "That will help," I said, and he held out a spoonful for me to test. Not that it needed testing. My father's spaghetti and Bolognese sauce has been my favorite meal since I had teeth.

I made sure I had time to run an errand and headed for the door.

"Where to?" he asked, and I told him the hardware store down in Hilleville.

"I need some supplies."

"No paint." Dad used his teacher-voice. "No gray, especially. I want to help choose the color."

I promised the painting part of this project was a long way off, grabbed my purse, and walked outside. And straight into Maxine Tibbitts.

I stopped short and took notice. She had planted herself directly under the kitchen window. The open kitchen window. Within easy ear-shot of where Dad and I were just talking. She held up her i-Tablet and took my picture.

"Would you stop doing that!" I snapped, and she snapped another. "Maxine! A trip to Hilleville Hardware does not merit documentation." I jerked my head at the kitchen window. "And of course you know where I'm headed."

I darted around her, but she followed me to the driveway.

"I didn't mean to overhear," she lied. "But I was hoping you'd have time for a chat. Now that you're off your ladder."

"Go away," I said and kept moving. "No chats."

"Have you heard from Gabe?" She was still right behind me.

"No! No chats." I got into my car and started moving. The woods along Leftside Lane looked beautiful in the late afternoon sun, but I snarled anyway. No chats with Gabe Cleghorn.

Insert colorful words . . . Here.

***

"I don't suppose Gabe called?" I asked as I climbed the stoop to the porch.

My father, Joe Wylie, and Charlie shook their heads.

I dropped the bag from Hilleville Hardware at my feet. "Where's the wine?" I said and headed to the kitchen. Joe followed.

"Anything else to unload?" he asked from the doorway.

"Lots of primer. But I don't need your help."

"Yep," he said and left.

"Go ahead and make yourself useful," I muttered. I poured myself some wine from the bottle on the counter, registered "good stuff," and read the label. The Malbec was way nicer than anything my father and I would have bought for ourselves.

"Maybe he is useful," I told Charlie, and as if on cue, Joe stood in the doorway holding two five-gallon buckets of primer.

"Where do you want these?"

I gestured to the porch, gave the spaghetti sauce a stir, and grabbed the wine.

I refilled everyone's glass, Joe set the primer in a corner, and we sat down in the rocking chairs on either side of my father. Conversation went immediately to the dead redhead.

"What do you know about her?" Joe asked me.

"How about nothing, nothing, and nothing?"

"No," he said. "I bet you know more than you think you do. For instance, what was she wearing?"

I sipped my wine and pictured her. "Cut-off jeans and a tee-shirt," I said. "Nothing special."

"What about the tee-shirt? Did it have a logo?"

"Like the sweatshirt you were wearing this morning?" Dad added helpfully.

I watched a few ducks float by. "It was gray," I said.

Dad stopped rocking . "Like the color you're painting the house?"

I nodded. "Yes, actually."

"What!?" Joe exclaimed, and I jumped a little. "You're painting the house gray!?"

"Gray," I said firmly. I pointed at my father. "Not one word, old man."

Bobby smirked, and Joe told me how much he liked the Kelly green. "It's so jolly!"

I blinked at Joe. I turned and blinked at my father. "So exactly how long did you guys rehearse that?"

When they stopped high-fiving each other, Joe cleared his throat and insisted he really was serious about the dead woman's tee-shirt. "A logo could be a clue," he said.

I thought back. "You know what? It did say something." I shook my head. "But I don't know what. I was too flustered."

"That's okay," Dad told me.

"No, it isn't," Joe said. "What made you so flustered?"

"I get flustered around death."

"An understatement," Dad mumbled. "Don't even ask what she did when her mother died."

"What did you do when your mother died?"

I rolled my eyes. "Can we get back to the redhead, please?"

"Okay, so how did you know she was dead?" Joe asked, but he stopped me before I went ballistic. "I'm not implying she wasn't dead. But what made you so sure?"

"She was staring straight into the sun, and she was almost as gray as her tee-shirt."

"Maybe she drowned," Dad said. "Maybe we should have the lake dragged."

I argued that wouldn't help at all. "Whether or not she drowned, she was in a canoe." I caught sight of our canoe and stood up. "Come on," I said. "Let's try an experiment."

Dad reminded me dinner was almost ready, but I reminded him he should like experiments. "Mr. Science Fiction Writer." I tilted my head. "And Mr. Mad Scientist." I pointed to our canoe. "Let's put that in the water."

They obeyed, and I settled in.

"She was on the floor." I scooched onto the floor, trying to imitate the redhead's position. "And her arms and legs were sprawled out all over." I spread my arms wide and tried to get my knees to extend to the sides of the canoe like hers had.

"That's not a very flattering pose, girl."

"The redhead didn't look so good either." I tucked my legs back to a semi-normal position and stared at my knees. "She was way taller than me."

"What a surprise," Dad said. "She was over five feet."

"Five feet, one and a half," I corrected and looked up at the two men standing on the dock.

My father's a small, tidy, dapper sort of guy. He's pushing seventy, but other than his bald head, you'd never guess it. Bobby has big brown eyes like me, a baby face like me, and is pint-sized like me. He's taller than five-one, but was nowhere near dead-woman height.

I checked out my neighbor. Twenty years younger than my father, and a giant in comparison. Blue eyes, more rugged features, brown hair, some gray. Bambi says hunky-boo—

"Girl." Dad waved to get my attention. "What are you thinking about?"

"Size," I said. "What are you?" I asked Joe. "Five-ten?"

"Ten and a half," he said with half a smile. "I'm no giant."

"No, but you'll do." I ignored another half-smile, climbed out of the canoe, and pointed. "Sit down dead-woman style, please."

"Put your arms like so." I knelt down on the dock and pulled on his left arm. He arranged his right arm to match.

"And my legs like this?" He stretched out, and his knees popped up over the edge of the canoe like hers had.

I stood up. "Perfect," I said. "She was five-ten."

"Her canoe could have been a different size," Joe argued.

"That's right," Dad said. "Science experiments should be exact. No uncertain variables."

"Says the retired English teacher." I told Joe to wait and dragged my kayak into the water.

Then we each paddled out, and Joe sat still while I banged my kayak into the canoe, trying to mimic my actions of the morning. The only new "variable" was Charlie. He thought this game was super fun and swam back and forth between Joe and me, deftly avoiding our paddles.

"It was a regular old metal canoe, like you see everywhere around here." I deliberately smacked into the bow of the canoe, and Joe flicked a paddle to splash me. "And." I splashed him back. "Her canoe was the same size as this one."

"You'd be a good scientist," Joe told me. "Good experiment."

"But I'm still missing something." I stopped splashing and frowned at the canoe. "Some crucial variable."

Chapter 9

Joe didn't have to ask me twice. When he pointed to his pontoon boat and suggested we take a trip over to Mallard Cove, I put down the stack of plates I was clearing from the picnic table and headed off the porch. "Let's go."

"Cassie wait," Dad called after me.

"For what?"

"You don't need to go down there and upset yourself."

"Yes I do, Dad. I need to figure out that missing variable."

Joe shrugged at Bobby. "It can't hurt to explore," he said. "To make some observations."

"Maybe it'll help me remember something," I added. "And I want to ask Joe a few questions." I glanced at Maxine's house. "Out of earshot."

"Well then, you kids go," Dad said. "Charlie and I will hold down the fort."

I ignored the kids comment, and Charlie ignored the fort comment. He raced across our yards and ended up the first on board.

"Out of earshot," I repeated as Joe maneuvered his boat around a group of kayakers.

He told me Lake Bess is over three hundred acres. "We'll steer clear of everyone." He turned left, toward the north end of the lake. "And we'll take the long route."

"Good," I said. "Because I have lots of questions. I want all the dirt on everyone who lives in Mallard Cove and Fox Cove."

"We'd need ten trips around the lake to cover all the dirt on the B and B."

"So condense." I waved to the Gallipeaus as our pontoon boats passed each other. "But don't skip anything about Arlene and Pru," I whispered. "Or the ghost. Haven't I heard something about a ghost?"

"Do you believe in ghosts?"

"About as much as I believe in Whoozit."

"Whatzit?" Joe asked, and I reminded him about Bobby's sci fi world.

"How about you?" I said. "Do you believe in ghosts?"

"No. But some spooky stuff happens at the Fox Cove Inn."

"What exactly? Who's the ghost?"

"Ghosts," Joe corrected. "And I thought you wanted the condensed version."

***

A speakeasy or a bordello. A speakeasy and a bordello. A speakeasy then a bordello. Whatever the exact timing, the history of the Fox Cove Inn was chock full of spooky stuff and dirt.

"It was a speakeasy during Prohibition," Joe said. "But the bordello phase lasted well into the seventies."

"As in the 1970s?" I was incredulous. "Where was the sheriff?"

"Taking bribes. I was only a kid, but even I know Fred McGuckin wasn't nearly as conscientious as Gabe Cleghorn. He didn't shut the place down until someone got shot and killed."

"Is he the ghost?" I asked.

"Ghosts," Joe reminded me, but he waited until we were past the public beach to say more. "Most people assume the ghosts are the dead Mr. Pearsons. And they weren't shot, they were poisoned by their wives."

I looked at Charlie. "Bobby doesn't know what he's missing," I said, and Joe told us Arlene isn't the first Pearson woman with a bad temper.

According to the ghost stories, the Pearsons ran the bordello for several generations. And with each new generation, some Pearson wife decided her Pearson husband was bad for business.

"How many ghost-guys are we talking about?" I asked.

"Three, I think. Supposedly they roam the hallways groaning and complaining of stomach cramps." Joe held his index finger to his lips as we passed the Lake Store.

Tater Ott, a kid who makes Dennis the Menace look tame, was fishing off the dock. He waved enthusiastically, and Charlie looked to me for permission to jump in and go visit.

"No," I said firmly, and he sat back down.

Tater kept waving. "Maybe I'll catch your dead lady," he called out. "Wouldn't that be wicked, Ms. Baxter?"

"Wicked," I agreed, and Joe kept us moving. He set a course for the eastern side of the lake, and I asked about Arlene and Pru's father. "Is he one of the ghost-guys?"

"No, but their grandfather supposedly is. After the shooting that closed the place down, Grandma needed some income. Legend has it she poisoned Grandpa for the life insurance."

My mouth dropped open. Charlie's mouth dropped open. And the ducks we were passing changed direction to follow us and hear more.

Joe continued, "Soon after that, their son Arty—that's Arlene and Pru's father—ran away to Boston. That's where Arlene and Pru were born and raised."

I thought about everyone's general age. "Did you know Arty?"

Joe shook his head and said he was just a little kid at the time. "And Arty never came back home. After Arty's mother died Sheriff McGuckin boarded up the Fox Cove, and it sat there for decades."

"Great for ghost stories," I said. I asked how Arlene and Pru ended up at Lake Bess.

"They inherited the place after Arty died," Joe said. "Supposedly they knew nothing about the Fox Cove until the estate attorneys tracked them down."

"So they moved up here?" I asked. "Sight unseen?"

Joe shrugged. "Lake Bess is a good place to live, Cassie. Maybe they wanted a fresh start."

"Maybe," I said. "Or maybe they didn't know about the speakeasy, bordello, poisonings, shootings, and ghost-guys."

***

"Are we brave enough to venture in?" Joe asked as we made it down to Fox Cove.

"We must," I said. "In the name of scientific observation."

We got situated at the mouth of the cove and stared across the water at the Fox Cove Inn.

"Here's what I'm observing." I gestured toward the terrace where several guests were enjoying the evening. "They definitely have a view of Mallard Cove."

"So do the Poquettes." Joe pointed to Oden's farm, located up the hill behind the B and B, and I noticed Rose and Ruby at the edge of the property chowing down on some poor innocent plant.

"They had an even better view this morning." I reminded Joe the goats had been in Mallard Cove at five a.m.

"The Honeymoon Cottage also has view of Mallard Cove," he said, and I glanced at the quaint little building in the middle of the B and B's garden.

I nodded. "So anyone over here could have seen what happen—"

"Get off my property!" Arlene Pearson emerged from the Honeymoon Cottage, and everyone in every direction jumped ten feet in the air. The people on the terrace wrestled each other to get through the French doors leading off the patio, and out of Arlene's way. And poor Charlie tried to make himself invisible beneath Joe's captain's chair.

"She doesn't own the lake," I told the dog. But when Arlene headed toward the water's edge screeching my name, I also considered hitting the deck.

"Why did you bring her over here?" she screamed at Joe. "You're ruining my business. Get! Out!"

"On it," Joe said under his breath. He started backing away when Arlene caught sight of Rose and Ruby and went truly ballistic. The goats disappeared around the back corner of the inn, and Arlene raised a fist and ran after them.

"And people think I'm crazy?" I asked.

"That woman is spookier than the ghost-guys," Joe agreed.

Chapter 10

"Mama Bear, Papa Bear and Baby Bear," I said as we arrived in Mallard Cove. "The first time I kayaked down here, I gave these houses nicknames."

Joe pointed to the smallest house. "Evert Osgood's is Baby Bear?"

I nodded and gestured to the largest house, in between the other two. "The La Barge place is Papa Bear, and Fanny Baumgarten's is Mama Bear."

I glanced around. It didn't appear that any of the bears were home that evening. "The La Barges don't really live here, right?" I asked. "I know they have a big house in Montpelier."

"It's probably better for Ross's political aspirations to live in the state capital," Joe said. "But Lake Bess is a good place to raise children. Their son Travis grew up here."

I mentioned that I'd seen Travis at the Lake Store a few times. "He's always buying beer."

"That's Travis. He still lives here. He takes care of the place for his mother." Joe nodded at Papa Bear, and I noticed an upstairs shutter dangling forlornly from its hinges.

"Any La Barge dirt?" I asked.

Joe raised an eyebrow. "Don't you already know enough about the La Barges?"

A valid point. Unfortunately, Ross La Barge is a Vermont celebrity. Better known as Ross the Boss, he owns a used car lot outside of Montpelier, and his TV commercials are legendary for their stupidity.

For instance, every Thanksgiving, Ross dresses up like a turkey, and encourages us to, "Gobble! Gobble! Gobble up a pre-owned vehicle from Cars! Cars! Cars!" Another classic, for his annual tribute to Valentine's Day, Ross the Boss dresses up as Cupid and dances around in the bed of a bright red pickup truck.

It gets even worse every four years when he embarks on another round in his never-ending quest to become governor. We Vermonters are then treated to incessant campaign commercials, featuring Ross's wife Janet bragging about her husband's maturity, good taste, and sound judgment.

Never say never, but I'm guessing I'll never vote for a man I've seen dressed in a pink diaper.

Joe asked if I'd seen the latest commercials. Lucky me, I had. Because lucky Vermont, Ross was already starting his gubernatorial campaign for the coming November.

"I assume Janet won't shoot any of her vote-for-my-husband commercials here." I waved at Papa Bear, and in particular, at the raggedy hammock tied between two maple trees in what might once have passed for a garden.

"That's where Travis sleeps off his hangovers," Joe said.

I glanced sideways. "Am I sensing dirt?"

"Dirt, problems, whatever you want to call it. Travis drinks. And I think he does drugs." Joe frowned. "He graduated from Hilleville High with my daughter Paige."

"I take it they weren't friends?"

"No, thankfully." He frowned some more. "But Travis does have some talent. He has a lot of potential."

"It can't be easy being Ross the Boss's son," I said.

"Yep, and it's even harder being Janet's son." He nodded toward Baby Bear. "What do you know about Evert?"

"I know his house looks a lot tidier than he does."

"Don't let looks fool you," Joe told me. "Evert's a good guy."

Easy to believe, since lots of Vermonters look pretty darn rugged. All those months of surviving the seriously cold winters make people up here a little rough around the edges. Let's just say Evert Osgood's edges are very rough.

"He seemed friendly anytime I've talked to him at the Lake Store," I said. "But he's always so messy-looking."

Joe explained that I'd probably caught Evert on his way home from work. "He's the dynamite expert for the state highway department. He blasts rock. When you talk to him, speak up. He's half deaf from his job."

"So the dirt on Evert is actual dirt," I told Charlie. "Which can probably also be said about Miss Rusty," I added as I remembered Evert's basset hound.

"That dog is cute as a button." Joe said, and Charlie and I had to agree.

I glanced at Mama Bear. "I'm guessing there isn't any dirt on Fanny?" I asked, and Joe agreed it was highly unlikely.

Like Ross the Boss, Fanny Baumgarten is a local celebrity. But in a good way. Fanny was the sole teacher at Lake Elizabeth Elementary School for half a century. Yes, you read that right. Lake Bess has a one-room schoolhouse where Elizabethan children attend kindergarten through third grade. After that they get bussed into Hilleville for the remainder of their K through twelve education. And the reason this system still exists is Fanny Baumgarten.

In the late 1970s when state authorities decided one-room schools were obsolete, Fanny fought to save her school. She produced all kinds of statistics proving that every student who ever attended Lake Elizabeth Elementary went on to graduate from high school. Yes, you read that right also. Every. Single. Student.

But Fanny didn't stop there. She called in the troops—namely her former students—and dozens of doctors, lawyers, teachers, engineers, and a well-known actor came out of the woodwork, down from mountaintops, and across continents to testify in front of the Vermont State Board of Education on behalf of their elementary school.

Fanny won the battle. Her victory made the *New York Times*, and the framed article about her sits atop the meat counter at the Lake Store.

"Was she your teacher?" I asked.

"Of course." Joe pointed to Baby Bear. "And Evert's." He pointed to Papa Bear. "And Janet's. And Oliver's, and Maxine's. Mrs. Baumgarten taught every Elizabethan over age thirty." He stopped smiling. "You know what happened after her retirement?"

"She went blind," I said. "I've seen her at the Lake Store with Lindsey. You know, her assistant, or aide, or whatever the right word is."

"Beautiful is the word," Joe said on reflex. He glanced at me. "Sorry."

"Why?" I asked. "She is beautiful."

An understatement. Lindsey Luke is drop-dead gorgeous—tall and buxom, with long dark hair, piercing blue eyes, and a pale complexion. She's stunning. And she certainly stuns any man who gets in her path. I've witnessed the profound effect she has at the Lake Store. Chester Stewart and Hollis Klotz are actually rendered speechless in her presence, Oliver drops things, and my father gets dizzy.

"Bobby has to hold onto me for support every time we see her," I said. "It doesn't help that he stands eye level with her chest." I glanced at Joe. "What profound effect does she have on you, Dr. Wylie?"

"I stutter. She probably thinks my name is Joe Why-Why-Why."

***

"Why, why, why?" I pointed to the sky, where storm clouds were rolling in.

Joe frowned upward also but steered us toward the cattails, anyway. "Let's take a quick look," he said and maneuvered the boat to hover over the dead-redhead spot.

I stared into the pool of darkening water, and Charlie came over to see what I was so interested in.

"Nothing," I said. "She was dead, and she was lying in a plain, old, ordinary canoe." I pointed to the three canoes at the three docks of Mallard Cove. Even Fanny had one.

"Think harder," Joe told me.

I took another peek at the cattails, and it actually came to me. "I know the missing variable!" I looked up. "There were no paddles! She had no paddles in that canoe, Joe."

"Someone was out here moving her around," he said.

"Either that or she was beamed up, Chance-Dooley style." I shook my head. "But my father insists this so-called beaming up business doesn't work."

***

"Rose and Ruby weren't the only ones watching you this morning," Joe said as we arrived back at his dock.

"Nope." I waited until my feet were on solid ground before responding. "The murderer was watching me."

"Murderer!" He glanced at Maxine's house. "Murderer?" he whispered.

"The redhead didn't die in that canoe, Joe. And she wasn't asleep. Someone killed her and put her out there. And when they saw me see her, they decided they'd better hide her."

"That's a stretch, Cassie. You're jumping to a lot of unsubstantiated conclusions."

I folded my arms. "Do you have a better hypothesis, Mr. Mad Scientist?"

Joe stared at me. "Okay, so maybe it's a remote possibility," he said. "Now what?"

"We test the hypothesis, right? Isn't that what scientists do?"

He reminded me I'm not a scientist. "Gabe Clegorn's the guy to test this hypothesis."

"He's not a scientist, either."

"No, but he is the sheriff."

"The sheriff who never called me," I said. "The sheriff who hasn't found the body, the sheriff who hasn't figured out anything."

"Patience is a virtue."

"How would I know?" I said as thunder clapped overhead. "Something sinister happened here," I shouted over the sudden downpour. "And I intend to find out what."

About then, lightning struck nearby and set off both Charlie and the FN451z. Charlie ran in nervous circles around me, and a totally frenzied FN beeped, burped, and chirped from inside Joe's house.

"Go home!" he shouted, and everyone ran for cover.

Chapter 11

I opened one eye, checked the time, and told my father he drives me nuts.

"Why? I let you sleep in."

FYI, it was 5:30, and Dad was, of course, sitting in the rocking chair next to my bed. That particular morning he had his laptop open and was busy typing. "What's another word for rudder?" he asked.

I looked at Charlie. "How about tail?" I sat up and patted the covers, and he jumped up to join me.

"You spoil him, girl."

I hugged the dog, and he spread his sixty-pound bulk across my lap. "Charlie protected me from the big bad thunderstorm last night."

"I hope he didn't protect you from Joe." Dad looked up. "Did lightning strike?"

"Spare me."

"You kids were out late."

"Keep wiggling your eyebrows like that, and this kid will tell you nothing."

The eyebrows halted mid-wiggle, and I told my father what I had learned from Joe.

"Ghosts?" Dad asked.

"But even more fascinating than the ghost-guys is that missing variable, right? The missing paddles."

"More proof something fishy was going on."

"I need to talk to the sheriff again," I said.

"But only after breakfast." Bobby closed his laptop and stood up. "Pancakes?"

***

"Brace yourself," Dad said when I entered the kitchen a while later.

I stopped short and stared at the *Hanahan Herald* lying on the table. Unlike the daily paper from Montpelier, which we pick up for ourselves at the Lake Store, the county newspaper gets delivered to our door every Wednesday morning. Tater Ott, the child who likes to go fishing, is our delivery boy.

"How bad is it?" I asked from a safe distance.

"There's a nice picture of you."

I gasped. "In my pajamas?"

"No. Maxine promised she wouldn't do that."

I stepped over to take a peek. "It's on the front page," I whined.

"I told you to brace yourself."

***

I slumped into a chair, and Dad brought me a cup of coffee with ridiculous amounts of milk in it. He hovered over my left shoulder. "It could be worse," he said.

"How?"

"It's a flattering photograph," he said, and I stared at a picture only my father could consider even remotely flattering.

"She took that when I caught her spying under our kitchen window," I said. "I'm snarling."

"But only a little."

I read the caption. "HELP!" it said. "Please help Cassie Baxter find her body!"

"Maybe no one will pay much attention," Dad suggested.

I glanced up. He cleared his throat and went back to flipping pancakes. "Read it to Charlie," he said.

Oh, why not? And so I read "Lake Bess Lore," Maxine's weekly column, out loud. "DEAD BODY SIGHTED!!!" I began.

"Oh, yeah," I told Charlie. "People are bound to skip right over this."

He wagged his tail, and I continued, "Never a dull moment at Lake Bess! According to my new neighbor, Cassie Baxter, we're missing a body! All the hullabaloo started bright and early Tuesday morning, when Cassie set out to stir up mischief in Mallard Cove. Why she insisted on kayaking at 4 a.m. is anyone's guess, and we Elizabethans are still trying to figure out why she went bird watching in her pajamas!?!?"

I got up to show my father. "What do you think of this punctuation, Mr. English Teacher?"

"I think Maxine would earn an 'F' on her essay. 'Hyperbole' I'd write in big hyperbolic letters in the margins."

I sat back down, and skimmed and paraphrased the part about the Lake Store dock. "I found a body. Commotion, commotion . . . I lost a body. Commotion, commotion . . . Wild goose chase, commotion, fire department, commotion, youngsters from the state park, commotion.

"Oh, but I must read this next part verbatim." I tapped the paper and read, "What with all the sirens and whistles, and with Cassie jumping up and down and screaming like that, it's a wonder folks down in Hilleville didn't hear!!!"

"Three exclamation points," I said. "And I did not jump up and down."

"Yes, you did," Dad said.

"I didn't scream."

"Yes, you did."

I kept reading. "Despite the commotion, no body was found! NO BODY!!!"

"More unnecessary capitalization, more exclamation points," I said.

"More hyperbole," Bobby said.

I continued, "Folks hereabouts are wondering what poor Cassie Baxter really did see in Mallard Cove. But never fear! Your reporter spoke to Sheriff Gabe personally, and we'd like to give poor Cassie the benefit of the doubt. We think she did see a redheaded lady, but the lady was taking a nap."

I looked up as Dad set a plate of pancakes in front of me. "I'm so relieved Sheriff Gabe and Maxine are in perfect agreement."

"Keep reading."

I took a deep breath. "Poor Cassie is spending every waking moment fretting about her dead lady," I read. "But Sheriff Gabe has proven his mettle on tougher cases than this. Let's hope he comes up with an explanation for poor Cassie real soon. In the meantime, anyone with any information should call me or the sheriff. Anything to help poor Cassie!!!"

I slammed down the paper.

"Maybe it's a good thing," Dad suggested. "It will get people's attention."

"Old man! Not two minutes ago you said no one would pay much attention. Which is it?"

"I was wrong earlier." Bobby sat down with his own plate. "Remember what happened when your mother died? A little publicity is a good thing."

"Yeah, right."

"I am right," Dad insisted. "Now people from all over the county will be on the lookout for your redhead."

"Yep," I said. "And now people from all around the county will think 'poor Cassie' is a complete lunatic."

"Whereas some of us know for sure."

***

Dad asked me to pass the maple syrup. "Anything else?" he asked, and I returned to "Lake Bess Lore."

"The Congregational Church is hosting a potluck picnic next weekend." I skimmed Maxine's list of upcoming Elizabethan birthdays and anniversaries. "Tater Ott turns twelve on Sunday, and Oden Poquette's goats destroyed Brooke Ferland's prize peony bush last Saturday."

I tapped the paper and read, "You may recall, the peonies from that exact same bush earned Brooke the blue ribbon at last year's county fair. What a shame!"

I scowled at Charlie. "Why is it so hard to keep those goats in one spot?"

"Don't ask Charlie," Dad said. "He's from Hoboken."

Chapter 12

"Well, well. If it isn't Miss Looney Tunes." The thirty-something receptionist at the Hanahan County sheriff's office adjusted her glasses and puckered her nose. "I almost didn't recognize you without your pajamas."

"You've never seen me in my pajamas."

"But your reputation precedes you, babe. Great article in the *Herald*." She snickered, and I noticed the nameplate on her desk. Sarah Bliss.

Perfect. I shook my head and asked to see the sheriff.

"Take a number." She pointed me to the deserted reception area, I assumed that made me number one, and sat down on a beige vinyl chair about as inviting as Ms. Bliss herself.

***

"Cassie Baxter!" Gabe Cleghorn finally emerged from the hallway.

I dropped the brochures about keeping kids off drugs I'd been feigning interest in and stood up. "Any news?"

"I've been meaning to call you."

"With news?"

Gabe tilted his head Sarah Bliss-ward and silently led me to his office. Along the way we passed a closed door with a scrap of paper taped to it. So Gabe actually had a deputy that week? According to the *Herald* this is a rare occurrence. The seriously low pay tends to keep the job open.

I took the chair Gabe indicated in his office and he moved around the desk. "Sorry about Sarah," he said as he sat down. "She comes on kind of strong, but she does a good job around here."

"She made me feel right at home."

Gabe cleared his throat. "What can I do for you?"

"You can tell me you found the body."

"No can do."

"Well then, hopefully these will help." I took a slip of paper from my purse and slid it across the desk. "I put some notes together after breakfast this morning."

"Waffles?"

"Pancakes," I said pleasantly and pointed to my notes. "It's a few things I thought of since yesterday."

"Five-ten, and wearing shorts and a tee-shirt," Gabe read. "Not much here."

"But the fact that there were no paddles is significant. Somebody had to put her out there, right?"

Gabe looked up.

"And she couldn't remove herself from the lake without paddles, either," I said.

"You must not have seen the paddles."

"Because there were none."

"That you noticed."

I took a deep breath. "Maybe you should tell me what you learned," I suggested.

"Nothing." He put down my notes. "I spent all day yesterday trying to verify your story. I got nowhere."

"Someone's lying to you, Gabe. I'm convinced someone killed that woman."

"What, like murdered?"

"Yes. Like murdered."

He picked up a pen and started clicking it on and off. "How?"

"I don't know, but somebody sure does." I hesitated. "Maybe somebody at the Fox Cove Inn?"

"Nope." Click, click. "No one at the B and B saw anything."

"Maybe you should try again," I said. "I think Arlene Pearson lied to you."

Gabe stopped clicking. "Are you accusing her of murder?"

I bit my lip. Was I?

"Probably not," I said. "But she's hiding something. I have it from a reliable source that the Fox Cove must be involved in this."

"Oh, really? What source?"

"Josiah Wylie. He's my neighbor."

Gabe laughed out loud. "Figures," he said. "Since Joe has such an unbiased opinion of the Fox Cove."

"What are you talking about?"

"Ask Joe."

"Okay, I will," I said. "But what about Mallard Cove?" I asked. "Did you learn anything there?"

"Nothing." Gabe explained that no one had even been home at the La Barges since Ross the Boss was campaigning down in Woodstock, Janet was in Montpelier, and Travis was staying there, too.

"But he lives in Mallard Cove, right?"

"Yes, but he works at Cars! Cars! Cars! On the days he works back-to-back he 'crashes,' as he put it, at their house in Montpelier."

"You talked to him?"

"I did my job." The sheriff started clicking his pen again. "I called Travis. And before you ask, I talked to Fanny Baumgarten and Evert Osgood in person." Click, click. "Evert was awake, you know. He's working on Interstate 89 this week, so he was up at the crack of dawn to drive down to Richmond."

"Terrific. Did Evert see anything?"

"I already told you. Nothing. He's half deaf, but he claims he heard his dog bark."

"Miss Rusty?" I sat forward. "Maybe she was barking at the dead woman. Or the murderer."

"Nooo. She was barking at the goats. Did you hear her?"

I reminded him I'd been kind of flustered.

"Figures," he said. "So that leaves Fanny Baumgarten."

"Did she see anything?"

"Excuse me?"

I grimaced and apologized for my choice of words.

Gabe nodded. "Fanny's old and blind," he said, "but she does alright. She spends most of her time on her upstairs porch overlooking Mallard Cove. Unbelievable, but she was awake, too." He clicked his pen. "And she heard something."

"Miss Rusty?"

"And you." Click, click. "Fanny Baumgarten heard you talking." Click. "To the supposed dead woman."

***

I stared at the pen and swallowed a few colorful words. "I told her to move," I said.

"About twenty times," Gabe said. "Why didn't you mention this yesterday?"

"I didn't remember until now."

"Why were you talking to someone who was supposedly dead?"

I held up an index finger. "Better question. If she wasn't dead, why didn't she move when I told her to?"

"Because she was out cold. And she did move, didn't she? After you left."

"Come on, Gabe!"

"No, you come on. You don't know what you saw or heard. You didn't notice Fanny, you didn't hear Miss Rusty—"

"I saw a dead woman."

Gabe took a deep breath. "Listen," he said. "I've checked for missing persons, I've checked for abandoned cars, I've questioned people." He clicked his pen. "I've done everything I can, Cassie."

"Ga-aabe! You can't just drop this!"

He raised an eyebrow and dropped the pen.

Chapter 13

Dad looked up from his computer. "No body?" he asked.

I stepped into his office and plopped into a rocking chair. "Nothing," I said. "No one knows anything about anything." Charlie sauntered over for a pat on the head. "Actually, I take that back. Miss Rusty knows something. And the goats. But Gabe refuses to talk to them."

"You're nuts."

"Wacko and Looney Tunes. Gabe promised to keep his eyes and ears open. And meanwhile I'm supposed to relax."

"You're not very good at that."

"No kidding." I pointed to the computer. "So distract me. What's up with Chance Dooley's propulsion pistons?"

Dad frowned at his computer. "Nothing good there, either. Chance thought he found a mechanic on Whoozit who could help him. But it turns out Zach Cooter doesn't know a turbo thrust propulsion piston from a plain old reciprocal reverse performance piston. The technology of the Spaceship Destiny is simply too advanced for your average Whooter."

"Zach Cooter, the Whooter?" I giggled at Charlie. "Does he usually work on scooters?"

"Ooooo. That's good, girl. Can I use it?"

"Of course," I said and stood up. "You and Chance can keep working on the Spaceship Destiny, and Charlie and I will work on the Jolly Green Giant." I tapped my thigh. "Come on, boy."

"Cassie, wait."

"For what?"

"You should call Fanny Baumgarten. She called while you were out."

"Da-aad!" I lunged for the phone on his desk. "Why didn't you tell me?"

"I just did." He handed me a slip of paper with the number on it. "I even tried your cell, but I couldn't get through."

"You could have texted," I said while I punched in the number.

"That doesn't always work, either. Communicating with planets beyond the Crystal Void is easier than reaching anyone around here by cell ph—"

I waved him to be quiet and spoke to Fanny. She claimed she was anxious to talk to me, but I guess anxious means different things to different people. She asked me to stop by at two.

It was ten o'clock.

"I'd be happy to come by sooner," I said brightly. "In fact, I could stop by right now."

"No," she said. "Two is better. Travis should be awake by then."

I scowled at my father. "Gabe told me Travis is in Montpelier."

"No. He's here in Mallard Cove now. And we want to talk to him, don't we?"

"Why?"

"Because he's responsible for the dead girl, isn't he?"

Suddenly, I had many, many, questions. "You believe she was dead?" I asked.

Fanny hesitated. "You believe she was dead?"

"I know she was dead."

"Well then, so do I. You're not blind, are you?"

***

I arrived at Mama Bear at 1:59 sharp, and it started raining at 2:00.

Luckily, Fanny called down to me almost immediately. "Come on up, Cassie."

I found my way inside and to the upstairs porch, and we exchanged the usual pleasantries.

"This is a great spot," I said as I glanced around. We were sheltered from the rain but still had a nice view of Mallard Cove, Papa Bear, and Baby Bear. I frowned at my blind hostess. Make that, I had a nice view.

"Let's have our tea." Fanny pointed in the direction of a tray laid out with a teapot and three cups, and I expressed some surprise at how delicate things looked.

"If I'm careful I can still do these things," she said. "Although I will ask you to pour."

"Is the third cup for Travis," I asked as we sat down.

"No. Travis isn't much of a tea drinker." She explained the extra cup was for her assistant. "I thought it might be Lindsey when you pulled up, but your car sounds different."

"And then we'll go see Travis?" I asked, but Fanny had gotten distracted, and I heard a car pull up behind the house.

"We're on the porch, Love," she called out, and Lindsey Luke soon appeared. She greeted me and bent down to give Fanny a kiss, inadvertently flashing enough cleavage to stop a speeding locomotive.

"Love made this tea set," Fanny told me as I poured. "She's so talented!"

"I just do pottery is all."

"Just pottery!" Fanny tapped her knee. "You do beautiful work."

Lindsey reminded her she can't actually see it. "And Cassie isn't here to talk about me, anyways," she said. "She wants to talk about the dead lady."

"And Travis," I added. "I want to talk about Travis La Barge."

"No kidding." Lindsey pulled a copy of the *Herald* from her purse and told Fanny that Maxine had outdone herself.

"Love reads me the *Herald* every Wednesday," Fanny explained. "It's our favorite thing."

"But Maxine doesn't mention Travis," I said. "What's this about Travis?"

Somehow, no one got the hint that I wanted to talk about Travis, and instead we discussed Maxine.

"Maxy Tibbitts has been a gossip since kindergarten," Fanny said. "But she doesn't know everything, does she? For instance, she doesn't know about those missing paddles."

I stopped short, my teacup halfway to my lips. "How do you know about the missing paddles?"

"I heard you talking to Joe last night," she said. "I was getting ready for bed, but my windows were open."

Lindsey must have noticed my confusion. "Fanny's eyesight stinks," she said. "But she hears everything."

I spoke to Fanny. "And yesterday you heard Travis?"

"Not exactly."

"But over the phone you said—"

Lindsey tapped Fanny's knee. "Tell Cassie what you heard yesterday morning."

"Oh, yes. Now, let's see." Fanny put down her cup. "The birds, of course. The ducks quacking, the loons calling, the geese honking. Oh, and the robins, and the crows, and—"

Lindsey glanced at me. "Fanny's a stickler for details."

"Terrific," I said. "So then you heard Travis?"

"No," Fanny said. "I heard you. You kept telling someone to move, move, move."

I groaned.

"I didn't know it was you at the time," she continued. "And I certainly didn't know anyone was dead."

"Why didn't you say something?" I asked.

"I did. But you must not have noticed."

I groaned again. Gabe Cleghorn was right—I missed a whole lot while I was busy being flustered. "And then you heard Travis?" I asked.

"No. Then I went inside to make coffee, and when I came back out, I heard Miss Rusty." She pointed in the general direction of the "Doggie Treats" jar on a side table and smiled. "We're good friends. Miss Rusty comes over for treats every evening."

"What about Evert?"

"We're good friends, too, but Evert feeds himself. Except on holidays. We've had Thanksgiving dinner together for years. And Christmas, and Easter, and—"

"Fanny," Lindsey interrupted. "Cassie means did you hear Evert yesterday."

"Yes, I did. He scolded Miss Rusty for barking at Oden's goats."

"And then you heard Travis?" I asked.

"No. Then I sat here like a bump on a log until the sirens started." She waved a hand. "Noises from every which way. I'm afraid I couldn't keep track of it all."

I shook my head. "So exactly when did you hear Travis?"

"I never heard Travis."

***

Fanny slapped her knees and stood up. "Now then, let's go talk to him, shall we? Get this cleared up."

"Fanny, wait." I jumped up.

"For what?"

I whimpered a little. "I don't understand. Travis was in Montpelier, right? Which is why he's the only person, or creature, you didn't hear. Did not hear."

"That's what Sheriff Gabe thinks, too," Lindsey said. "But Evert and I agree with Fanny."

"If something bad happened in Mallard Cove, Travis was involved," Fanny said.

"But do you have any proof?" I asked.

"That's what Sheriff Gabe asked, too," Lindsey said.

Okay, so I actually had to agree with Sheriff Gabe.

"No, Cassie." Fanny was firm. "I've known Travis his whole life."

"And I've known him since high school," Lindsey said. "I was a couple of years ahead of the jerk."

"The jerk?" I asked.

"He's been hitting on me since he was fifteen."

Fanny sighed. "Travis does seem to require some supervision."

"More like a lot of supervision," I said. "He's dangerous. He must have killed that woman."

"What!?" They both jumped.

I shrugged. "Sorry, but I'm convinced someone killed her. And now you're telling me Travis is responsible."

Fanny reached for Lindsey's hand. "Travis wouldn't do something like that."

"He's not violent," Lindsey agreed.

"So is he involved, or isn't he?" I asked.

"Let's find out." Fanny rapped her cane and told me to come along.

"Fanny, wait!" Lindsey jumped into her path. "You stay here. Cassie and I will go."

"No, Love," Fanny argued. "Travis bothers you too much. Cassie and I can handle this. Isn't that right, Cassie?"

I assessed our little tea party. Me—middle-aged and miniscule. Fanny—old and blind. And Lindsey—tall, young, and absolutely the toughest of the bunch.

"Right," I mumbled.

Chapter 14

"You-hoo? Anyone home?" Fanny called out.

We navigated the last of the wet lawn to Papa Bear, and she knocked repeatedly while I picked up the *Hanahan Herald* still laying on the doorstep.

When Travis finally answered, he held up a beer and burped in Fanny's face. "Want a brew-ski?" he asked.

I was stunned, but Fanny took it in her stride and politely declined.

"You're not getting any tea." He burped again. "My mother isn't here."

"We know that, dear. We're here to see you."

"Got news for you, Mrs. Baumgarten. You don't see-eee anyone."

I was moving beyond stunned, but again Fanny remained calm. While she tried to get her foot in the door, I took a closer look at Travis. His hair was rumpled, and his clothes were wrinkled, but let's face it, you could say the same about mc and lots of other Vermonters. He had a short compact physique and came about eye level with Fanny. I had to look up at both of them.

Eventually, Fanny got sick of pussy-footing around. She used her cane to push him aside, I shoved his newspaper at him and followed, and Fanny led the way into the den. Not exactly my style, but Janet La Barge was probably responsible for the formal furniture and expensive-looking art. Travis, however, had to be the owner of the mess. Sneakers and flip flops littered the floor, tee-shirts and dingy towels hung over every other chair, and an impressive collection of empty beer cans cluttered the coffee table.

I jumped forward before Fanny's cane collided with those beer cans and helped her into an armchair. Travis plopped down on one of the couches and opened up the *Herald*, and I took a spot on the opposite couch. I tried to ignore the stench of stale beer wafting up from the coffee table while Fanny formally introduced us.

"I know all about Cassie Baxter," he said without looking up.

"Do you know she and her father live in the old Tumbleton place?" Fanny asked.

Travis dropped the newspaper. "That ugly green house?"

"I'm re-paint—"

"You're Paige Wylie's neighbor? We're buds, you know. I'm buds with her father, too."

"Buds? With Jo—"

Fanny interrupted to remind us we weren't there to discuss the Wylies. "We're here to talk about you, Travis."

"Yeah? What about me?"

"We want to know what happened yesterday."

"Too late. I already took care of yesterday."

I sat forward. "What do you mean, you took care of yesterday?"

"I mean, I talked to Sheriff Gabe." Travis suddenly remembered his beer. He poured what was left of it down his throat and let out a prolonged belch. "Breakfast," he said proudly.

I was getting kind of nauseous, but Fanny soldiered on. "What did you tell Gabe Cleghorn?" she asked.

"Duh. Someone planted that chick out there to get me in trouble and make my father look bad."

"So you admit there was a dead woman?" I asked.

"Nooo, Miss Looney Tunes." He leered and sneered. "She was only playing dead to mess with my father."

"Why?" Fanny asked.

"Duh. To help the big shots. The Democrats, the Republicans—they're all scared Dad's gonna win this time."

And people think I'm crazy? Trust me, neither Democrats nor the Republicans take Ross the Boss that seriously. He runs for governor as an independent every four years, and he must waste gobs of his own money in the process.

"Let's get back to you," Fanny said. "Why did you tell the sheriff you were in Montpelier?"

"Because I was. I worked at Cars! Cars! Cars! on Monday, had a few brew-skis at Mandy's that night, and then crashed at my parents' house. Then it was back to work yesterday." He leered at me and almost fell off the couch. "Work, work, work."

"You're lying," Fanny said. "You were here."

"Yeah? You have proof?"

"I know what I know," she said.

"Yeah, and I have proof I wasn't here. My mother's vouching for me. And the loser-manager at Cars! Cars! Cars!" Travis tried to drink more beer, found the can empty, and slammed it onto the coffee table.

"Where did you hide the body?" Fanny asked him.

"How about the bathtub?" He stood up and kicked her cane away. "Go check."

"That's it!" I jumped up, grabbed the cane, and told Fanny it was time to go. I helped her to her feet and tried leading her out, but she didn't budge.

"Relieve an old lady of one worry." She was nose to nose with Travis, and it was gratifying to see him back up a step. "Did you kill that girl, Travis?"

"No, Mrs. Baumgarten." He actually swallowed his next burp. "I didn't kill anyone."

Yeah, right.

Chapter 15

"You-hoo," I hollered through the screened door. "Anyone home?"

Dammit, this was not the plan. I had wanted to march over to Joe's, bang on the door, and maybe give it a few kicks, until he was forced to open up and face me.

"You-hoo," I repeated.

The FN 451-z beeped, burped, and chirped. But evidently Joe couldn't hear me over the racket.

I muttered a colorful word and walked in. "Are you up there?" I shouted at the ceiling.

"Cassie?" I heard a bunch of clinking and clanking, and Joe rushed down the stairs. "What a nice surprise," he said as he reached the landing.

I folded my arms. "You know Travis La Barge," I said. "And so does Paige."

"Didn't I mention that last night?" He gestured me farther into the room, but I stood still. "Are you mad about something?" he asked.

"Very good! I just got back from a little visit with Fanny Baumgarten." I raised an eyebrow. "And Travis."

"How is Fanny? I haven't seen her in a while."

I rolled my eyes. "She's fine. She heard the whole thing yesterday."

"But that's fantastic." He waved me toward the couch. I gave up and took seat. Joe took the easy chair opposite.

"I'm not here to discuss Fanny Baumgarten," I said. "I'm here to talk about you. You and Travis, Paige and Travis, what Travis said about you, what Gabe said about you." I pointed. "You, you, you."

He blinked. "Why don't you start with what Travis said about me?"

"He said you're buddies!" I practically jumped out of my seat. "Buds to be exact. He told me he's 'buds' with Paige also."

"None of us are 'buds.' Would it mean something if we were?"

"Yes it would!" I threw up my hands. "Last night you said he and your daughter were not—not!—friends. And now I figure out he's a murderer at the exact same time I find out you're friends with him? Yes!" I said, and Joe flinched. "It does mean something!"

He stared at me. "Have I missed something? Why don't you tell me about your entire day."

"Okay, fine!" I snapped. I gave a summary of my infuriating visit to Gabe, my enlightening visit with Fanny, and ended up back at Travis. "He's a complete jerk," I concluded.

"Was he sober?"

I thought about it. "I think we caught him on his first beer of the day," I said. "So he was quite clear when he told me he's 'buds' with all you Wylies."

Joe shrugged. "Paige went to school with him—K through twelve. First at the Lake School, and then at the schools in Hilleville."

"So they were good friends."

"No, but you have to understand small towns, Cassie. Their kindergarten class had seven children in it, and their senior class at Hilleville High only had something like sixty kids."

"They know each other well," I said.

"Yes. But they're not buddies."

"Travis thinks they are."

"Travis is dreaming." Joe got up, took a photograph from the mantle, and handed it to me.

"She's cute as a button," I said.

"No kidding." He sat back down. "She was also the valedictorian of her senior class, and at the top of her class at MIT, and she's doing just as well in graduate school."

"She has some internship in Boston this summer, right?"

"A Pendergrass internship." Joe waited until I looked up. "And what was Travis doing today?"

"Drinking beer and belching."

"Figures. I don't mean to brag, but Paige is out of his league. She doesn't tell me everything, but we're close—

like you and your father. If she were 'buds' with Travis, I'd know."

"And you?" I asked. "Are you 'buds' with Travis?"

"No, but I know everyone around here. I've lived here my whole life, except for when I was at MIT."

"Ah-ha!" I sat back and folded my arms. "You went to MIT."

"Undergraduate, graduate, and post-doc." He tilted his head. "Is that a problem?"

"It's in Boston. And isn't it interesting that Arlene and Pru Pearson are from Boston?"

"Why?"

"Jo-ooe!" I jumped. "Try following me, here! I think you're buddies with Arlene Pearson. More than buddies."

He laughed. A lot. "You're kidding, right?" he asked. "Didn't you hear her last night? She hates me."

"Why? Was it a bad break up?"

More laughter. "Who put this idea into your gorgeous head?"

I gave him my most withering look until he apologized. "Who put this idea into your average, run of the mill head?" he asked.

"Gabe Cleghorn."

"What?"

"Gabe told me you're biased when it comes to the Fox Cove Inn." I nodded. "Why is that?"

Joe stared at me a long time.

I stared back. "You have skeletons in your closet, Dr. Wylie."

About then, the FN451z let out a cacophony of beeps, burps, and chirps.

I kept my eyes on Joe and pointed to the ceiling. "And that's one of them."

***

"Wine?" Joe pointed to the clock. 5:02.

"Why not?" I said. "It might help me pry something useful out of you."

"You can try." He left for his kitchen, and I stood up to replace the picture of Paige on the mantle.

It was crowded up there—pictures of Paige skiing, Paige hiking with friends, Paige playing the piano. I moved two steps sideways and looked at some older shots—Paige at about ten, laughing with her mother Helen on their pontoon boat, Helen and Joe, also on the boat, Helen and Joe, their wedding photo.

"I've thought of taking some of those down."

I jumped and turned.

"But Paige likes them."

"I don't blame her." I took the glass he offered, he tapped mine with his, and we each took a sip. Whatever the skeletons in this guy's closet, they were resting beside a very nice stash of wine.

We returned to our seats, and of course Joe shifted the subject away from himself. "Fanny really thinks Travis was involved yesterday?"

"She's does. But she refuses to say he murdered the woman." I sighed. "And she didn't actually hear Travis, and obviously she didn't see him, and therefore Gabe Cleghorn doesn't believe her."

Joe scowled. "At the risk of making you angry—"

I held up a hand. "I know, I know. You agree with Gabe. So did I until I talked to Travis. What a jerk."

"At the risk of making you angrier, Travis isn't violent."

"Oh, come on! So you agree with Gabe, then? He was in Montpelier?"

Joe held up a hand. "Not necessarily, okay? But we need proof, other than Fanny's intuition, that he was in Mallard Cove."

"Well, don't count on the sheriff," I muttered. "Until the body shows up and tap dances on his doorstep, Gabe's dropping the case."

"That's what he says, but Gabe will figure it out. He's a smart guy."

"I've already figured it out. Travis killed that woman."

"What if she wasn't murdered?" Joe asked.

"What!?" I put down my wine. "I thought we already established that fact. Last night on your pontoon boat. No oars, remember?"

"But let's look at the facts." While I sputtered and pouted, my annoying neighbor calmly stated the facts. "We know she was dead, and we know someone moved her around. But we can't know much more until there's a body, and an autopsy."

"Travis La Barge knows," I said. "Miss Rusty knows, and Rose and Ruby know."

"Do you know you're nuts?"

"Wacko and Looney Tunes," I added. "What can you tell me about Lindsey Luke?"

"She's gorgeous."

"Terrific, but what else? She told me she also went to high school with Travis. Which means she went to school with Paige, right?"

Joe pointed to the ceiling. "Let's go upstairs."

"Whyyy?"

"Trust me," he said. He stood up and gestured for me to do the same.

I reminded him I most definitely did not trust him and followed.

***

Quantum Physics in the Nuclear Age: Theoretical Considerations, *Trouble-Free Calculations of Equilibrium Linear Velocities*, *The Big Book of Sudoku Puzzles: Level 5*. I read the titles on Paige Wylie's bookcase and concluded we had nothing in common. Even if we both lost our mothers when we were children and had both been raised by our fathers.

The FN451z beeped from somewhere down the hall, and I shot a sideways glance at Joe. And even if our fathers are both really, really, quirky.

He knelt down and pulled out a stack of yearbooks—four Hilleville High *Highpoints* from the bottom shelf. "What are we looking for?" he asked, and I reminded him that checking his daughter's yearbooks was his idea.

I sat down cross-legged, and he pushed two yearbooks my way. "Let's try pictures of Travis," I said and began paging through a book. "And Lindsey. And Paige, of course."

"Here's Travis." Joe handed me a book and tapped at a picture. Personally, I wouldn't have recognized the kid. He was in some sort of shop class, and wearing goggles.

"That's his talent," Joe was saying. "Travis is good at fixing things. In particular, he's a great electrician."

I wondered if the redhead had been electrocuted, shuddered, and kept looking. But we didn't find much more on Travis. The caption under his graduation photo told us he liked the Boston Red Sox and "partying."

Paige Wylie was everywhere in all four yearbooks—drama club, debating team, chess club, cross country skiing, cross country track.

"I don't see anything on Lindsey," I said eventually. "She told me she's a little older than Travis."

Joe hadn't noticed anything, either, so we re-checked the books for Lindsey Luke. Nothing.

"That's weird," Joe said.

"But does it matter?" I closed the book on my lap. "Even with pictures, I haven't learned anything useful. Other than you have a amazing daughter."

"Then it was useful." He was replacing the books on the shelves when we heard my father calling from below.

"You-hoo," he yelled. "Anyone home? Have you seen Cassie, Joe?"

"She's up here with me," he called down.

I sprang into standing position and went for the stairs.

Dad was smiling up at me. "What are you doing up there, girl?"

Chapter 16

"Quick dinner tonight," Dad said as I shoved him out the door and toward our own house. "It's Bingo night."

"I'm not going to Bingo, and you can wipe that smirk off your face," I said.

"What smirk?" he asked from behind the smirk. "Of course you're going to Bingo."

"I plan on staying home and pouting until further notice."

"You'll do no such thing." We walked inside, and Bobby directed me to the kitchen table. He set out two plates of leftover spaghetti. "Eat."

While we ate, we argued. My father had some bizarre notion that I had promised when I moved to Lake Bess that I'd always go to the Wednesday night Bingo game with him. I myself had no such memory.

"We haven't missed a Lake Bess Bingo since you moved here," he said.

"But I can't face all those Elizabethans. Everyone thinks I'm nuts."

"You are nuts. And you've been facing Elizabethans all day. You faced Fanny Baumgarten. You faced Joe Wylie." He waited until a looked up. "Should I even ask what you were doing in his bedroom?"

I put down my fork. "If you must know, we were in his daughter's bedroom."

"Kinky!"

"Da-aad! We were looking at her yearbooks."

He winked at Charlie. "How disappointing."

"Yeah, right." I picked up my fork. "Would you stop worrying about my love life? Start worrying about murder, instead." I described my conversations with Fanny and Lindsey, and Travis, and Joe, and my father lost any remaining residual smirk.

"Girl!" he said. "You can't go around accusing Travis La Barge of cold-blooded murder."

"It's not like anyone believes me." I twirled the last of the spaghetti onto my fork. "Everyone insists he's not violent."

"But what if he is? You could have been in danger."

"Fanny was with me."

"And she'd be a big help if the guy turned violent." Dad pointed to the dog. "Even Charlie would be better protection."

Charlie thumped his tail and dropped his tennis ball at my feet.

***

Dad pointed to the clock and stood up. "Let's walk," he said. "It stopped raining."

I told Charlie we'd play later, loaded the dishwasher, and Dad and I took off for Elizabeth Circle.

The dirt road was a mess from all the rain we had gotten, but Rose and Ruby didn't seem to mind. We waved to the gals, and then to Oden Poquette when he jogged by in pursuit.

"I should ask Oden to look for the dead woman," I told my father. "He has more energy than I do."

"Speaking of energy, or lack thereof," Dad said. "Maurice tells me Celia Stump is our new Bingo caller."

"Isn't she the woman with the energy level of a slug?"

"That's Celia."

"What possessed Maurice to pick her?" I asked.

Desperation was the answer. Maurice and Mimi Gallipeau, the couple who live on the other side of Joe, are in charge of Lake Bess Bingo. Their biggest challenge is keeping a Bingo caller on board. Every few weeks they recruit a new volunteer, and each volunteer promises to be faithful and show up every Wednesday, until death do they part. But it never works out, and Bingo callers around here are about as permanent as deputy sheriffs.

"When Celia quits, you should volunteer," Dad said.

"I'm too new."

"Nooo. You're a bona fide Elizabethan, just like me."

"Maybe I don't want to be an Elizabethan."

"Girl! That's blasphemy. And besides, you'd be the perfect Bingo caller. Proceeds go to the Lake School, and you're a teacher yourself. And you're reliable. You certainly won't run away to join the circus."

My father was referring to the Simon Haley Bingo debacle. According to legend, Simon had used his hallowed position as Bingo caller to rustle up dates. One night he picked up a female trapeze artist who was staying at the campground, and the two of them haven't been heard from since.

***

I love Mimi Gallipeau. She's one of the few people on Planet Earth who have to look up to catch my eye. And that night I loved her even more, since she gave me a great big smile as I entered Town Hall. "I'm glad you showed up," she told me as I paid the two dollar entrance fees for my father and me. "Show these folks what you're made of."

I thanked Mimi for the encouragement, and a hush fell over the crowd as I stepped into the room to show the folks what I was made of. Dot Stewart was collecting money for bingo cards, but when she saw me she couldn't seem to lift her hands to take my money. I waited, and eventually she got a hold of herself. Then all eyes followed as Dad and I found seats toward the back of the room, as far from Maxine Tibbitts as possible.

Unfortunately Evert Osgood and his dog were sitting with Maxine—Evert on a metal folding chair like the rest of us, and Miss Rusty at his feet. And yes, Evert brings his dog to Bingo. Evert brings his dog everywhere.

I was deciding how to talk to Evert, but still avoid Maxine and the swarm of children taking turns petting Miss Rusty, when Maurice leapt onto the little stage.

Our Bingo emcee, Maurice encourages the crowd to get excited about Lake Bess Bingo. Considering the prizes consist of really cheap toys or one of Mimi's homemade pies, this is no easy feat. But Maurice does his best. Whenever people start getting bored, he revives our enthusiasm by juggling, walking on his hands, or jumping rope. For a man about my father's age, he's surprisingly agile.

Maurice got us started with one of his painfully awful jokes, which invariably involves a Vermont farmer, a cow, and a civil servant, and then Celia Stump shuffled up to the stage. She plopped down on the Bingo caller's seat, yawned for a solid minute, and at some point mustered up the energy to call out the first number, I-17.

We searched our cards and waited, and within the next five minutes Celia called out the second number, B-2.

On and on it went. When Prissy Ott, who is five years old, raised her hand and asked Celia if she could please go faster, Maurice knew the crowd was getting restless. He took two hula hoops from the pile of prizes and started hula hooping, one at his waist and one on an arm.

Dad nudged me. "You should volunteer."

***

"You-hoo! Cassie! Bobby!" It was Maxine Tibbitts. It was Bingo intermission. It was hell. "Did you see my column this morning?" she called out as loudly as humanly possible.

"Yes!" all the Bingo players called back.

Like I said. Hell.

Everyone was in the parking lot, making their way over to the Lake Store for whatever snacks or sodas they needed to stay motivated for round two. And of course everyone stopped to stare as Maxine landed at my side.

My father patted my arm and stepped away. Using his teacher-voice and child-herding skills, he directed people toward the store, reminding them they only had fifteen minutes.

But Maxine blocked my path.

"What?" I snapped.

"My column!" she said. "I was pleased my editor ran it on the front page. Weren't you?"

"I was thrilled," I said, but of course Maxine didn't catch the sarcasm. I tried again. "And thanks for including the picture," I said. "Now everyone in the whole county will recognize me."

"Isn't it wonderful? It'll get lots of attention!" Maxine reached out to shake me. "You're so cute!"

"I was snarling in that picture."

"But only a little." She kept on smiling. "Now everyone will want to help you. They'll be on the lookout for your redhead."

"And you had to mention my pajamas?" I asked.

"Oh, absolutely!" Maxine shook me again. "That was part of the human-interest angle. Folks will be remembering you and your pajamas for days. Weeks! Maybe even months!"

***

Maybe Maxine shook me one too many times. Maybe she told me how darn cute I am one too many times. Or maybe I'm nuts. But an idea occurred to me, and I managed to shrug her off.

I marched into the store and elbowed my way through the Bingo players to get to the cash register.

Oliver looked up. Actually, everyone did.

"Can I have your attention?" I announced loud and clear. "I need everyone's help." I ignored the look on my father's face and spoke to the crowd. Loud and clear. "Everyone knows what I look like," I said, and everyone nodded. "But it's the dead redhead I need help with. Who was she?"

I described her in as best I could and glanced around at all the expectant faces. Evert Osgood was paying attention, as was Miss Rusty. But no one spoke up.

I sighed and turned to Oliver. "Do you have any ideas?" I asked a lot more quietly. "You know everyone around here, right?"

He shrugged modestly. "There's a family of redheads in Stone City," he said. "But no one in their twenties. You sure she was in her twenties?"

"Yes." I turned around again. "In fact," I continued, loud and clear. "She was about the same age as Travis La Barge. Isn't that interesting?" I asked, and my father stared at me, aghast.

I pursed my lips and stepped back to contemplate the moose head above the cash register. And something else occurred to me.

I waved to my father. "I'm leaving."

"Now?"

"Yes, now. I have to go home. But you stay." I thanked Oliver for his time, pushed Chester Stewart aside, and left in a great big hurry.

"Cassie, wait," Dad called from the porch. "What about Bingo?"

I told him the game would go on without me and kept walking. I had made it past the Congregational Church when Evert Osgood's truck pulled up.

"Want a lift?" he asked.

***

Evert didn't have to ask me twice. He did, however, have to convince Miss Rusty.

"Miss Cassie gets the people seat," he insisted. He gave her rump a good solid push, and with enough heaving and ho-ing, the dog finally got the hint.

She may have been reluctant to give up the passenger seat, and she may have taken up the entire area where my feet were supposed to go, but Miss Rusty was still totally lovable. She rested her snout on my left knee, and stared up at me with those basset hound eyes.

"Miss Rusty and me had an all-teerior motive for skipping the rest of Bingo," Evert told me as we began moving.

I stroked the dog's enormous ears. "The dead redhead?" I asked.

"I don't know who she was," he said. "But I know Fanny's right. Travis is to blame."

"He claims he wasn't even here. And Gabe Cleghorn believes him."

Evert downshifted to make it through one of the muddiest sections of the road. "Sheriff Gabe's real smart," he said. "But Fanny's smarter, if you know what I mean."

I did. I asked Evert if he had spoken to Fanny that evening. "Did she mention my theory?"

He nodded, but he also insisted Travis was not a murderer.

I swallowed a colorful word and stared out the window.

Evert glanced over. "I did me some thinking during Bingo," he said. "Came up with a theory of my own."

I shifted around. "You did?"

"Mm-hmm. Miss Rusty's a clue."

I looked at the dog. "You saw the murderer, didn't you?"

"We don't know about that," Evert said. "But the more I think about it, the more I'm sure Miss Rusty wasn't barking at them goats. She likes Oden's goats."

"She was barking at the murderer," I said.

"Nope. She was barking at Travis."

"She doesn't like Travis?" I asked.

"Oh, yes she does. Miss Rusty likes most everyone, and Travis gives her treats." Evert shifted again. "She visits Fanny when I get home from work, for her evening treat. And for her midnight treat she goes to Travis. I have a doggy door, so she comes and goes as she pleases while I'm asleep."

I thought about Miss Rusty's treats schedule. "But this was way past midnight," I said. "It was closer to 5 a.m."

"Yep. And there's my theory. Travis must have fed her twice—her midnight treat, and then again to stop her from barking that morning. Miss Rusty didn't eat her breakfast, if you know what I mean."

"Not really."

Evert reached out his hand, and Miss Rusty gave it a lick. "Miss Rusty's always hungry," he said. "I can't recollect her ever missing a meal before."

He pulled into Leftside Lane. "So there you have it," he said as he came to a stop in the driveway. "Solid proof Travis was home yesterday morning."

I scowled. "Because Miss Rusty didn't eat breakfast."

"I told you she's a clue."

Chapter 17

"You-hoo? Anyone home?" I let myself in Joe's screened door.

"Cassie?" he called from above. "Aren't you at Bingo?"

"No, I'm in your living room. And I need to see those yearbooks again."

"What are we looking for this time?"

"Not what, who." I met him on the top tread. "We're looking for the dead woman. Why didn't we think of it this afternoon?"

I slipped past him and headed for Paige's room. "But I was thinking about the redhead during the Bingo break, and then I was looking at that moose head over Oliver's cash register, and it was like, he spoke to me."

"The moose told you the redhead went to school with Paige?" Joe asked as we plopped ourselves on the floor again.

"I know it's crazy." I grabbed a couple yearbooks. "And don't worry—the moose didn't really talk to me. But he did inspire me." I was flipping through the pages pretty quickly, and Joe suggested I slow down. I flipped to the front and started again. "Did Paige go to school with any redheads?" I asked. "Flaming redheads?"

"The only flaming redheads I know are the McCrea family in Stone City."

"Oliver mentioned them."

"But none of them will be here." Joe tipped his head toward the yearbook in his lap. "Trisha's the youngest, and she's closer to my age than my daughter's."

"Look anyway," I said. "There has to be more redheads around here than one family in Stone City."

Joe looked up. "That's where Lindsey Luke lives."

"In Stone City? What's the population there—like fifty?"

"Probably closer to a hundred and fifty." He blinked. "Coincidence?"

"Oh, come on." I shook my head and reminded him he's a scientist. "Fact—it's not against the law to live in the boondocks. Or in the same town as these redheaded McCreas." I reached out and tapped his yearbook. "Keep looking."

He blinked again. "Paige reminded me about Lindsey when we talked. I'm sorry I didn't think to ask her about redheads."

I skipped a beat. "You talked to Paige about this?"

"I called her after you left for Bingo. I thought she might have insight on Travis."

"Did she?"

"Yes. But let's talk about Lindsey, first."

"So talk," I said. "Talk, talk, talk."

Joe held up a hand and told me to hold on. "Paige gave me some gossip, okay? But first she scolded me. She reminded me we scientists stick to the facts."

"Facts, gossip." I waved a hand. "I'm not a scientist—I'll take whatever I can get. Even the testimony of Miss Rusty."

"Excuse me?"

"What did Paige say about Lindsey?"

"She used to be Dean Taylor's girlfriend."

"Who?"

Joe leaned over and took the yearbook away from me. "This is the third time today I've looked at this thing," he said and shuffled through the pages until he found the picture of the Student Council from Paige's sophomore year.

"Dean Taylor was Senior Class president that year." He pointed out Dean and then showed me his graduation shot. "Looks pretty clean-cut, no?"

"He wasn't?"

"He was arrested for dealing drugs the summer after he graduated."

My mouth dropped open. "By Gabe?"

"Yep. It made headlines in the *Herald*. But until Paige reminded me, I'd forgotten all about it."

I asked if Lindsey had been arrested also, but Joe didn't think so.

"There's more," he said. "But remember we should separate facts from gossip."

"Separate what? What, what, what?"

He took a deep breath. "According to Paige— according to the Hilleville High gossip at the time—Lindsey had lots of boyfriends."

"Travis?"

"Yes, Travis." He held up a hand when I jumped. "Paige doesn't know that for a fact, okay? But apparently the guy likes tall women."

"Lindsey's tall," I said.

"And it's common knowledge Travis uses drugs."

While we searched again for pictures of Lindsey, Joe wondered out loud if she and Travis might still be friends.

"Not the impression I got today," I said. "But what else did Paige tell you about Travis?"

"Nothing good. Drugs and alcohol. But she insisted he's not violent."

I put down the yearbook, which still contained zero pictures of Lindsey Luke. "Why does everyone stick up for him? You Elizabethans make me bonkers."

"You're an Elizabethan, too," Joe said.

"Hardly."

We went back to redhead hunting but found nothing.

I leaned back against the bed and sighed. "So much for Mr. Moose Head's inspiration."

Joe sat back to join me, and we listened to the rain that had just started up, and to the FN, which had been beeping, burping, and chirping all along. I studied Paige's bookcase and wondered if I'd find a picture of propulsion pistons in *Practical Modeling of Multi-Component Mass Transfer Coefficients*.

"How was Bingo?" Joe asked.

"Why weren't you there?"

"Did you miss me?"

I gave him a withering look, and he mumbled something about a guy can dream. Then he told me he'd been working. I made the mistake of asking for details and thus learned everything I ever wanted to know about re-calibrating the FN451z.

"She's not cooperating," he said. "So I'm taking her down to Manchester tomorrow. She has a sister machine there. Hopefully she'll get straightened out."

"She?" I said. "Her? You really are a mad scientist."

"Yep."

"Speaking of crazy people, I need to go get Bobby." I glanced at the ceiling, and we listened to the rain. "We walked to Bingo."

"Maxine was there, wasn't she? She can drive him home."

"I'm sure she'd love to get Dad in her car."

"Among other places."

Say what? I glanced up, and Joe was staring at me. Was he actually leaning forward?

I quick grabbed a yearbook, but he reached over and took it away. "Come with me." He stood up and pulled me to my feet. "I want to show you something.

***

"I can't believe it's so big!" I stared, aghast.

"No, Cassie. That's the generator." Joe turned me around. "That's the FN451z."

I stared, aghast again, and the FN blurted out the usual beeps, burps, and chirps.

"I can't believe it's so small!" I said. "How can anything that little make so much noise?"

Joe smiled. "Lots of little things pack a big punch."

Chapter 18

"Beverly Crick is going bra shopping today," Dad informed me.

"And I need to know this at 5 a.m.?"

"It's 5:20."

Since it's impossible to roll your eyes when they're closed, I resigned myself to waking up. I sat up and yawned at my father, who was, of course, seated in the rocking chair next to my bed.

"Let me guess," I said. "Beverly won the grand prize last night."

FYI, the grand prize at Lake Bess Bingo is always a fifty-dollar gift certificate to Xavier's Department Store in Hilleville.

"See what you missed by leaving early?" Dad said.

"Evert Osgood left early also," I said. "He made a point of giving me a ride home."

Dad stopped rocking. "Oh, no."

"Oh, yes. Miss Rusty saw something, Dad." I patted the bed for Charlie to join me. "So now, if I can get her to corroborate her story with Rose and Ruby—"

"You're nuts."

"Speaking of lunatics." I raised an eyebrow. "Did Maxine give you a ride home?"

Dad scowled. "Why are you looking at me like that?"

"Joe thinks she likes you."

"As you would say, spare me." My father gave me the same look I was giving him. "You're spending a lot of time with Joe lately."

"Spare me."

"Why aren't you married, Cassie?"

"Da-aad. It's way too early to get into that again."

"Joe would make a good husband."

"Spare me!" I shooed Charlie away and got up. And while Bobby lamented his woeful, grandchild-less state, I rummaged around in my closet and came out with a handful of wrinkled stuff. "I'm going kayaking," I said. "I'll paddle over to the store for the newspaper."

"Why didn't you marry Kyle?"

"Kyle Caprio is a pompous ass."

"Joe Wylie isn't a pompous ass."

"Nope. He's a mad scientist."

"And you're cute as a button, intelligent, and charming. You're quite a catch, girl."

I showed Charlie the ratty old Hawaiian shirt I was holding. "Next thing I know, he'll be saying I'm a snappy dresser."

Dad shrugged. "One minor flaw. And you do have that problem with patience. But still."

"Why aren't you married?" I asked. "You're cute and smart. And you really are charming, and a snappy dresser, and patient." I winked at Charlie. "No wonder Maxine has a crush on you."

"I'll tell you who has a crush on whom."

"I do not have a crush on Joe."

"Well, you should. He has a crush on you."

"Spare me." I stood in my bathroom doorway, but my father still didn't get the hint.

"Why do you think he's over here all the time, girl?"

"Because you invite him. And can we please stop talking like we're sixteen? Crushes. Sheesh!"

"You're right." Dad got up and called to Charlie. "Joe's far too dignified to harbor a crush."

"What's that supposed to mean?" I called after them.

"You're a big girl. Figure it out."

***

"How do I look?" Dad asked as he came down the stairs.

I glanced up from loading our Cheerios bowls into the dishwasher, he stood at attention, and I assessed his outfit. Bobby wore linen slacks, a blue linen sport coat, and his favorite bow tie—the one with R2D2 and C3PO on it. "As Bambi would say, hunky-boo."

"Girl," he scolded. "Do I look like a successful author? Do I look professional?"

"Absolutely." I smiled and assured my father he had risen to the occasion, as usual.

But the occasion itself was a bit unusual. Dad was driving to Albany, New York for a science fiction convention. And even more exciting than me getting a whole day to myself, he was finally going to meet his favorite author, Lucille Saxby. He'd been looking forward to it for weeks, and was one of three lucky fans to win a private interview. Of course he planned on telling the amazing Ms. Saxby all about Chance Dooley.

"I'm so nervous!" Dad said as Charlie and I walked him out to his car. "Lucille Saxby. In the flesh!"

"You have all the books you want her to autograph?" I asked, and he tapped his satchel. "And some copies of your stories to show her?" Tap, tap. "Be sure to mention Chance's propulsion pistons problem," I said. "Maybe she'll have some suggestions."

"Good Lord! Do you think she'll be that interested?"

"Absolutely." I opened the car door and handed Dad a thermos of coffee. He gave me a peck on the cheek and climbed in.

"Cassie, wait." He held the door open and asked about my plans for the day.

I pointed to the Jolly Green Monster.

"You'll stay out of trouble?"

"Promise," I said and crossed my fingers behind my back.

"Uncross your fingers," he told me.

***

Sarah Bliss wasn't exactly trouble, but she was troublesome. And she was, of course, guarding the entrance to the sheriff's office. "This is becoming a bad habit," she said.

I agreed wholeheartedly and asked to see Gabe. And for the second morning in a row, endured that uncomfortable vinyl chair and Sarah's uncomfortable stares, before Gabe rescued me.

"What's up?" he asked as we took our seats in his office.

"Travis La Barge," I said. "I think he's behind all this."

Gabe frowned. "What happened to your Fox Cove Inn theory?"

"I've changed my mind. I've talked to more people."

"Figures."

I cleared my throat. "Fanny Baumgarten, Lindsey Luke, and Evert Osgood all agree that Travis is somehow responsible."

"He was in Montpelier."

"No. He was in Mallard Cove."

"Then how come no one saw him? How come you didn't see him?"

"I was flustered."

"Figures."

I took a deep breath. "Fanny's convinced he was there," I said. "And everyone knows Fanny's always right. And you yourself told me Miss Rusty barked at something. Evert thinks she barked at Travis, and he fed her something to shut her up. Miss Rusty had no appetite for breakfast that morning."

Gabe shook his head. "That's your proof? You need to stop harassing your neighbors, Cassie. I'm getting complaints."

"Oh, please. From who?"

"Who do you think? From Travis. From his mother." Gabe picked up a pen and started clicking. "Do you know Janet La Barge?"

"Not personally. But I've seen her campaign commercials for her husband."

"She's threatening to get me fired unless I rein you in."

"You're an elected official, Gabe."

"Even so." Click, click. "I need you to cool it, Cassie."

I stared at the pen. "You realize Janet's behavior fits with what I'm saying? She's protecting her son because he murdered that woman."

"Or the opposite," Gabe said. "Travis has nothing to do with it, and his mother's upset he's being accused of murder."

It took me a minute to think of a comeback. "How about this?" I sat forward. "Since we can't prove he was at Mallard Cove, let's prove he wasn't in Montpelier. Have you checked with Cars! Cars! Cars! to verify his story?" I asked. "Or Mandy's?"

He stopped clicking. "Who's Mandy?"

"Ga-aabe! It's the bar in Montpelier. Travis claims he was there Monday night. Can't you at least check his alibis?"

"No can do."

"What? Why?"

"Think, will you? Without a body, there is no crime." He dropped the pen. "I can't spy on private citizens for no good reason. It's illegal."

"Yep," I said. "And so is murder."

Chapter 19

"You're kidding me, right?" Bambi asked.

"No. I'm serious."

"You're seriously, right now, in Montpelier, spying on the La Barges?"

"Someone has to." I glanced at the mansion across the street from where I was parked. "The sheriff says it's illegal for him to do it."

"Perfect! The sheriff said no, so you rushed straight over to confront someone you just told me you suspect of murder."

"I don't intend to confront anyone right this minute. And I didn't rush. I drove home to let Charlie out, first. And then Mr. Hooper's cows delayed me some more."

FYI, the drive from Lake Elizabeth to Montpelier normally takes about twenty minutes. But this is Vermont, and normal is a relative term. The drive takes a lot longer if the cows at the Hooper farm decide they need a change of scenery while you happen to be driving by. Traffic in both directions waits while the herd of Holsteins walks in cow time—which is slower than Celia-Stump time—across Route 19 and into the pasture on the other side.

"I stopped to smell the cow manure and tried calling you," I said. "To warn you ahead of time."

"Let me guess. Your cell phone didn't work."

"Mr. Hooper's cows performing a synchronized dance step would have been more likely."

While Bambi made some not-so-encouraging noises, I reminded her how lucky it is that cell phones do work within Montpelier city limits. "And luckily, I figured out where the La Barges live."

"You're brilliant," Bambi said. But in case you haven't quite caught on, she was being sarcastic. Montpelier is the state capital, but it's a very small city. And considering Crabtree College is there, and I lived there for twenty years, I know my way around, and knew where to find the fanciest neighborhood in town.

"I looked up their address, and here I am," I said.

"I know I'm going to regret asking this. But what are you doing? How illegal are you?"

"Zero illegal. I'm simply parked out front, watching."

"Not obvious at all, I'm sure."

I decided to back up a bit. "They don't know my Honda." I stopped the engine again. "And I'm hiding behind a maple tree."

"Cassie! What exactly do you expect to see? Is the missing body propped up on the front stoop?"

"Nooo." I stared in front of me. "The only things I see are the three or four thousand Ross the Boss for Governor posters decorating the front lawn."

Bambi groaned.

"I'd love to go inside and snoop around," I said. "Take a peeky in the closets, check under the beds. You know, to see what turns up."

"You're nuts."

"Wacko and Looney Tunes. And after I'm done here, we'll go to Cars! Cars! Cars!"

"We?"

"You're coming with me."

"Remind me why I answered the phone."

"And after the car lot, we'll go to Mandy's for lunch. My treat."

"Remind me why I answered the pho—"

"Holy moly!" I hunkered down. "You will never guess who just drove up!"

"The dead redhead?"

"Nooo! It's Travis." I watched him park and walk inside. "I'd love to take a peeky in his car," I said. "Do you think I'd get caught?"

"Do you think at all?"

***

"Ross the Boss for governor! A car in every garage!"

Bambi and I stared at the banner hanging over the entrance at Cars! Cars! Cars! Unlike that sign, or the American flag that can probably be seen from Whoozit, we were being discreet. We had parked in the strip mall across the street, and we were gathering up our nerve.

"What does that slogan even mean?" Bambi asked.

I grinned. "It means Ross the Boss is busy on the campaign trail and not here."

"Would he recognize you?"

I doubted it. But I still felt better knowing he was preoccupied elsewhere.

"So what's the plan?" she asked as I started the car.

"Easy." I said. "I'll pretend to be looking for a used car, and you'll pretend to help me."

"Cassie, wait." She put a hand out, and I killed the engine.

"For what?"

"We need a clearer plan—a more precise experiment."

"You sound like Joe Wylie."

"Ooo! That's good."

"What is?"

Bambi pointed to the car lot. "We'll say you're buying your boyfriend Joe a truck for his birthday—"

"Joe's not my boyfriend."

"And I'm here to help since you don't know anything about trucks."

"And you do?"

"My brother has one."

I rolled my eyes, and Bambi said something about aliases.

"I'll be Barbara Smith. And you're Cassandra Jones."

I tilted my head. "Is your full name really Barbara?"

"Do you think I'd use Bambi if it were?"

I started the engine again, but she grabbed my arm.

"What now?"

"Patience is a virtue," she said, and I rolled my eyes again. "I mean it, Cassie. The more time we spend in there, the more we find out. We need to browse, and you need to act very indecisive and confused."

"That won't be hard."

***

A group of salesmen swarmed my car, but only one of them won the battle.

He opened my door and yanked me out. "How are you ladies today? It's a fine day, isn't it? Might be some rain later on, though. Larry Suggs here. What can I do to put you ladies in the car of your dreams?"

I backed away, but Bambi seemed perfectly at ease. She came around from the passenger side and introduced herself. "I'm Dr. Barbara Smith." She held out her hand. "And this is Dr. Cassandra Jones."

"Lady doctors!" Larry leered. "Want to take my temperature?"

I curled my lip while Dr. Smith told the fool we were college professors. "Dr. Jones is looking for a truck for her boyfriend," she explained. "Joe wants a big truck for his birthday. Isn't that right, Cassandra?"

I squeaked something incoherent, and Larry led us to the trucks, where we proceeded to "browse."

Pussy-footing around is more like it. I spent at least ten minutes listening to Larry and Bambi-Barbara debate the ins and outs of bed capacity and four-wheel drive before interrupting.

"So, Larry," I said as we inspected a gigantic red truck. "Does Ross the Boss think he'll win this fall?" I ignored Bambi's frown and smiled sweetly. "He's exactly what Vermont needs—someone with good solid business sense."

"Mr. La Barge usually gets what he wants," Larry said. "And Mrs. La Barge always does. Now then." He rubbed his palms together. "Which of these beauties can I interest you in, little lady?"

Little lady—I kid you not.

Bambi stepped forward before I slugged the guy and patted the red truck looming over us. "You seem to like this one, Cassandra." She ignored my frown and smiled sweetly. "Do you think Joe would like it?"

"Of course he would!" Larry said, and before I could stop him, he opened the door and hoisted me inside.

I glanced around. That truck would dwarf the Spaceship Destiny. And it definitely dwarfed me. The steering wheel was only slightly smaller than a Ferris wheel, and the gas pedal looked ready to devour my size-five foot for lunch. But no worries there. No way I could ever reach the pedals.

I asked Larry if he didn't have a nice little scooter I might try, but he ignored me. "Let's take it for a spin!" he chirped.

"No," I said firmly and suggested Dr. Smith get behind the wheel, instead. "You might even reach the gas pedal," I told my tall friend.

But obviously my tall friend thought it would be great entertainment to watch me drive the ridiculous truck. "Two against one," she said and hopped into the back seat. And yes, of course the Jolly Red Giant had a back seat.

While Larry scurried off to get some peddle-lifts, I yanked the rear view mirror down to where I could actually view something at my rear. "I hate you," I said.

Bambi looked up from buckling her seat belt. "Joe is going to love this truck."

Larry came back, got me situated, and buckled himself into the passenger seat.

I started the engine. "Off we go!" I said and hit the gas.

***

First things first. I drove over two curbs.

Larry screamed, Bambi hissed a colorful word, and I drove off—literally off—the Cars! Cars! Cars! lot.

Luckily, I did better once we were on the open road. Never mind what Bambi claims.

But managing the Jolly Red Giant took all my concentration, and I couldn't ask Larry anything about the La Barges. And Bambi was no help since she was too busy cursing the fates and praying for dear life.

Larry was kind of distracted, too. He clutched the dashboard and kept assuring me the truck was fully insured for test drivers.

After what Bambi still insists were the five most terrifying minutes of her life, we made it back to the car lot, and I parked the thing. Well, maybe not parked, exactly. But I did stop the engine, and Larry took the keys away from me.

He and Bambi seemed in a hurry to escape from their side, but when I opened my door it was a long drop down to the pavement. Larry rounded the truck and hovered below, and I jumped.

"Let's crunch the numbers!" he said once he had me settled on my own two feet. He began outlining the "excellent" financing options available at Cars! Cars! Cars!, but I interrupted.

"Could you give us a minute?" I asked him. "This is a big decision."

"It's a big truck!"

"I think we've proven that," Bambi mumbled.

Larry took a few conciliatory steps back, and Bambi leaned forward. "I almost wet my pants when you aimed for that flagpole," she whispered.

"I missed the flagpole by at least three inches," I whispered back.

"Try one."

I took another look at my parking job. "One and a half," I said. "And that's not the issue. Travis is the issue, and we haven't even mentioned him." I jerked a thumb at the truck. "How the heck am I going to get out of buying this thing?"

"Give phony bank info."

"Really?' I asked. "Larry won't catch me?"

"Not today, he won't. He'll call you tomorrow. You can think about that tomorrow."

"Like Scarlett O'Hara?" I asked, but Bambi was already waving to Larry.

"We'll take it!" she said.

***

Like everything else at Cars! Cars! Cars!, the showroom was enormous. We settled ourselves at a large desk at the back wall, and Larry handed me a stack of paperwork and began fiddling with the computer.

He paused, his fingers poised above the keyboard. "Your address and phone number, Dr. Jones?"

Bambi elbowed me, and I remembered my name. I thought fast and gave my old apartment address but decided it wouldn't hurt to use my actual cell phone number. He'd never reach me on that.

Larry had other questions, but I ignored him and concentrated on the photographs of the sales staff lining the wall above his head. Ross the Boss presided over everyone else. And Travis was up there, too. Right in the middle of the row of pictures below Ross.

"Is that Ross the Boss's son?" I pointed to Travis's photograph. "The family resemblance is striking. Father and son are such handsome men."

Bambi looked at me as if I had lost my mind, and Larry also frowned. He handed me a list of "Upgrade Options" and explained why the sticker price on the truck was only a rough estimate.

Bambi leaned over to take a look. "You mean she has to buy the tires separately?" she asked, and Larry assured us they were top of the line.

"But back to Ross's son," I said. "Why haven't I ever seen him in the Cars! Cars! Cars! commercials?" I pointed again. "Especially since he works here."

"Supposedly works here." Larry snorted. "Mr. La Barge won't ever flaunt that kid on TV."

I caught Bambi's eye. "Why's that?"

Larry jerked a thumb over his shoulder. "That's as clean and sober as I've ever seen Travis."

I feigned shock. "Ross the Boss allows his son to drink at work?"

Another snort. "No worries there, little lady. Travis has been here maybe twice in his whole life."

About then, an older guy in glasses joined us, and Larry started clicking furiously at the keyboard.

"You ladies getting everything you need from Larry?" the guy in glasses asked.

"We're on a roll," Bambi said.

***

"Staff meeting in five minutes!" a female voice announced from behind us, and the paperwork on my lap went flying.

"Oh, no," I mouthed to Bambi as the two of us shifted slightly to take a peeky.

"Oh, yes," she hissed. She grabbed my arm, and we hit the deck as Janet La Barge swept across the room. We were feigning great interest in gathering up the paperwork when she stopped in front of us.

Insert colorful words . . . Here.

Chapter 20

"Do you think she recognized me?" I asked.

"Do you think at all?" Bambi said. "What possessed you to run away like that?"

"Fear, panic." I stared past my dashboard at Cars! Cars! Cars! "Terror."

Bambi admitted Janet was a little scary. "But you're not on TV, like she is. And you've never actually seen her at Lake Bess, right? So she wouldn't recognize you, right?"

"Not unless she's seen the latest *Hanahan Herald*."

Bambi groaned. "And she had to notice how we high-tailed it out of there. Larry screaming, 'Wait, Dr. Jones! Wait!' wasn't exactly subtle."

"Speaking of which," I said. "Why, oh why, did you tell him we're college professors?"

"We are college professors. I thought our doctor titles would give us an air of authority."

I started the engine. "There's a first time for everything."

***

"Dr. Baxter?" Keith Wheeler hollered from behind the bar. "Is that really you?"

"There's a first time for everything." I waved to my former student, and Bambi and I made our way over.

Mandy's is a Crabtree College hangout, so it made sense that I'd know the bartender. And I guess it also made sense Keith would be shocked to see me. Mandy's is a student hang out, not faculty.

"I can't believe it's you," he said.

I told him even teachers have to eat and introduced him to Dr. Vixen, and Bambi and I took two bar stools as he continued staring. "Our burgers are good," he said.

We agreed to burgers, Bambi ordered a beer, and I took a Diet Coke.

"Can he be trusted?" she whispered as he left to place our orders.

I sure hoped so. But Keith was back with our drinks before I had time to think about it.

"Anything else?" he asked.

"Yes," I said before I lost my courage. "I need your help."

"I haven't seen your dead girl," he said, and Bambi choked on her beer.

***

Being authoritative college professors, we recovered. "I take it you saw this week's *Hanahan Herald*?" I asked Keith.

"Hanahan Who?"

Bambi helped me out and asked him how he knew about the dead woman.

"Oh, everyone knows."

I made the mistake of asking who everyone was and quickly discovered that the Crabtree College grapevine was alive and kicking, even during the summer. Keith had heard the story from a student named Frank Hershey. Frank had heard from another student, Heather Something, who had heard about it from a Reba Something.

"And Reba has a cousin, or brother, or something in the Lake Elizabeth Fire Department," Keith said. "Did you really find her naked?"

"Nooo," I said. "She wasn't naked."

"Umm, that's not what I meant, Dr. Baxter."

I hesitated, but had to ask, "What did you mean?"

"Everyone's saying you were naked."

I shoved aside my Diet Coke and ordered a beer.

***

While I sipped bad beer, Bambi enlightened Keith on the basic facts, and a waitress brought our lunch.

He waited until she stepped away. "You were in your pajamas?" he whispered.

I put down a French fry. "My outfit isn't the issue." I used my teacher-voice. "The missing woman is the issue. And I think you might know something."

"Me!?"

"Yes, you. You work here, don't you?"

"You think the redhead hung out at Mandy's?" Keith asked. "I don't think so, okay? I'd remember a girl like that."

I shook my head and told him I had something else in mind. "I think you might know someone who knew the redhead."

"Me?"

Bambi tapped my knee. "Subtlety," she whispered.

But in case you haven't quite caught on, subtlety isn't one of my better skills. I had no idea how to find out about Travis without actually mentioning Travis. I mentioned Travis.

"How do you know Travis?" Keith asked. "He doesn't go to Crabtree."

I ignored the question and asked my own. "Was Travis La Barge in here on Monday?"

Keith gave it some thought. "No," he said. "Mondays are our slowest night, so I'm pretty sure I'd remember him. Especially if he was with that redhead." He squinted. "Did Travis know the dead girl?"

I ignored that question also. "What about drugs?" I asked, and Keith jumped ten feet in the air. I waited until he landed. "I'm curious where he gets his drugs."

"Umm, let me get that bill for you," Keith said and ran away.

Bambi looked up from her lunch. "Subtlety is your middle name," she told me.

I didn't have to respond, because about then, my cell phone rang. "There really is a first time for everything," I said. I didn't recognize the number, but it was from Hilleville. Hoping it was Gabe, I answered.

"Cassie! It's Maxine!" She didn't wait for a response. "I am so glad you answered! I'm at the library, and I called your house, but no one answered, and I was afraid I didn't have this number, but I finally found it, and then I was afraid it wouldn't go through, because you know how cell phones work around here, and then I was afraid—"

"Maxine!" I interrupted. "I'm busy. What is it?"

"It's the dead woman, Cassie. They found her."

Chapter 21

"What!? Who? Where? When?" I looked at Bambi. "How?"

"I don't know," Maxine said. "It just came over the newswires, and my editor at the *Herald* called me. I hung up on him to call you."

"Did Gabe find her?"

"I don't know," she whined. "But wherever you are, turn on a TV. Channel 9 is your best bet. This should get a special report."

I hung up, gestured to Keith, and pointed to the TV overhead. "Channel 9."

***

"That's a lot of mud," Bambi said.

"That's a lot of state troopers," Keith said.

I shushed them both, and we watched the TV.

A Channel 9 reporter and a bunch of state troopers and other official-looking people were wandering around in the mud at Golden Rock—a popular hiking spot just outside Montpelier.

The reporter interviewed the trooper in charge, and we learned some hikers had discovered the body of a woman that morning. The reporter asked for details.

"We know very little right now," the cop said. "But we suspect foul play."

"No kidding," I said, and Bambi reached over for my hand.

"It seems likely the body has been here a few days," he said.

"No kidding again."

The reporter asked if the woman had been identified, and the trooper said not yet. "But we estimate she was in her twenties, and she had red hair."

"No kidding, no kidding, no kidding."

"We're asking anyone with any information to contact their local authori—"

I squeezed Bambi's hand. "Can you get a ride home?"

"Go," she said, and I ran for the door.

***

"What do you want?" Sarah Bliss was her usual cordial self.

"I want to see Gabe," I said. "I don't intend to put up with your garbage. And I don't intend to wait."

"He's not here."

"Well where the hell is h—" I stopped and took a deep breath. This was a good thing, right? Gabe had better things to do than pussy-foot around with me, right?

I changed my tone. "He's heard the news, hasn't he?" I asked. "Is he in Montpelier?"

"How should I know? Why Montpelier?"

"Sarah! Because that's where the body was found. That's where Trav—" I stopped myself again. "Is Gabe at Golden Rock?" I asked.

"It's out of his jurisdiction."

"Pardon me?"

"Golden Rock is in the next county."

"What!? Are you actually telling me Gabe doesn't care because she was found in the next county?" I flapped my arms, and jumped up and down, and pretty much went nuts.

"Would you calm down?"

"No!" I screamed, and she flinched. "If I don't get some satisfaction I swear I will jump over this counter and strangle you, you stupid—"

She held up a hand. "Maybe I'll let you talk to P. T."

"Who's P. T.?"

She reached for her phone. "You'll see."

Unfortunately, I did. Almost immediately, a very young deputy sheriff popped out from the hallway and lunged for my hand.

"P.T. Dent at your service!"

***

I'll spare you the stupid conversation about the stupid weather, and how long it took the deputy to lead me to the door with the stupid paper nametag. But eventually, we were sitting in his office, and P. T. was fumbling to find paper and pen.

"What can we do for you today, Ms. Baxter?"

"I know about the body they found at Golden Rock."

A blank stare.

I tried again. "Do you know about the body they found at Golden Rock?"

Another blank stare, but I assume he noticed the steam that was coming out my ears. "It's supposed to be my day off," he said. "But Sheriff Gabe called me in. He left in a real hurry and told me to man the ship."

"But he didn't tell you why?" I said. "Sarah didn't tell you why? You really don't know why?"

"Why?"

I explained why.

"You think the woman at Golden Rock is the person you saw in Mallard Cove?" he asked.

"I know she is."

"But it's a different county. And your woman was only sleeping."

I walked out before I strangled him.

***

I considered going to the Hilleville Police Department, but I wasn't in the mood for a fender bender, right then. So instead I headed back to Montpelier—this time to the State Troopers office. Why I hadn't thought of that in the first place, I don't know. But I knew where the headquarters were, parked my car, and marched in.

"I want—I demand—to see the person in charge," I told the trooper who greeted me. "I know about the woman at Golden Rock."

He looked me up and down. "Curly blond hair, teeny-tiny." He caught my eye. "Are you Cassandra Baxter?" he asked. "Captain Sterling's been looking for you."

Chapter 22

Captain Jason Sterling didn't pussy-foot around. By the time we got settled in his office, he knew I'd seen him on TV, and I knew he had heard about me from Gabe.

"Cleghorn gave me your contact info, but not much else," Sterling said. "I left a message at your home, and I tried your cell, but you know how that works." He pulled out a legal pad and about a dozen pencils. "Now then," he said. "What happened Tuesday? I want all the details."

I did my best.

"Did anyone else see anything?" he asked as I finished up.

"Miss Rusty."

"Rusty." He wrote down the name. "First name or last?"

"She's a dog."

Sterling looked up. "Excuse me?"

"Miss Rusty is Evert Osgood's basset hound. She barked at something that morning. No," I corrected myself. "She barked at someone. I think she saw Travis La Barge, and he fed her to shut her up, and—"

Sterling held up a hand. "Other witnesses?"

"Rose and Ruby."

"More dogs?"

"Nope. Goats." While Sterling wrote down their names, I explained Oden Poquette's goat problem. "I know it sounds crazy," I said. "But Rose and Ruby saw even more than Miss Rusty did."

Sterling told me not to feel bad. "This can't be the first crime in Vermont witnessed by livestock."

"It gets better," I said. "My other witness is Fanny Baumgarten."

"Is she a cow?"

"No. Fanny's a lovely old lady."

"That's good."

"She's blind."

He cringed. "That's bad."

"No kidding."

He returned to his notes and asked how to spell Baumgarten.

"Fanny's old and blind, but she's actually an excellent witnesses," I said. "She's very alert."

"Blind people have to be," he agreed and asked if there was anyone he should talk to. "Humans, preferably."

I mentioned the Fox Cove Inn. "They were close enough to see something, but supposedly no one did."

"You're not convinced of that?"

"You should talk to the owners," I said. "Arlene Pearson, in particular."

Sterling squinted. "Pearson, as in the ghosts? Please don't tell me a ghost saw something."

"All the ghost-guys are male. Arlene's female. And you should definitely talk to Travis La Barge. I'm almost positive he's the guy responsible."

Sterling broke a pencil in half. "Cleghorn warned me you've been harassing La Barge."

"Somebody had to," I said. "Since Cleghorn, as you call him, refused to take me seriously. The Cassandra Syndrome strikes again."

"Excuse me."

"No one believed Cassandra, and look at what happened to Troy."

"Troy?" Sterling asked. "Does he live in Mallard Cove, too?"

I rolled my eyes and suggested we concentrate on Travis. "If he's half as arrogant with you as he was with Fanny and me, you'll arrest him on the spot."

"You and the blind old lady talked to him?" Sterling broke another pencil. "When?"

"Yesterday. And I've done some more investigating today."

"You confronted him again?"

"Nooo. I was completely stealth. Travis didn't even see me at his parents' house."

The cop blinked. "Excuse me?"

"His parents live here in Montpelier," I said. "Although his mother might have recognized me at Cars!

Cars! Cars! But Bambi and I decided that's highly unlikely and headed on over to Mandy's."

"Mandy? Bambi?"

"Mandy's Bar and Grill and Dr. Bambi Lovely-Vixen." I waved a hand before he could even comment. "I know, I know. Bambi doesn't sound so smart, but she is. And she's terrific at this sleuthing stuff. She came up with aliases for us and everything."

Sterling broke two more pencils. "I know I'm going to regret asking this," he said. "But why did you need aliases?"

"At Cars! Cars! Cars! of course. You do know Travis La Barge is Ross the Boss's son?"

Captain Sterling started groaning in an odd way.

"We didn't use aliases at Mandy's," I continued. "It wouldn't have worked, since the bartender knew me."

Several pencil pieces went flying.

I glanced up and caught what was raining down in my direction. "Actually, I've saved you a lot of trouble," I said. "I've disproved both of Travis's alibis. He simply was not in Montpelier earlier this week. But the ironic thing is, he's here now. Which is quite convenient for you. The La Barge house can't be more than a five minute drive."

Sterling stared, aghast.

"I can go with you, if you want."

***

Let's just say Captain Sterling wasn't thrilled with that idea.

"Okay, then." I stared at the pile of pencil rubble. "Maybe we should move on to the details I don't know."

"Are there any?"

"Very funny." I smirked. "What about the dead woman? Who is she, how did she die, who found her?"

He shoved the pencils in the trash and told me two hikers had found her. "I can't believe they were out there with all the rain we've been having. The trail is a muddy mess."

"Who are they?" I asked. "I'd like to thank them."

Sterling wouldn't give me their names, but he did tell me they were two women from Hilleville. "And they knew all about you," he said. "Something about your local paper?"

I groaned.

"Well anyway," Sterling said. "They saw the body and thought of you. They called 911 as soon as they had cell coverage."

"She was just lying there?" I asked. "On the trail?"

Worse, if possible. Sterling told me the body was discovered only a few yards from the trailhead. "She was in pretty bad shape." He toyed with another pencil. "Some animals found her before we did."

"She'd been there since Tuesday," I said quietly.

Sterling waited until I looked up. "Thank you for your help."

I sighed. "Maybe Travis planned on hiding her better."

"Maybe whoever." He emphasized the whoever. "Couldn't make it further into the woods due to the conditions."

I asked if "whoever" had left any tracks, but any evidence had been washed away in the rain. I asked what killed her, but the autopsy report wasn't finished.

"Natural causes seems unlikely," Sterling said. "And we've ruled out gunshot wound, but we haven't rule out other violence."

"She wasn't stabbed, and she wasn't beaten up," I said firmly. "There was no blood."

Sterling made a note and thanked me again.

"Maybe it was a drug overdose," I said. "Travis uses drugs."

"You have details on that?"

I shook my head, and Sterling assured me the medical examiner would look for drugs. "We're also working on ID," he said. "She doesn't fit any missing persons reports."

"Well, why not?" I asked. "Doesn't anyone care about her? Other than me?"

"If she has a criminal record, we'll be able to ID her through DNA."

"And if she wasn't a criminal?"

Sterling insisted someone probably did care and would come forward as soon as they saw the police sketch. He pulled a sheet from the file on his desk and slid it toward me. "All the news outlets are going to run this," he said. "Does it look accurate?"

I stared at the black and white drawing for a long time. "She had green eyes," I said quietly.

Chapter 23

"A big truck for a little lady!" Larry the car guy left the first of the hundred or so phone messages waiting for me when I arrived home. "Your beau is going to love this truck!"

"Beau?" I asked Charlie. "Little lady? What century is this guy from?" I thought some more. "And how did he get this number?"

Larry had other concerns. He knocked three hundred dollars off the price and threw in a complimentary ice scraper if I called him before the end of the business day.

I hit delete.

Maxine had left a message before she found my cell phone number, and Oliver called to tell me how happy he was that the redhead had been found. I could hear Chester and Hollis in the background insisting they believed me all along.

"It's what kept me going," I told the machine, and Charlie and I listened to Gabe's message.

He told me the news and assured me he was working with the state troopers to identify the mystery woman.

"About time," I said and moved on to Captain Sterling's message. He had called about twenty minutes before I showed up at his office, asking me to contact him ASAP.

"Done," I said and hit delete again.

The last two messages were also interesting. Fanny Baumgarten was elated with the news, and Pru Pearson sounded—I glanced at Charlie. "She sounds scared," I said.

Whatever their moods, both women invited me to stop by that afternoon. And to make the idea of me visiting the Fox Cove Inn even remotely plausible, Pru promised Arlene wouldn't be home.

"Let's go," I said and walked to the door. But Charlie sat still, and I remembered I had a call of my own to make.

***

I tried to keep my voice from cracking. "They found her, Dad."

"What!? Where? When?" He thought a second. "How?"

I explained all I knew.

"It's a good day, girl."

I smiled. "Yes it is, old man."

"I've had a good day, too," he said. "Lucille Saxby likes Chance Dooley! She asked me out to dinner to discuss his propulsion pistons."

I rolled my eyes at Charlie. FYI, Lucille Saxby is a very attractive, sixtyish woman. "You actually have a date with Lucille Saxby?"

"Nooo. This is business." Dad reminded me it's a four hour drive from Albany and told me not to wait up. I suggested he stay the night, but he insisted he'd come home. "If I didn't, who knows what you'd imagine."

***

"You are such a dear to come by," Fanny said.

I jumped and looked up, and she standing was at the railing of her upstairs porch. "How did you know I was down here, Fanny?"

"I heard you."

"But I'm walking."

"Do you have someone with you?" she asked.

I shook my head. Leave it to Fanny Baumgarten to hear Charlie, the quietest dog on Planet Earth. I made sure he was welcome upstairs, and by the time we got there, Fanny was digging into the Doggie Treats jar.

"I'm sure Miss Rusty won't mind sharing." She held out her hand, and Charlie seemed to agree. After she finished with Charlie, she invited me to sit down. "I wish I could give Maxy Tibbitts a treat," she said. "I used to scold her for her gossiping, but her story worked, didn't it?"

"I guess it did," I said. "The hikers knew what they had found this morning. And it was nice of Maxine to call me as soon as she heard the news." I looked around and asked Fanny how she had heard. "Did Lindsey tell you? Where is she?"

"Love's at home today." Fanny clapped her hands. "Preparing for tomorrow."

"What's tomorrow?"

Evidently, Lindsey Luke had an important art show in Woodstock the next day. A well-connected art dealer was interested in her work.

"Ms. Ingleby has connections in Boston!" Fanny said. "Isn't that exciting? I can't wait to meet her."

"You're going also?"

"Love says she needs my moral support."

I thought about Paige Wylie's yearbooks. "Lindsey must be very talented," I said. "Where did she go to art school?"

"She's self taught." Fanny smiled and shook her head. "Lindsey's such a love. She's so busy today, but she's still making time to call me regularly. To keep me posted on the news."

Fanny told me she'd also had the TV on most of the afternoon. "And I'm sure I'll learn even more from Captain Sterling. You've spoken to him, Cassie?"

"I have."

"He's promised to stop by this evening to talk to Evert and me. Hopefully Travis will be back by then, too."

I told Fanny I liked Sterling, and that I was thrilled he wanted to talk to her. "This guy means business."

"And of course Gabe's been awfully busy, too."

I blinked. "He has?"

"Oh, yes. He's stopped by several times looking for Travis." She shook her head. "I still can't bring myself to accept that Travis harmed that girl, but no one's seen hide nor hair of him all day."

"Because he's in Montpel—"

"There he is," Fanny interrupted. And about then, I heard a car also.

"Travis?"

"No, that's Gabe." She stood up and walked to the porch railing, and Charlie and I followed. "He's still not home, Sheriff," she called down.

Gabe had the same question as I. "How do you know it's me?"

"I know the sound of that car of yours, don't I? You've got a belt lose somewhere."

"I guess it's better than having a screw lo—" What a shocker, the sheriff stopped smiling when he noticed me.

I waved, and he frowned some more. "I thought we agreed you'd stop harassing the neighbors, Cassie."

"Cassie's not bothering me," Fanny said. "I invited her. And she knows where Travis is. Isn't that helpful?"

The look Gabe shot upwards gave me the strong impression he didn't think I was helpful, but I told him anyway. "Travis is in Montpelier."

"Correction. He was in Montpelier."

"So you've talked to Captain Sterling again?" I asked.

Gabe told us every cop in the state of Vermont was talking to Sterling that day. "But no one has talked to Travis La Barge. We can't find him."

"Did you search his parents' house?" I asked.

Gabe put his hands on his hips and glared upward.

"You should," I mumbled.

Gabe spoke to Fanny. "You'll call me, Fanny?" he asked. "If you hear Travis come home?"

"The minute," she promised.

He looked at me. "And you'll go home and stay out of trouble?"

"I'm on my way," I said. Luckily, no one but Charlie could see my fingers crossed behind my back.

Chapter 24

I poked my head inside and looked both ways. No Arlene. I double-checked the front desk. No Arlene.

"The coast is clear," I whispered to Charlie, and we stepped inside the Fox Cove Inn.

We tiptoed into what was probably called the drawing room and checked behind the three largest pieces of overstuffed Victorian furniture. No Arlene. But no Pru, either. In fact, the place seemed deserted.

"Over here," someone said, and I turned to see Pru standing in the doorway behind the front desk. Like her sister, Pru Pearson is tall. But Arlene has short hair and always wears black leggings, and Pru has long hair and always wears paisley-print dresses.

She waved me forward, but I hesitated and asked if Charlie was allowed. "He can protect me if your sister catches me here."

Pru looked down. "He doesn't look like much protection."

"He's all I've got."

She slapped her thigh, and Charlie led me into the office—a far different place than the cop offices I'd been getting used to. No beige vinyl for the B and B. Pru pointed me to an elaborately carved chair in front of an elaborately carved desk, and I took a seat as she shut the door behind us.

She ignored the desk and sat in the chair facing me, and all three of us stared at the closed door to our right. Charlie got bored first, and decided to take a nap while Pru continued looking at the door.

"She's not suddenly going to turn up, is she?" I asked.

"She already has!"

"Arlene's here?" I jumped up. "Then I can't stay here! Your sister hates me, and I've already had a long day." I headed for the door, and Charlie followed.

"Sit!" Pru said.

We sat.

"I wasn't talking about Arlene," she said. "I'm talking about the dead woman. Why did she have to turn up?"

"It's good she turned up," I said, and Pru let out a word I didn't expect from her. I scowled. "What's going on?"

"Umm. Well." Her eyes kept darting to the closed door.

"What?"

She grimaced. "That artist's drawing they keep showing on TV? Have you seen it?"

"You recognized her, didn't you? She was one of your guests, wasn't she?"

"Nooo!"

I rolled my eyes. "Well then, what?"

"Umm. Well. Was the police picture missing any, you know, details?"

"What details?"

"From when you saw her the other day." Pru pointed toward the lake. "What did she look like when you saw her?"

"Like the police drawing, except in color. Why?"

"Umm," she said. "Was there any red?"

"Her hair."

"No. I mean was there any, you know, blood?"

"Nooo." I waved a hand. "There was no blood."

She again said that word I didn't expect. Actually, she said it a few times.

"No blood is good, isn't it?" I asked.

Pru started shaking. "She was poisoned, wasn't she?"

***

"Both culprits are AWOL," I told Bambi the second she answered her phone. "Travis and Arlene."

"Who? What? I thought Travis was at his parents' house."

"Yes, but apparently Gabe, Sterling, and all the cops in Vermont can't accomplish what I managed on my own this morning. No one can find him. And why do I know Arlene won't be around when Sterling finally gets over there?"

"Over where?" Bambi asked. "Who's Arlene? Who's Sterling?"

I stopped pacing. Clearly a lot had happened since I ran out of Mandy's. I plopped down in the purple rocking chair and started with the news from Golden Rock and my conversation with Captain Sterling.

"The guy we saw on TV?" she asked. "What a hunky-boo. Did you notice?"

I reminded her Sterling and I had discussed a decomposing corpse. "It wasn't exactly romantic."

"Is he married?"

"No ring."

"So you checked."

"Spare me. He's about six-four."

"So you checked."

"Would you spare me? I'd need a step ladder to kiss the guy."

"Handy that you're painting your house. You have step ladders all over the place."

I rolled my eyes and moved on to my conversations with Fanny and Gabe. "If you suggest Gabe Cleghorn's a hunky-boo, I'll hang up."

"Promise?"

"Unbelievable, but he didn't annoy me nearly as much as Pru Pearson did. She's the queen of pussy-footing around."

I realized Bambi knew zero about the Fox Cove Inn, the Pearson sisters, or the ghost-guys. I summarized.

"So now you think Arlene's the culprit?" Bambi asked.

"Not necessarily, but Pru sure does. Supposedly Arlene had a fling with Travis."

"Didn't you just say Arlene's about your age?"

I had. But according to Pru, Arlene and Travis had both been bored over the past winter. "You know how cabin fever drives some people nuts come January," I said. "And evidently, they saw a lot of each other since he was working over there."

"He sold them a car?"

"No. But supposedly he's a great electrician." I got up and stared out at the lake. "I'm not sure why I haven't heard this before, but supposedly Travis helps people in the neighborhood. He's even worked for Maxine."

"And he worked at the B and B?"

"He fixed the faulty wiring in their upstairs hallway."

"And ended up in this woman's bedroom."

"Not quite. Supposedly they met in the Honeymoon Cottage, which is on the grounds. But then he dumped her in the spring, and since then, she's become an insomniac. Pru says it's good for business."

"Excuse me."

"It's reinvigorated the ghost stories. Guests hear Arlene wandering the hallways and assume she's a ghost. The guests like ghosts."

"Perfect," Bambi said. "So the wandering insomniac wandered over to Mallard Cove and killed this woman?"

"Poisoned her. In a fit of jealousy."

"You're nuts."

"Wacko and Looney Tunes." But I reminded Bambi this wasn't my cockamamie theory, but Pru's.

"How about some facts?" Bambi the scientist asked. "Did Pru actually see her sister wander over to Mallard Cove?"

"No."

"And was the woman actually poisoned?"

"The cops don't know yet."

"And if it was poison," Bambi kept going. "Where did Arlene get it?"

"I don't know. But history dictates the Pearson women have a ready stock of the stuff. And supposedly Arlene has some history with poison. According to Pru, she poisoned her ex-husband's dog a few years back." I petted Charlie for reassurance and reported that the dog survived. "But the ex-husband put out a restraining order, and that's the main reason the Pearson sisters left Boston."

"Remind me why I answered the phone," Bambi said.

"To help me figure this out. Ask me some more questions."

She thought a minute and asked about the body disappearing. "Does Arlene keep a bottle of magic disappearing potion next to her jar of poison?"

I had wondered about that, too. "I asked Pru if Arlene somehow dragged the body out of the lake and hid it in the

Honeymoon Cottage, until she somehow, without anyone noticing, got the body off the premises and up to Golden Rock. I meant it to be facetious," I said. "But Pru took me seriously."

"Unbelievable."

"It gets worse. Pru admitted she doesn't know how Arlene got rid of the body. But she wouldn't have put it in the Honeymoon Cottage because the contractor who's building the new ski resort down in Thornley is renting it. And—this is a direct quote—'Mr. Chase would have noticed the dead woman. I'm sure he would have complained.'"

"Pru Pearson sounds even loonier than you."

"You noticed?"

Bambi asked if Pru had mentioned her cockamamie theory to the cops, and of course the answer to that was no.

"I guess Gabe stopped by the B and B earlier in his desperate search for Travis. But it sounds like the queen of pussy-footing around pussy-footed around."

Bambi asked if I planned on telling Sterling, but Pru had sworn to me that she'd tell him.

"He's due at the B and B this evening." I got up and peeked out the back window. Obviously my father's car was still gone, but one of our neighbors was back home. "In the meantime I have another errand," I said and hung up before I lost my nerve.

I rummaged around in the cupboard, grabbed the nicest bottle of red I could find, and headed out.

Chapter 25

"Do you have time for a chat?" I asked when Maxine answered her door.

She glanced at the bottle in my hand. "I think I might even have a corkscrew," she said. She asked me to do the honors and found two juice glasses in her cupboard, and we took seats on her deck.

I leaned over to tap her glass with mine. "Thank you."

"What for? I don't even have proper glasses."

"Thank you for tracking me down this morning."

"Silly! We Elizabethans look out for each other."

I took a deep breath and said it. "And thank you for your article in the *Herald*."

She sat up. "It did help, didn't it? I am so glad! Have they identified her? Have you talked to Sheriff Gabe?"

I said I'd talked to a lot of people, but finding the body hadn't solved everything. "We still don't know who she was."

"Gabe will figure it out."

"Or the state police. But it's getting complicated." I waved to the Gallipeaus as they floated by on their pontoon boat. "The more I learn about Lake Bess, the more I don't know."

"What do you want to know?" Maxine asked. She reminded me she's a lifelong Elizabethan, a librarian, and a journalist. "Chances are I know everything," she said with a smile.

"This is unofficial, right?" I watched her drink her wine. "Nothing goes into your column?"

"Do you see my i-Tablet?"

I glanced around the deck. No, actually. I took a chance, drank some wine, and told Maxine Tibbitts I was curious about the people in Mallard Cove and Fox Cove.

"Fanny didn't do it."

"Gee, thanks," I said. "But what about Evert Osgood?"

She scowled. "You don't suspect Evert?"

"No, but I don't know much about him."

122

"Well, I do," she said. "We went to school together, you know. Kindygarten through twelve. Evert wouldn't hurt a fly—not unless it was harming Miss Rusty."

"So that leaves us with the La Barges." I noticed Maxine's glass was empty and poured her a refill. "With Travis to be exact."

"Your suspect."

"Maybe." I shrugged all nonchalantly. "I understand he's an electrician. In fact, I understand he did some work for you?"

Maxine seemed puzzled. "Who told you that?"

"Umm, I think it might have been Pru Pearson. I understand he did some work at the B and B also."

"And Pru told you Travis worked for me?"

"She said he did some electrical work for my neighbor."

Maxine sipped her wine. Actually, she was sipping at a pretty fast clip.

"Ohhh!" she cried eventually. "Oh, oh, oh! That wasn't me, Cassie. That was Joe." She waved a hand Wylie-ward. "Travis worked with the FN451z. Something to do with electricity."

***

"What else did you and Pru talk about?" Maxine asked, and I tore my gaze from the Wylie house.

"What do you know about the B and B?"

"Probably more than I want," she said. "Let's start with the electricity. Which has been a problem since the bordello days." Maxine sighed. "Arlene and Pru thought they'd inherited a fine mansion. But when they got here they found a ramshackle place with unsafe wiring."

"So they hired Travis."

"No. Travis was no more than ten when those first renovations got started. But the electrical system has continued to be a headache for the Pearson sisters."

I assessed the half empty wine bottle. "What about the Pearson sisters?" I asked. "Do you know anything about their history? You know, before they moved here?"

She sighed again. "I assume Pru told you about the ex-husband's dog? You realize it never happened."

"Say what?"

"I'm saying." Maxine drank some more. "That Pru Pearson is fishy. You can't trust everything she says, especially when it comes to her sister."

"Oh?"

"Oh, yes." She nodded. "I've had a few chats with Pru, and Arlene always comes out looking bad."

"That certainly was true this afternoon," I said.

"I know Arlene isn't the most charming creature on earth," Maxine kept going. "But I looked them up."

"You're kidding me?"

"Well, nooo. When they moved to town, I did some research."

I squinted. "What exactly did you learn?"

"Exactly nothing." She shook her head. "I couldn't verify anything Pru told me about her sister. No nasty divorces, no restraining orders. I don't mean to brag, Cassie, but I'm pretty good at research. Oh, let's face it." Maxine giggled. "I'm very good at research."

I watched a loon dive beneath the surface of the water and thought about my own chat with Pru. Was she trying to protect her sister? Or maybe incriminate her sister?

Maxine interrupted my thoughts as the loon re-emerged. "I wouldn't be surprised if Pru accused her sister of murder." She held out her glass, and I poured. "And unfortunately, people tend to believe Pru because of all the legends."

"The ghost-guys." I nodded. "Joe told me."

"I'm surprised at that."

I assured her Joe doesn't believe in ghosts. "But he told me the stories—all those Pearson wives poisoning their Pearson husbands."

Maxine hiccupped. "Did Joe mention the other ghost?"

"Don't tell me there's a girl-ghost?"

"No. But there is a non-Pearson ghost."

I shook my head and suggested maybe we'd had a little too much wine. But Maxine wasn't listening. She drank some more and stared off to our left. "He's away today?" she asked.

"Bobby's in Albany."

She turned back to me. "I meant Joe."

"He's away also," I said.

"Well then, I suppose it's safe to chat about it." She hiccuped again. "The other ghost at the Fox Cove is Joe's father."

I put down my glass and stared at Maxine. "Start. Chatting."

***

"It happened back in the bordello days, of course," Maxine said.

"Of course," I squeaked.

"And of course the ghost might be a fabrication. But Nate Wylie was definitely shot and killed. Evidently, he stepped out on his wife fairly often." Maxine shrugged. "It caused quite a bit of gossip. I was a teenager at the time, and my parents didn't want me to hear it." She shrugged again. "But of course I did."

"How old was Joe?"

"He was just a little guy. Probably around three."

I asked for more details, but Maxine claimed there weren't any. "They never figured out who killed Nate, or over what woman. Sheriff McGuckin looked into it, but the gun was never found." She frowned. "It's probably still at the bottom of the lake."

"A lot of crime goes unsolved around here," I said.

"Because we're so small," Maxine said. "The sheriff never has enough manpower. Have you met Deputy Dent?"

I groaned in answer and stared Wylie-ward.

Chapter 26

"Her name was Nancy Finch."

I jumped ten feet in the air, but somehow managed to land on the dock, and not in the water. I greeted Captain Sterling.

He smiled and waved to the dozen or so boats hovering close by. "Her name was Nancy Finch," he hollered, and several people called out that they'd believed me all along.

Meanwhile Charlie swam into shore with his tennis ball. As usual, he rejected my toss in favor of a better arm, but I was kind of interested in what Sterling had to say. I called a halt to the game of fetch, and hustled the dog and the cop inside.

"You have quite a fan club," Sterling said as I shut the door.

"I swear some of those people have been out there since Tuesday." I waved him toward the blue rocking chair and offered coffee or tea, but he wouldn't even accept a glass of water. We sat down, and I watched him study his surroundings.

"I'm painting the exterior gray," I said.

He looked up. "But this house is so jolly."

"Nancy Finch," I reminded him.

"Was identified by her sister this afternoon. She saw the artist's sketch on TV and drove in from Burlington."

"Thank you, sister."

Sterling nodded and told me both Finch sisters lived in Burlington, but they had found Nancy's car in Montreal. "At a strip joint in the red light district."

"So much for Mandy's."

"Excuse me?"

"Montreal is in Canada," I said brilliantly.

"Which is why your sheriff never located the car. Why would he check with the Mounties?"

"And why would she end up here?" I asked. Lake Bess is at least an hour's drive from Burlington. And even farther from Montreal. "And where does Travis La Barge fit in? You've talked to him?"

"Not yet."

"Oh, for Pete's sake! Why not?"

"We still can't find him," Sterling said. "I was just at Mallard Cove—he's not there. And Cleghorn's been searching all day."

"Hello-o! He's at his parents' house." I threw my arms up. "I told you that hours ago."

Sterling frowned, and once I sat back a little, he told me that he had, of course, checked. "Ross is out of town, and Janet La Barge swears she hasn't seen Travis all day."

"She's lying."

Sterling agreed that maybe she was, but also insisted he had to "justify cause" before he could get more assertive.

"You need to barge in on the La Barges," I argued.

"No can do."

"So what can you do?"

"I can tell you the results of the initial autopsy report."

"What, what, what?"

"It's inconclusive. So far we have no concrete cause of death."

I got up to pace. "This is not how it works on TV."

"No, it isn't." Sterling watched me. "And you won't like this, either, but there's a chance we may never know how she died."

Insert colorful words . . . Here.

***

Sterling waited for me to make another rotation around the living room to inform me the medical examiner had come up with at least one interesting finding. "Nancy Finch had sexual relations right before she died."

"With Travis!" I pointed to the front door. "Go. Arrest. Him."

Sterling offered a firm "Negative" to that and waited for me to sit down. Then he explained something about DNA evidence, and how they needed to get Travis's DNA. But to do that legally, he had to prove Travis met Nancy in Montreal that night. "Then we'll have just cause to pursue La Barge more aggressively," he said.

"So go prove he was in Montreal." I again pointed to the door. "Get out of here!"

I think Sterling laughed. But he did tell me he was headed up there next. "Someone at that nightclub must have seen La Barge with the victim. Border Patrol can also help—they had to stop and show ID." He caught my eye. "Any other questions?"

Oh, please.

"What about Pru Pearson?" I asked. "Did you talk to her?"

"I talked to both the Pearsons, a few minutes ago."

"Arlene's back?"

"Back from where?"

I rolled my eyes and asked Sterling what he had learned at the Fox Cove Inn.

"Nothing," he said. "Neither Prudence nor Arlene know anything. Just like they told your sheriff the other day."

"Oh, for Pete's sake! Of course they know something! Pru knows all kinds of things!" I frowned at Charlie. "But Maxine says maybe not."

Sterling stood up. "So maybe Pru knows something. Or maybe Arlene knows something. Or maybe Maxine, whoever she is, knows something."

"Exactly." I followed him toward the door. "Maybe someone knows something. Maybe we should get them all in one room together, and let everyone tell you everything they know. Maybe I should be there with you to help."

Sterling stared.

I sighed. "Maybe you should go to Montreal."

"Maybe."

***

I awoke with a start and checked the rocking chair. No Dad.

I checked the time. Midnight.

"He's not home yet," I told Charlie and closed my eyes again.

But who could sleep with all that growling?

My eyes popped open.

Growling.

Charlie was growling.

I sprang up and switched on my reading light. Charlie stood rigid next to the bed, the fur along his spine bristling at attention.

Holy. Moly.

"Charlie?" I whispered.

At the sound of his name, he shifted ever so slightly. But he never took his eyes from my bedroom door. And he did not stop growling.

About then, I heard it, too.

"It's only Dad," I whispered. "He must be home."

So why was I whispering? And why was Charlie growling?

I bit my lip and listened to the boogey man prowling around below.

God help me—the boogey man was climbing the stairs! Shit!

I scanned the room for something to use as a weapon.

Nothing. Nothing on the floor, nothing thrown over the chair. No scattered shoes, no junk mail, no sledgehammer. Nothing! Nothing, nothing, nothing!

And meanwhile, the boogey man had made it to the second floor landing and was heading up.

Well, I wasn't going to stand there and be slaughtered! I lunged for the phone. The bedroom door opened. And Charlie sprang into action.

I hurled the phone with all my might. Someone screamed, and I took a giant leap toward the doorway.

***

I tripped over Charlie and the prone body of the boogey man, fell down the stairs, and stopped at the second floor landing. Actually, the bottom half of me stopped there. My head and shoulders made it a little farther.

But evidently I was still alive.

I tried breathing. When that worked, I backed up onto the landing, and eventually I stopped shaking enough to notice all the sore spots. Nothing felt broken, but my left shin hurt like hell. I lifted my pajama leg and fought back a wave of nausea. With only the dim light coming from my bedroom, I could still see a welt the size of Charlie's tennis ball.

About then, I registered the barking and glanced up.

"I thought you were Travis," I said.

"Son of a bitch," Janet La Barge replied.

Chapter 27

"This is the first time he's ever barked," I said.

"I'm thrilled," Janet said. "Get him off me."

I closed my eyes and smiled.

"Now!" she said.

Don't ask me why, but I crawled up the stairs to where Charlie had her pinned to the floor. "Good boy!" I told him.

He stopped barking and wagged his tail.

"Get. The dog. Off me."

"Stay," I said, and Charlie worked on making himself comfortable on top of Janet.

I stood up and yelped in pain, but somehow managed to limp over to the hallway light. Then—don't ask me why—I pulled Charlie off our guest.

"Holy moly!" I knelt down and took a closer look. A gash on Janet's forehead made the bruise on my shin seem minor. "How did that happen?"

"Son of a bitch."

About then, the phone I had whacked her with began beeping near her feet. I reached over to turn it off, and that's when I noticed the gun.

"Son of a bitch!" I said, and she informed me she needed ice. "Were you going to shoot me?"

"Ice!" she snapped.

"There's no need to get all testy about it," I snapped back.

Don't ask me why, but damned if I didn't limp down to the kitchen. I was wrapping ice cubes in a dish towel when Ross the Boss popped in through the kitchen window.

"Are those your pajamas?" he asked."And why are your doors locked? Really inconvenient." He made a show of brushing off his shoulders and glanced around. "Where is she? Is she okay?"

I refused to answer. Instead, I hobbled over to the window. Someone—Janet—had pushed in the screen. Moving very slowly in order to irritate Ross as much as humanly possible, I set the screen aside and shut the window.

"Do you even know who I am?" I asked.

"Cassie Baxter. Your picture was in the *Herald*. You're even cuter in person."

If the downstairs phone had been within reach, I swear I would have whacked him, too.

***

"Son of a bitch." Janet groaned from above, and Ross flew through the living room and up the stairs.

I gathered up the ice pack and was about to follow, when something else occurred to me. I limped over and unlocked the front door. You know. In case Travis decided to join us.

"Give me that!" Ross grabbed the ice pack as I made it to the third floor and knelt beside his wife. "Baby Doll," he cooed. "What happened?"

Janet whined. "This woman attacked me, Rossy. She and her stupid dog." She waved a hand at Charlie, who wagged his tail and licked her outstretched fingers.

While the La Barges discussed whether or not Charlie should be put down, I sat down on a stair and re-evaluated the damage to my shin.

"Tell you what, Ross," I said eventually. "Instead of picking on an innocent dog, why don't you ask your wife why she's in my bedroom." I pulled down my pajama leg. "And while you're at it, ask her about the gun lying at your feet."

I stood up. "Come on, Charlie," I said, and he walked across Janet to follow me.

***

"Where's the wine?" I muttered to the empty kitchen. I tossed Charlie two of his most special treats and opened a bottle of red while Ross helped Janet down the stairs.

He placed the gun on the coffee table, just so, and then worked on getting his wife settled on the couch. Eventually, he noticed me. "What are you doing?" he demanded.

"Drinking. You want some?"

I meant it to be facetious, but Ross took me seriously and said something about preferring bourbon on the rocks.

Janet looked up from smoothing her hair and rearranging herself. "And while you're serving, I'll take a touch of sherry."

Son! Of a bitch!

I slammed some glasses onto the counter. "No problem, Janet! I always serve sherry to my would-be assassins!!"

"There's no need to get all testy," Ross said. But when I threatened to hurl some stemware at him, he hustled over to help me.

I found the bourbon and shoved the bottle at him. "I'm out of ice," I lied. I pointed to the ice pack his wife was dabbing at her temple, and then rummaged around in the same cupboard for my father's cooking sherry.

Hoping it was the rankest stuff ever distilled by mankind, I poured Janet a big old glass, hobbled over, and handed it to her. "Enjoy!" I chirped.

Ross brought me my wine, and I found a rocking chair. He took a seat next to his wife, and Charlie also decided to stick close to Janet. He sat on her feet.

She tried kicking him away.

"Kick him again," I said slowly. "And that gash on your forehead will be the least of your problems."

She slammed the ice pack down on the coffee table and glared.

"That's it!" I jumped up and threw the ice pack across the living room, past the kitchen counter, and into the sink.

Anger drastically improved my aim, but my left leg crumbled beneath me, and I plopped back down. "I want an explanation, or I'm calling Gabe Cleghorn. Now!" I screamed at her stupid, stupid, smirk.

Ross patted her knee. "What were you doing with the gun, Baby Doll?"

"Protecting our son, you idiot!" She pointed to me. "This creature was in Mallard Cove yesterday! Questioning poor Travis. At the crack of dawn!"

"It was 3 p.m.," I said.

"Whateverrrr," Janet said. "And today she went to Cars! Cars! Cars! pretending to buy a car."

"A truck," I corrected, and Ross asked what model I was interested in.

"A four-wheel drive is just the ticket around here," he said. "I can help find you the pre-owned truck of your drea—"

"Shut up, Ross," Janet and I said.

I addressed Janet. "You recognized me?"

"Duh. Travis showed me your picture in the *Herald*."

"He showed me, too," Ross said. "You're cute as a button."

"Shut up, Ross," Janet and I said.

"Dr. Jones, my foot," she spat.

"I have a PhD in Ancient History."

She curled her lip. "It's not like you're a real doctor."

I admired the gash on her forehead. "What were you doing at Cars! Cars! Cars!?" I asked.

Janet raised an eyebrow. "Unlike some people, I had a legitimate reason to be there. I was reminding everyone of Travis's work schedule." She recited the supposed schedule. "He worked at the showroom all day Monday, went to Mandy's for a short time that evening to unwind, slept at our home in Montpelier, and went back to Cars! Cars! Cars! bright and early Tuesday morning." She nodded. "My son was nowhere near Lake Bess or the supposed redhead. End of story."

"Story's a good word for it," I said. "Are the people at Cars! Cars! Cars! actually going along with these lies?"

"If they want to keep their jobs, they are."

"What about Mandy's? Are they willing to lie for him?"

"Oh, please. It's Travis's word and my word against some drug-addicted barkeep." She gestured to her husband. "Rossy will verify everything, too. Won't you, Rossy?"

Rossy considered that. "May I speak now?" he asked me.

"Don't try to sell me a car."

***

He didn't. But Ross did try to convince me he'd been happy about the attention the state troopers had given him all day. "We Vermonters are so fortunate to have such a fine, dedicated group of law-enforcement professionals—"

"Get on with it!" Janet snapped.

Ross cleared his throat and told us the state troopers had chased after him on the campaign trail, asking after Travis and his whereabouts.

"He was home with me," Janet said. "The poor thing is a nervous wreck."

"Good," I said, and she informed me I'm a bitch.

Ross continued, "I didn't know where he was, but I cut my trip short to find out. When I got back to Montpelier I found him pacing a hole in the carpet. It took forever, but I finally got a semi-coherent story out of the stupid kid."

"Our son is not stupid!"

"Shut up, Janet," Ross and I said.

He smiled at me. "That's when Travis showed me your picture."

"Tell me I'm cute again, and I'll shoot you."

"Not before I do," Janet mumbled.

Ross leaned forward and casually moved the gun out of his wife's reach. "Travis told me where you live," he said. "And he told me Janet was here 'handling things.'"

"I'm only taking the necessary precautions," she said.

"By shooting Cassie?" Ross was incredulous, but I told him it was actually worse than that.

I pointed to Charlie. "That dog would have died protecting me. And my father. Trust me, Rossy. If my father were home, your 'Baby Doll' would have had to go through him to get to me."

"Necessary precautions," Janet repeated, and Ross finally snapped.

"What the hell were you thinking, woman!" he screamed.

"Someone has to think!" she screamed back. "They found that ridiculous girl! We've got to get Cassie to change her story, or they'll pin this on Travis!"

Ross watched his wife watch the gun. "Please tell me he didn't kill that woman," he said.

"Of course not. He was just having a little fun is all. You know Travis."

"She's dead!" Ross and I said.

"She was no one," Janet said.

I was deciding what else to throw at her when Charlie started barking.

"Why are all the lights on?" my father called from the porch. "Whose cars are those in the drive?" He turned the doorknob. "Why is this door unlocked, girl? And that can't be Char—"

Charlie rushed over.

"—lie."

Chapter 28

"He barks," I said as my father decided what exactly to stare aghast at.

He took in his dog, his daughter, and Ross the Boss, but somehow settled on Janet. On her forehead, to be specific. "What happened to you?" he asked, and her husband shot up.

He extended his hand. "Ross La Ba—"

"What the hell?" Dad asked. In case you haven't quite caught on, he had just noticed the gun.

"It's Janet's," I told him.

"Well I know it isn't yours, girl! Where's the wine?"

I stood up and limped toward the kitchen, but Ross jumped ahead of me. "Allow me!"

Whatever. When I turned around, Dad noticed the limp. "Sit!" he ordered, and Charlie and I both sat.

"What happened to you?" My father knelt in front of me, and I showed him my boo-boo. He poked at it. "Does that hurt?"

I yelped, and Charlie barked, and about then, Joe Wylie walked in.

"Is everything o—"

He dropped the black case he was carrying. "—kay?"

***

I guess it depends on what you consider okay.

Ross was at the kitchen counter pouring drinks, Dad was kneeling on the floor poking at my leg, Charlie continued enjoying the barking phenomenon, and Janet was barking orders at her husband to serve her more sherry, pronto.

Have I forgotten anything? Oh, yes. The gun.

"May I take care of that?" Joe asked.

"Please," I said, and he picked it up and walked back outside.

I didn't see him do it, but I know where that gun landed.

Ross handed my father his wine as Joe came back inside. "That's a Glock," he told him.

"Correction. It was a Glock." Joe pointed to Dad's glass. "May I have some?"

"She's got bourbon," Ross said.

"Even better."

"And I'm still waiting for more sherry, if anyone cares," Janet said.

No one did.

"You guys know each other?" I asked, and Janet snarled.

"Mr. Wylie, the mechanic," she said.

"Engineer," Joe corrected. "I have a PhD, Janet, as you know."

"And I suppose you think you're a real doctor, too? Just like Miss Looney Tunes." She pointed at me, and Joe glanced over.

"Are those your pajamas?" he asked.

About then, the FN451z decided to belt out a little ditty from inside its carrying case. Everyone jumped ten feet in the air, and Charlie resumed barking.

"Son of a bitch," Janet hissed, and Ross took a gulp of bourbon straight from the bottle.

Joe scowled at Charlie. "You bark?" he asked, and everyone but Charlie told him to get with the program.

I waved at the black box. "I thought she used electricity?"

"Or batteries." Joe seemed pleased with my interest and glanced around the room. "Any other questions?"

"What is it?" That was Ross.

"It's the FN451z." Surprisingly, that was Janet.

"Is it legal?" Ross asked.

"You-hoo?" Maxine Tibbitts called from the porch. "Anyone home?"

Why she was wondering, I really can't say. I also can't say why she chose to snap my picture when she came through the door. Because, trust me, there were plenty of other things to catch her attention. And by now you can probably list them with me—Charlie barking, the FN burping, Janet son of a bitching, Ross and Joe swigging bourbon at the kitchen counter, Bobby jabbing at my bruise.

"Are those your pajamas?" Maxine asked me. She snapped another shot before turning to Ross. "Oooo!" she said. "Is that sherry?"

***

Okay, so Maxine got her sherry. Janet got a refill, Dad and I had our wine topped off, and Ross and Joe, the bartending duo, divvied up the remains of the Jim Beam between themselves. Oh, and Charlie got a rawhide bone, which he proceeded to devour on top of Janet's left shoe.

Everyone found a seat and turned to me. "Explain," my father ordered as if it were all my fault.

I did my best.

"Charlie was growling?" Dad said.

"Janet tried to shoot you?" Joe said.

I pointed to her forehead. "Tried," I said, and Janet muttered her usual.

"About then, Ross showed up," I continued. "And Janet informed us killing me was a necessary precaution to protect Travis."

My father stood up and yanked Janet's sherry from her hand.

"No harm done!" Ross said. "Your daughter's fine, Bobby."

Dad confiscated his booze, too.

Ross frowned. "We're very sorry," he said. "And we've learned our lesson, haven't we, Baby Doll?" He patted Janet's knee. "No harm done."

I was once again fantasizing about hurling something at them, when Joe slipped behind my chair and freshened my wine.

"Smile!" Maxine said and aimed her i-Tablet. She beamed at the others. "Tonight's party should get my column on the front page of the *Herald* again next week!"

Let's just say Ross and Janet weren't thrilled with that idea.

"Cassie doesn't want to make the headlines again. Do you, Cassie?" Ross smiled at me, and I gave him my most withering look.

"Here's a shocker," I said. "But at this point I really don't care what gets into the *Herald*. As long as Travis is held accountable for his actions."

"Never!" Janet hissed. "It's your word against his."

"That sherry must be really potent stuff." I waved at the roomful of people. "What about all these witnesses? What about everyone in Mallard Cove? And the goats, and Miss Rust—"

"What about Travis?" Ross interrupted. He glanced around the room. "Please, please, believe me. The kid's a fool, but he's never been violent."

"That's right," Janet said.

"I agree," Maxine said.

"Me, too," Joe said.

"You see?" Janet told me. "You're so Looney Tunes, even your own boyfriend doesn't believe you."

"Boyfriend?" Joe asked.

"That's what she told everyone at Cars! Cars! Cars!" Janet smirked. "Cassie wants to buy you a big red pickup truck."

Ross caught my eye. "I can give you a good deal on that."

Chapter 29

"Look at this." My father and Charlie burst into the kitchen, and Dad tossed the newspaper on the table. "Nancy Finch is on the front page."

I pushed my coffee aside to take a look. "She was pretty." I stared at her picture. "But even alive, she seems—" I searched for the word.

"Haunted," Dad said. "That's what Oliver and I decided. He sends his regards, by the way. As do Hollis and Chester. They insist they believed your cockamamie story all along."

"It's what kept me going," I mumbled while I read. "Thanks for going out for this. And for not waking me up at the crack of dawn."

"We didn't get to sleep until the crack of da—"

"Wait a minute." I tapped the paper. "It says she died of heart failure. But what about Travis?" I skimmed some more. "There's no mention of Travis."

"The papers couldn't cover what they didn't know yet."

"But still. What if Ross sees this and changes his mind?" I got up to get my father some coffee, and he assured me Ross the Boss wasn't going to change his mind.

"He gave us his word last night that Travis would turn himself in first thing this morning." Dad took the cup I handed him. "He's probably with Gabe right now."

"But what if Janet gets her way?" I said. "She wasn't exactly keen on this plan."

"And I'm not exactly keen on Janet. If she stalls this operation, we'll fish her stupid gun out of the lake and let her explain that to Gabe." Dad pointed to my shin. "You should see a doctor."

I glanced down. "It looks worse than it feels," I lied, but decided maybe shorts weren't the best option for the day.

"At least take it easy," Dad said, but I shook my head and reminded him about the Jolly Green Giant.

"Girl! You can't be on a ladder today! I forbid it."

I promised to work only on the first floor. "But I can't sit still. Not with all this stuff going on."

"All this stuff is about to be settled." He pointed to a chair. "Sit."

I sat, and Charlie, who was already sitting, laid down.

I smiled at the dog. "It's ironic, but before Janet showed up last night, I was actually formulating a new theory."

"A Travis-free theory?" Dad asked.

"Not exactly." I explained my conversation with Pru Pearson. "But then I talked to Maxine, and she contradicted everything Pru said."

Bobby scowled. "You spoke to Maxine? On purpose?"

"I know it's crazy, but we had a nice chat. Maxine was a font of useful information—most notably about Joe Wylie and his deep dark secrets."

"The FN451z is legal, girl."

"The FN is only the tip of the iceberg, old man."

My father wiggled his eyebrows. "You seem quite interested in Joe Wylie these days."

I grabbed some of the newspaper. "I'm mad a Joe."

"You weren't mad at him last night."

"I was flustered last night. I forgot to be mad."

"Well, get over it. He's coming over tonight."

I protested, but to no avail. Bobby found the sports section and pointed out the ball game scheduled for that evening—the Red Sox versus the Yankees. FYI, my father is a diehard Yankees fan, and Joe's a diehard Red Sox fan. So of course they had to watch the game together.

"I hope the Red Sox lose," I said.

"No kidding. We Baxters have always been Yankees fans."

I rolled my eyes and reminded my father that this Baxter isn't a fan of baseball at all. "But this Baxter is mad at the Red Sox fan."

"We have a bet going," Dad said and explained the three-game series. "Tonight, tomorrow, and Sunday. If the Yankees win, Joe's cooking for us on Sunday. If the Red Sox win, we make dinner for him."

"We always make dinner for him. I refuse to cook for him."

"You never cook. And don't worry. The Yankees will win, and Joe will cook."

"I refuse to eat his cooking."

"But you will drink his wine."

"I'm not nuts."

"Debatable." Dad informed me we were having French toast for breakfast. He got up to start the process, and I set aside the newspapers.

"I was so flustered last night I forgot to ask about your date," I said. "How did it go with Lucille Saxby?"

Bobby kept his attention on the eggs he was cracking.

"Dad?" I asked. "Was it okay?"

"She says I need a love interest."

I laughed out loud. "I'm sure she did."

Dad frowned until I stopped laughing. "In my stories," he said firmly. "LuLu says Chance needs a love interest."

"Him, too."

***

"LuLu?" I asked, but Dad pretended not to hear me.

I winked at Charlie and got up to pour more coffee. "So which lucky Whoozit woman gets Chance Dooley, hunky-boo of the entire Hollow Galaxy?"

"It's a little tricky." Dad whisked the eggs and added some cinnamon. "You know Zach Cooter?"

"The Whooter scooter mechanic." I asked if Zach had a sister.

"No, but LuLu and I did some brainstorming, and we decided Zach doesn't exist anymore. Poof! He's gone."

"It's a dog eat dog world on Whoozit," I told Charlie.

"LuLu says we authors must be ruthless," Dad continued. "But you'll like Zach's replacement—her name's Evadeen Deyo."

"Good name."

"LuLu came up with it just like that." Bobby snapped his fingers. "She's such a pro."

I asked when the pro let him start calling her LuLu. Dad again ignored the question and informed me Evadeen Deyo is the best mechanic on Whoozit.

"Evadeen's exactly what Chance needs." He started dipping the bread in the egg batter. "Speaking of which, LuLu needs something from you."

"My blessing?"

"Yes, actually. She wants to use your story—but set it in outer space."

"You told her about the dead redhead?"

"That's right." Bobby got out the frying pan and started cooking. "LuLu says your story would be perfect for her next Paladia Fleming novel. Instead of goats and basset hounds, she'll use Ewalds and Enyons—those are the farm animals on Planet Zoar. And she'll put Paladia in her pajamas when she ventures out to the Pink Waters of the Odoric Sea in her trusty Kizito."

I shook my head and reminded my father I was functioning on limited sleep. "Should I know what a Kiziti is?"

"Kizito, girl. It's a little shuttle thing, something like your kayak. Paladia will find, and then lose, a dead body of a Nezbidian Neot. She'll become the laughing stock of the entire galaxy. But of course LuLu will give it a happy ending. Sooo?" Dad set a plate of French toast before me. "Can LuLu use it, Cassie? What do you say?"

I said LuLu sounded even loonier than me.

Chapter 30

Dad poked his head out a window and looked down. "Someone named Larry Suggs is on the phone for you."

I kept scraping paint. "Tell him I'm not interested."

Dad's head disappeared for a second and popped back out. "He says he's the car guy. He's says he has a big red beauty for a little blond beauty."

"Not interested."

Bobby disappeared again and popped back out again. "He's willing to take another five hundred off the price and throw in a complimentary microwave oven."

"Not. Interested."

"But we could use a new microwave."

I rolled my eyes for the umpteenth time. "Hang up," I said. I dropped my scraper and limped toward the porch.

I needed to call someone else. Someone way more important than Larry the car guy.

***

What a shocker, Sarah Bliss was in a bad mood. And she refused to let me speak to Gabe.

"He's busy?" I asked hopefully.

"We're all busy, thanks to you. I love being called in on a Saturday to do extra paperwork." She hung up.

I looked at my father. "Sarah just answered my question—Gabe's busy."

"With Travis," Dad said.

I pulled out Captain Sterling's card and started punching in another number. "Let's make sure."

***

Captain Sterling was way more pleasant than Sarah Bliss. He even let us put the phone on speaker while he gave Dad and me the update. Travis La Barge had indeed turned himself in to Gabe that morning.

"Cleghorn's still trying to get a few more details out of him," Sterling said. "La Barge won't budge on what prompted him to come forward today, after doing such a good job hiding yesterday."

Dad and I blinked at each other.

"But whatever the reason," Sterling continued. "The case is now officially closed. Your input helped a lot, Ms. Baxter. The State of Vermont thanks you."

"Would the State of Vermont please call me Cassie?"

"Thank you, Cassie. Other than the crucial fact that La Barge didn't actually kill Nancy Finch, you were right about everything. Right down to the dog and the goats."

"Say what?"

"The animals saw everything."

"Nooo," I said impatiently. "What about Travis? Who killed her, if he didn't?"

"No one."

"What? Travis wouldn't have moved her around unless he was responsible for her death."

"That's just it—he thought he was responsible. He thought she died of a drug overdose, but the cause of death was a heart attack. The final autopsy report came in late last night."

Needless to say, Dad and I had lots of questions, and Sterling agreed it was unusual for someone as young as Nancy Finch to die of a heart attack.

"Ms. Finch's heart condition confused Paula Spear, our medical examiner, too," he said. "She couldn't quite put her finger on it, so she called in a cardiologist from Dartmouth-Hitchcock Hospital, and he confirmed Paula's suspicions." We heard some papers rustling, and Sterling came back on the line. "Nancy Finch had something called Hypertrophic Cardiomyopathy."

"Never heard of it," I said.

"Because it's very rare. It strikes teenagers and young adults. No known cause, but it may be genetic."

Dad asked about heart medications, and Sterling told us Nancy had probably been on several. "According to the cardiologist, she should have had surgery to correct the abnormality."

"No wonder she looked so scared in that picture in the newspaper," I said.

"I'm not making excuses for her," Sterling said. "But this might have been what led her to drug abuse. Cocaine and heart disease don't mix. Finch would have known the risks. La Barge really can't be blamed."

Dad asked if she and Travis had the same drug dealer, and Sterling explained about the strip joint in Montreal. "They met each other there on Monday night."

"She was a stripper?" I asked.

"Correct. She left work with La Barge, and they crossed the border at around one, and got to Lake Elizabeth soon after that.

"And then she died," I said quietly.

"And Travis panicked," my father said. "What was he thinking?"

"He wasn't." Sterling reminded us Travis had been seriously high. "He told Cleghorn he was passed out in the yard—there's a hammock out there—until you woke him up, Cassie. He sobered up pretty quickly after seeing your reaction and decided a canoe wasn't the best place to hide a body."

"So he brought her to Golden Rock?" I shook my head. "He had to know she'd be found there, too."

"No one's claiming La Barge has any brains."

"Is he under arrest?" I asked. "Dragging a body around can't be legal."

"No, it can't," Sterling agreed. "Cleghorn charged him with unlawful tampering with a corpse and obstructing a police investigation."

Dad asked how long he'd be in jail, and Sterling told us he was already out. And I said that sounded way too lenient.

"His parents posted bail immediately," Sterling explained. "And the arraignment is already scheduled for next week. Until then La Barge isn't allowed to leave Hanahan County."

We asked what would happen then, and learned that the charges against Travis would likely be dropped if he cooperated with the authorities.

"A list of his drug dealers will go a long way toward helping us poor slobs trying to get a handle on this stuff,"

Sterling said. "After that, his parents will likely put him in rehab."

I took a few deep breaths. "That is good news, isn't it?" I said, and Dad smiled.

"Isn't it reassuring to know your neighbor isn't a murderer?" Sterling asked. "And an added bonus—his father's giving up on the governor's race."

"You're kidding?"

"Nope. Ross La Barge has a press conference scheduled for tonight."

"But there's a Red Sox-Yankees game tonight," Dad said.

"Proof positive that smarts don't run in the La Barge family."

***

Dad switched off the phone. "Can you relax now?" he asked me.

I smiled. "Yes, old man. I think I can."

In fact, it felt like all the nervous energy I'd been thriving on for days drained from my body in one fell swoop.

I limped out to the porch and sat down. Dad and Charlie followed and the three of us watched a nuthatch on the white birch trunk nearest the porch. Nuthatches have this upside down approach to life. I stared at the little bird and thought about the upside down goslings in Mallard Cove that Tuesday morning. I thought about Nancy and Travis.

"How scary life would be for a twenty-something stripper with a bad heart," I said.

"Pretty scary for Travis, too," Dad said.

I rocked back. "Do you think I could have changed this outcome?"

"No," my father said firmly. He reminded me Nancy was dead before I even knew she existed. "And Travis will be better off once he gets help for his addictions. And think about his mother."

"Must I?"

"You could have reported her little stunt with that gun last night. Janet should be grateful to you for agreeing not to."

"The La Barges have enough problems right now."

Dad reached over and patted my knee. "You've done all you can, so now help me with Chance."

"I refuse to help you with his love scenes, old man."

"But what about his propulsion-pistons pickle?"

"Wasn't Evadeen Deyo going to take care of that? I thought she was going to solve all of Chance Dooley's turbo thrust issues."

Dad told me it wasn't that easy. "In fiction you want to keep the reader guessing, anticipating the climactic scene."

I glanced at Charlie. "Climax?"

"Get your head out of the gutter, girl. I'm happy to report Evadeen Deyo is no pushover." Dad sighed. "Which brings us to the problem. She's so stubborn. She refuses to fix Chance's propulsion pistons."

"But I thought she was the best mechanic on Whoozit."

Bobby nodded. "She's the best in the whole Hollow Galaxy. But Evadeen hasn't worked as a mechanic for years. Instead she's been bartending at the Loozit."

I giggled. "The Whoozit Loozit? Let me guess. Where Evadeen Deyo serves up Whoozit Boozit?"

"Oooo, that's good, girl! Can I use it?"

"Of course," I said, but I reminded my father I was truly exhausted. "So why's Evadeen the wonder mechanic masquerading as a bartender?"

"I don't know! That's why I need your help."

I noticed the nuthatch was still there.

"Okay, how's this?" I said. "Maybe Evadeen's life was turned upside down by a sudden tragedy. Maybe a spaceship, or a propulsion piston she worked on long ago blew up. Maybe some Whooters were killed, and maybe she feels guilty."

Dad grinned. "Maybe you should be the writer."

"Nope. I'm going to relax, just like you told me to." I stood up and called to Charlie, and I limped, and he trotted over to the dock. I lay down in the sunshine, right on the bare wooden boards, listened to the water lap underneath me, and fell sound asleep.

***

"Excuse me, are you Cassandra Baxter?"

I woke up enough to roll over and greet whoever was calling to me.

Nancy Finch.

I blinked.

Nancy—insert colorful words here—Finch was standing in front of me.

I leaned over and threw up in the lake.

Chapter 31

I pulled myself onto my hands and knees and concentrated on breathing.

Charlie stayed close, and eventually I became aware of my father. Joe Wylie was there also. I remember being glad Maxine was at work. Because I really, really, wasn't up to facing her i-Tablet just then.

"But ghosts don't show up in photographs," I told the dock. "Or is that vampires? Or is it mirrors?"

"Cassie?" Dad said.

"Cassie?" Joe said.

I forced myself to lift my head and look at the Nancy-thing. "What. The hell. Are you?"

"Oh, for God's sake! Don't tell me you don't know about me!" She came at me, and I almost got sick again.

"I'm Nina," she said. "Nancy's sister. We're identical twins."

I closed my eyes again and took a deep breath. Identical—insert colorful words here— twins.

Bobby and Joe hopped onto the dock and lifted me to my feet. But when Joe suggested he carry me inside, I snapped out of it.

"I don't need help," I said loud and clear. Well, maybe not loud and clear. But I'm sure I said it. "Go home," I tried.

"But I just got here," the Nancy-Nina person-thing said.

I steadied myself and looked at Joe. "Go home," I repeated. That time I must have been loud and clear, because he backed off and my father said something about talking to him later.

I pushed Dad aside, too, and staggered my way up to the porch and into the kitchen.

My father, and Charlie, and Nina followed.

"Nina," I tried.

"I'm sorry I scared you," she said. "But this proves my theory, you know. You guys didn't even know I exist. It's a conspiracy to get that guy off. You can't fool me."

I splashed some water on my face at the sink, plopped onto a chair and put my head between my knees.

"You should be required to wear a name tag," I told the linoleum.

***

When I tuned in again, my father and Nina Finch were also sitting down. Dad offered his condolences, while Nina explained how she found us. Chester and Hollis at the Lake Store, of course.

"I had to meet you," she told me when I got myself more or less upright.

"Here I am."

"And this is the place." Nina stood up and looked out the window. "Where Nancy got killed."

"I'm sorry," I said.

Bobby waved her back to a chair, and she took her seat. "You have a sister?" she asked me, and Dad told her I'm an only child.

"But if you did," she continued, "how would you feel if she got killed in cold blood? You'd be pretty upset, right?"

I agreed that I would.

"Right," she said. "But the stupid state troopers keep telling me the jerk didn't kill her. Who gave her the drugs, then? Santa Claus?"

"We understand your sister died of heart failure," my father said. "Captain Sterling explained that to you?"

She turned to Bobby. "I don't care what Captain Sterling says, old man. Stop changing the subject."

About then, I remembered the heart defect Nancy had might be genetic.

"Did you know about your sister's health issues?" I asked gently.

"Nooo. I did not know about Nancy's freaking health issues!" She slammed the table with both palms, and my head throbbed. "Nancy didn't have any health issues," she said. "No one can tell me a twenty-five year old girl had a freaking heart attack!"

"Do you have a family doctor?" Dad asked gently.

"Stop changing the subject! We're talking about Nancy, not me. Sterling even had the nerve to tell me she was a stripper. Yeah, right! Like, I wouldn't know if my own sister was a drug addict stripper with a bad heart?" She looked back and forth between us. "You guys must think I'm a freaking idiot."

I promised Nina we didn't think that. "But we know you're upset."

"Yeah? How would you know?"

"Cassie's mother died when she was ten," Bobby said

"Yeah? And how—" Nina stopped. "Shit!" She slouched forward and hid her face in her hands. "Crap!"

She started crying. Charlie rested his muzzle on her knee, and she cried even more. "This isn't how it's supposed to go," she sobbed. "I've been practicing the whole way here what to say to you."

Dad caught my eye. "Why don't you try again," he suggested gently.

"I'm here to thank you." She looked up at me. "There! I said it. Thank you for finding Nancy. Thank you for giving a crap when no one else did."

Bobby got up to find some tissues, and I asked about her family. "Can your parents help you with this, Nina?"

"No. I never had a father, and don't ask about my mother, either." She took a handful of tissues from Bobby and seemed to calm down a little.

"The other reason I'm here is to meet the guy. I can't believe he's already out of jail." She reached back and pulled a scrap of paper out of her jeans. "Travis La Barge," she read. "The geezers at the store told me where he lives, too. I'll find it." She stood up to leave and knocked her chair halfway across the room, and it occurred to me that Nina shouldn't see Travis right then.

"Nina, wait!" I jumped up and sort of ran after her.

"No!" she said. She had already cleared the porch and was headed for the driveway.

"Wa-aaait!" I tried again, and I guess she saw me limping. For whatever reason, she stopped.

"What?" she snapped.

"Umm," I said. "Why do you want to see Travis?"

"Like, duh! Because he killed Nancy. I'd kill the bastard myself, if I had the guts." She kept walking.

"Nina, wait!"

"What now?"

I hobbled over and planted myself in front of her car. "You know Travis is in trouble with the law over this?" I half-expected her to pick me up and toss me aside. She didn't, so I kept going. "I seriously doubt he's home alone right now. And you don't want to be messing with his mother. Trust me."

"Why should I?"

"Because I'm trustworthy." I managed to find my teacher-voice. "Travis didn't kill your sister. You know that."

"He did too," she whined. "Nancy didn't do drugs. He must have forced her."

"Listen to me, Nina. I spent the entire week blaming Travis. And I agree he's a jerk, okay? But the cops say he didn't kill your sister. We've got to believe them."

"Why, because cops never lie?" She shook her head at me. "You know who this guy's father is? Ross the Boss has all kinds of money to pay people off."

I thought about the possibility.

She folded her arms. "You're thinking about it."

"Yes, I am," I said. "But, no. Captain Sterling isn't lying to us." I frowned at that head of red hair. "Although I do wish he'd told me about you."

Nina smiled a little. And she calmed down a lot. "I'm sorry I scared you."

"I know." I stepped aside and opened her car door. "And I'm sorry about your sister."

"I know." She climbed in and stared at the steering wheel. "I wouldn't buy a car from Ross and Boss if you paid me a million dollars."

"Tell me about it."

"And I won't vote for him. Ever."

I smiled at that, too. "If it makes you feel any better, he's withdrawing from the governor's race. He has a press conference tonight."

"I got to see that."

"Well then, go home and watch it. It's scheduled during the Red Sox game."

She shook her head. "What a jerk."

Chapter 32

"You're kidding me, right?" Bambi asked when I called to fill her in on the latest.

"No, I'm serious."

"The woman broke into your house, and came after you with a gun, so you served her sherry?"

"I was flustered."

Bambi laughed. "I guess so."

"Nina Finch was even scarier than Janet," I said. "But after I got over being sick at the sight of her, I kind of liked her. She's rough around the edges, but who wouldn't be?"

"Identical twins are often very close," Bambi agreed.

I asked Dr. Lovely-Vixen the biologist about Nancy's heart condition. "Do you think Nina has it, too?" I asked.

"I'm not a medical doctor. But I'd say probably. So, who else have you been bugging?"

I stamped my foot on the turret floor and winced. "Both Nina and Janet came to me," I protested. "I haven't bugged anyone. Fanny's off at an art exhibit, and Evert's at work, and I have no intention of talking to either Pearson sister again. Ditto with Maxine. My one 'chat' with her should last me a lifetime."

"What about Joe Wylie? I hope you're bothering him, at least a little."

"Nope. I'm mad at Joe."

"Oh, no."

"Oh, yes. He's way too evasive and elusive." I glanced Wylie-ward and listed all the secrets Joe had been keeping from me. "Well?" I asked Bambi. "He's scary, too, right?"

"Wrong. He's a hunky-boo."

***

"Why can't you guys watch the game at Joe's house?" I asked my father as I set paper plates and napkins on the coffee table.

"Because you'd miss us too much."

"Yeah, right."

"And you'd miss out on pizza from Santucci's."

156

"A valid point," I said. I went to find wine glasses while Dad fiddled with the remote and found the pre-game show.

The announcers were already arguing about the long standing rivalry between the Yankees and the Red Sox. And it got even noisier once Joe walked in, and he and Dad joined in the same old ridiculous arguments about who should have won that fateful game in 2003. Trust me, it will never be decided. At least not on Leftside Lane.

"Where's the wine?" I asked, but no one was listening. I shook my head and relieved Joe of the bottle he was holding. I also took the pizza from his other hand and set it on the coffee table.

"Should I even ask about your leg?" he asked.

"No," my father answered for me. "She's still limping, but she refuses to stop working on the house, and she refuses to go to the doctor."

I frowned and pointed to the pizza, and Joe started serving. "How about the twin sister?" he said as he handed me a plate. "Should I ask about her?"

I frowned again, but once again my father gave him all the details.

Joe looked at me. "She must be grateful to you."

"She is," Bobby answered. "Other than making Cassie sea-sick, we liked her, didn't we, girl?"

"We liked her a lot." I answered my father, but kept a withering glare on Mr. Wylie. "Because she was honest. Kind of brash, but honest and open." I raised an eyebrow. "And honest. She was very honest."

Joe studied me. I looked away and feigned interest in the kick-off, or whatever it's called. "You're mad at me," he said.

"No shit."

"She's pouting," Dad said. "She'll never outgrow it."

I told my father he drives me nuts, ate pizza, and pouted.

*****

Joe leaned forward and poured the last of the wine into my glass as Channel 9 cut away from the game for Ross's press conference.

He stood behind a podium trying to look dignified.

"At least he's not broadcasting from Cars! Cars! Cars!" Dad said.

"And at least he's fully clothed," I said. "I gag every time I see him in that pink diaper."

About then, I noticed Janet. Talk about gagging. She stood a few steps behind her husband and was also trying to pull off dignified. But her hairdo, obviously assembled to hide the bruise on her forehead, was almost as distracting as my recollection of Ross in his turkey suit.

"That bruise on her forehead looks pretty gruesome," Joe said. "Remind me never to make you angry."

"Too late."

Dad shushed us, and we listened as Ross officially stepped down from the gubernatorial race. He said all the right things, regretting this and regretting that. And most of all regretting that his son was such an idiot, although he didn't phrase it quite like that.

Then he opened up the floor to questions from the press, the first being exactly what charges Travis was facing.

"Tampering with evidence and obstructing a police investigation," Ross answered loud and clear, and Janet squirmed in the background

"He's being very honest and open," I said. "Unlike some people I know."

Ross continued, "I would like to point out that Travis turned himself in to the authorities of his own accord. And let me also be clear that my son was not responsible for that girl's death. She died of natural causes. Poor Miss Finch had a terrible heart disease."

He lowered his head to demonstrate his remorse, which I think was sincere. Janet—not so much.

But the reporters were more interested in Travis than Nancy. They wanted to know why he wasn't at the press conference.

"Travis is staying at our home in Hanahan County, where we posted bail," Ross said. "Until his arraignment on Monday, he can't leave the area." Ross gestured to Janet, who continued acting remorseful. "We're so disappointed he couldn't join us this evening."

"Okay, so maybe that wasn't so sincere," I said.

Someone asked Ross to comment on Travis's drug problem. "Is it true he and Nancy Finch were using drugs when she died?" he asked.

"I'm afraid that is true, Dave." Ross sighed. "Travis has struggled with his addictions for some time. However, we hope the judge will see fit to give him a suspended sentence in return for his cooperation. Travis is eager to do all he can to bring these villains who sell drugs to our children to justice. He promises to name all his sources to help the fine law enforcement officers of Vermont round up these criminals.

"After that," Ross continued, "if the judge is willing, Travis will enter a fine drug-rehabilitation program Janet's found for him down in Boston. We've already made the arrangements." The cameras focused on Janet, who shifted slightly.

Another reporter asked Ross about his own plans. "Will you run for office again?" she asked.

Ross attempted a chuckle. "I tell you what, Regina. I don't have any plans beyond tonight. Janet and I are hosting a gathering for our campaign staff in Montpelier after we finish up here." He gestured toward his wife. "We want to thank them for their tireless efforts on our behalf. But other than that, I honestly can't predict what the future holds."

It might have continued on, but Ross held up his hand to end the thing. "I want to conclude by extending my deepest sympathies to the Finch family. Travis, Janet, and I are all very sorry."

"Yeah, right," my father said with far more bitterness than I would have expected.

"Give him a break, Dad."

"I will not." He pointed to the TV, where Ross and Janet were holding hands and waving. "Those people threatened you."

"Only Janet threatened me. I know it's nuts, but I might have bonded with Ross a little."

"Excuse me?"

I shrugged. "But then again, he kept calling me cute. I hate that."

"You are cute," Joe said.

I put my glass down and stood up. "I'm going kayaking," I said and headed for the door.

"Cassie, wait," Dad said.

"For what?"

"Don't you want to see who's winning?"

I waited with my usual impatience until Channel 9 returned to the ball game, and we learned that the Sox had scored two runs while we were watching Ross.

"Vermonters will never forgive him now," Joe said.

Chapter 33

"How long have you been waiting for me?"

"Who said I'm waiting for you?"

"You're on my dock, Joe. And Charlie's with you."

Charlie paced back and forth as I pulled up to the dock, and Joe reached down to give me a hand, but I slapped it away.

"I don't need help," I said. "Who won?"

"The Yankees."

"Good." I climbed out of my kayak. "Looks like you'll be making dinner on Sunday."

"The Sox still have tomorrow and Sunday to redeem themselves."

"Good," I said. "I don't want to eat your cooking anyway."

"What's wrong, Cassie?"

"You!" I pushed him aside and yanked the little boat onto the lawn. It's an easy enough maneuver, but I was making a show of being testy. "You. Are secretive and dishonest."

"What have I been dishonest about?"

"You're kidding me, right? Where to begin!" I took an exasperated breath and plopped down cross-legged onto the dock. "Sit!" I ordered, and Charlie sat. "You!" I said, and Joe sat, too.

I pointed to his house, where, of course, the FN451z was chattering away. "Let's start with that, shall we? Everyone keeps asking you about the FN, and you never, ever, ever, answer the question."

"She's legal, okay? You want me to explain it again?"

"Nooo. I don't want to talk about your stupid machine."

"Well then, what?"

"How about your good buddy Travis La Barge? I had a chat with Maxine Tibbitts yesterday."

Joe groaned. "Oh, no."

"Oh, yes! I was too distracted last night, but I should have confronted you right then and there. Right in front of his parents."

"Travis worked for me."

"Now you tell me! But you never, ever, bothered to tell me before! Despite how often I've asked about him."

"He helped me with the FN451z. And you just told me you don't want to talk about my stupid machine."

"Well, guess what? I just changed my mind!"

Not really. But Joe took me seriously and explained the electrical work Travis had done for him. He might as well have been telling me how to fix Chance Dooley's propulsion pistons with a safety pin.

"Travis worked for me for two days tops," Joe said. "And this was over two years ago."

"Why did you fire him?"

"I didn't. He quit. He's not exactly a workaholic, and his mother disapproved."

"I thought Janet approves of everything her son does."

Joe shook his head. "She wants him to follow in his father's footsteps. Janet has very clear ideas, and Travis the electrician isn't one of them. She considers electricians laborers—beneath her son's dignity."

"She called you a mechanic last night," I said. "I think it was meant to be derogatory."

"You think?"

I raised an eyebrow. "She knew the FN451z by name."

"Come on, Cassie. Everyone who's spent any time at Lake Bess knows what I do. They may not understand what I do, but they know about the FN451z."

"Everyone's heard the stupid thing," I said, and the FN burped.

***

"So?" Joe tapped my knee. "We straight now?"

"Nooo. Maxine and I also chatted about the Fox Cove."

"Oh, no."

"Oh, yes. We discussed the ghost-guys. All the ghost-guys."

162

"Oh, no."

"Why didn't you tell me about your father, Mr. Wylie?"

"I didn't want to spook you."

"Yeah, right. Try again."

He took a deep breath. "You're right, okay? I should have told you, but maybe I was embarrassed. In case you haven't caught on, I'm a private person."

I made sure to catch his eye. "You're not your father."

"I don't even remember my father. I was three when it happened."

"And your mother?" I asked a little more gently, and he smiled a little.

"She was great," he said. "But she was a private person also, and the gossip got to her."

"Yet you continued living here?"

"Lake Bess is a good place to raise kids. And Mom definitely wanted me to go to the Lake School." He shrugged. "We ended up staying. I'm glad we did."

I asked where his mother lived now and learned she had died of cancer when Joe was in graduate school.

"Why do mothers always have to die of cancer?" I asked.

He didn't answer, but Charlie reached out a paw and plopped it onto my lap.

"Guns really spooked my mother," Joe said eventually. "Did you notice my reaction to that gun last night? Other than your father, I'm probably the only man in this town who doesn't own a hunting rifle."

I shook my head. "Believe it or not, Bobby does own one," I said. "He was so gung-ho about being a Vermonter, he considered going deer hunting last fall."

"No way."

"Correct," I said. "There's a brand new hunting rifle sitting in his closet collecting dust."

"Well anyway," Joe said. "I'm glad that bruise on your shin is the worst thing that happened last night." He waited until I would look at him. "Now it's my turn to ask questions."

"Oh, no."

"Oh, yes. What happened when your mother died, Cassie? Bobby keeps hinting that you did something—" He hesitated.

"Wacko, Looney Tunes, and nuts?" I suggested.

He smiled. "Yeah, that."

"I got on my bike and rode to my grandmother's house."

"That doesn't sound so wacko."

"She lives in Delaware."

He tilted his head. "And you were in New Jersey? Exactly how far did you bike?"

"It's 120 miles from Hoboken, New Jersey to Wilmington, Delaware." I frowned. "And before you even ask, I was ten, and my Grammie Maloney wasn't even in Delaware at the time. She was staying with us in Hoboken."

Joe's mouth dropped open.

I looked at Charlie. "Let's just say, I was flustered."

***

Let's just say, that's an understatement.

About ten minutes after my mother passed away, I asked my father if I could go for a bike ride. Poor Bobby was well aware of my nervous-energy problem and told me to go ahead. "Dad assumed I'd peddle over to the local park for a spin around the bike path. Instead, I got on the New Jersey Turnpike."

"That's nuts!" Joe said.

"Wacko and Looney Tunes," I agreed.

"No one noticed you?"

"Oh, all kinds of people noticed me," I said. "I was ten. And I had the silliest, girliest, bike on Planet Earth. Bright pink with purple and silver streamers on the handle bars." I smiled. "We Baxters have always liked bright colors."

While Joe continued laughing, I reminded him those were the days before cell phones. Somehow I managed to bike all the way down to Exit 1 without anyone reporting me.

"You made it to Delaware alone?" Joe was incredulous.

"Not exactly." I explained that my totally and completely distressed father had literally called out the National Guard to find me. It wasn't that hard. I may have known the way to my grandmother's house, but I forgot to take my allowance with me. When I reached the last exit on the Turnpike, the toll booth attendant wouldn't let me pass without paying. I threw my bike onto the roadside and paced back and forth on the curb and cried.

"That's where they found me," I said.

"But she refused to go home, even then," Dad said, and the three of us on the dock jumped.

"Da-aad!" I turned to see him waving from his balcony. "You've been spying on us!"

"Nooo. I just came out to, umm, to check on your progress, girl." He pointed to the banister. "You missed some yellow trim when you were scraping."

I'm guessing he could see the withering look I threw at him from two floors down and in the dark. "You drive me nuts, old man."

"Whatever." Joe waved to get my attention. "Did you, or did you not, make it to Grammie Maloncy's house?"

"Did," Dad told him and shook his head.

I reminded everyone that my intention had never been to run away from home, or from my father. "But I had to keep moving," I said. "I was flustered."

"Three National Guardsmen couldn't get her into their vehicle." My father kept shaking his head.

"I guess I was kicking and screaming a little," I told Joe, and Bobby muttered a colorful word.

I smirked upward. "Grammie says I showed some spunk."

"Your Grammie Maloney is loonier than you, girl."

"An understatement," I told Joe.

"Sooo?" he asked. "What did the Guardsmen do?"

They got on their bikes and escorted me to Wilmington, of course. And then they biked with me back to Hoboken.

"She made the national news," Dad added. He denies it, but trust me, he always smiles at this part of the story.

My mother's death, and the photos and film of me on my ridiculous pink bike captured the imaginations of thousands. To this day, the cancer center that treated my mother has never surpassed the donations that poured in that week.

Joe stared at me, aghast.

I shrugged. "Let's just say, I was cute as a button."

***

I waited until my nosey father finally, finally went inside. "So?" I asked Joe. "We straight now?"

"Nope, I have one more question." He grinned. "More current."

"Oh, no."

"Oh, yes." He kept grinning. "Did you really tell the people at Cars! Cars! Cars! I'm your boyfriend?"

I groaned and blamed Bambi for that stupid, stupid, idea. "Lucky me," I said. "Now the salesman keeps calling to pester me into buying the biggest, brightest, red pickup truck on Planet Earth."

"He called while you were kayaking."

"During the Red Sox game?" I asked.

"Bobby had me talk to him."

"Oh, no."

"Oh, yes. Larry described the truck for me. It sounds real nice."

"Go home, Joe."

"I could use a truck."

"Go home, Joe."

"And I like red."

"Go home, Joe."

Chapter 34

"I like this new routine," I said as my father and Charlie walked into the kitchen.

Dad dropped the newspaper on the table. "What's that?"

"You and Charlie go to the Lake Store for the paper and let me sleep in." I glanced at the headlines about Ross's press conference. "For two days in a row, I've actually slept until seven. Very civilized."

"We're losing our touch," Dad told Charlie. He refilled my coffee, poured some for himself, and sat down. And the two of them stared at me while I skimmed the article about Ross.

I looked up. "What?"

"Charlie and I have been discussing you and Joe."

"There is no me and Joe. And would you stop worrying about my love life?" I pointed to the stove and told him to think about breakfast, instead. "I'd like omelets, please. I have a full day of scraping paint ahead of me. I'm tackling the turret today."

"What!? You're not getting up that high on a ladder, Cassie. I forbid it."

"I have an alternative plan. No ladders involved."

"How? You can't fly, girl."

"You'll see," I said. "No worries."

"Yes, worries." Bobby shook his head and got up to crack some eggs. "But back to you and Joe. It sounds like he's very interested in that truck."

I slammed down my coffee cup. "You drive me nuts, old man! You kept spying on us? Is there anything you didn't overhear?"

"A little." He concentrated on beating the eggs and not looking at me. "But Charlie filled me in on those details."

Insert colorful words . . . Here.

***

The sirens started at nine.

I twisted myself around on the window ledge I was sitting on and squinted to see what was happening across the lake. I couldn't see much, but flashing lights were racing down Elizabeth Circle, headed toward Mallard Cove.

Oh, no.

"What in the world?" Dad said and I glanced down at his balcony two stories below.

"They're headed to Mallard Cove," I said.

"I meant you, girl. What are you doing?"

I was scraping the outside of my turret, of course. And I pointed out that no ladders were involved. Given enough sleep, I had come up with what can only be considered an ingenious plan. I could reach virtually every corner of my turret from the windowsills. The turret is an octagon, with the coinciding eight windows. Balancing my bottom on the window ledges wasn't exactly comfortable, but not nearly as precarious as it probably looked.

"Simple," I said, and tried smiling.

"Not simple," Dad argued. "Dangerous. And it's not exactly a flattering pose."

"Looks pretty good from my angle," Joe said, and I maneuvered myself around to see his head popped out of the FN451z's room. He pointed toward Mallard Cove. "But that can't be good."

The three of us, from our various spots at various levels, discussed what we could and could not see in Mallard Cove. From four stories up and literally hanging out of the Jolly Green Giant, I definitely had the best view. I told the guys to come join me. "Bring binoculars."

The guys, including Charlie, joined me in the turret about the same time the sirens were silenced.

"Wow." Joe looked around my space. "It's noisy up here."

"No kidding." I pointed toward his house—FN451z-ward to be specific.

I took the binoculars from my father and got myself back in position on the windowsill. And the guys poked their heads out the next best window and took turns using Joe's binoculars.

Even with three sets of human eyes, one set of canine, and two sets of binoculars, we couldn't see much, other than all the other Elizabethans, out on their docks with binoculars aimed at Mallard Cove. From all the shaking heads, we concluded no one could see anything.

I gave up on Mallard Cove and redirected my binoculars closer to home. "Where's Maxine?" I asked. "I can't believe she's missing this."

"She's at work," Joe said and reminded me of the library's weekend hours. I assumed Maxine still knew more about what was happening than the rest of us. Knowing her, she was probably, right then, on the phone with her editor at the *Herald*.

I squirmed through the window and back into the turret. "Why do I know something's happened to Travis?" I asked as I dusted myself off.

"But those ambulances could be for Fanny," Dad said. "Let's call." He left Joe and me in the turret and descended the circular stairwell to my bedroom to find my phone.

Joe looked around, literally, at the blue and lilac rocking chairs. "It's nice up here."

"I know."

He pointed to the coffee table stacked with novels and a few books on ancient Rome I'd been reviewing that summer. "This must be a great place to read."

I agreed with that, too, and told him I'd even gotten used to the FN serenading me. "Once school starts again, I'll grade essays and papers up here."

Joe was asking about my fall semester schedule when Bobby returned. From the look on his face, the news wasn't good.

"She wants to talk to you," he said. "She wants to tell you herself."

I took a deep breath, braced myself, and took the phone.

"He's dead, Cassie." Fanny sobbed. "Travis La Barge is dead."

Chapter 35

"I'm going over there," I told the guys when I could speak again.

"No." That was my father, of course. "Stay home," he told me. "You'll be in the way."

"Not at Fanny's, I won't. She's all alone, and she asked me to come sit with her."

"What about Lindsey?" Dad asked as I started shooing everyone out of the turret and down the stairs.

"I guess she's not there yet."

"Where's Evert?" Joe asked over his shoulder. "He should be with her. He and Fanny are good friends."

"I don't know, I don't know," I said impatiently. I continued shooing and finally got them through my bedroom and out the door.

I took a quick shower to free myself of lime green paint dust and yanked on a clean pair of shorts and a Hawaiian shirt. Uncharacteristic, but I actually thought a split second about my outfit, and switched to a gray polo shirt instead. I finger-combed my hair as I ran down the stairs and toward the door.

"Cassie, wait," Dad said.

"For what?"

"You're missing something." He held up my car keys and jiggled them, and I shook my head.

"Fanny told me to walk," I said. "Every emergency vehicle in the county is parked behind her house right now."

"You'll be in the way," Dad said, but I was already outside and racing up Leftside Lane.

***

I slipped past about three dozen emergency vehicles unnoticed, but of course Fanny heard me. She was on her downstairs patio and was talking to me before I rounded the corner of Mama Bear. We barely had time to share a good hug before Gabe Cleghorn joined us.

"What are you doing here?" he snapped at me. But he caught himself and apologized. "It's been a rough morning."

No one argued there, and the three of us took seats on the patio.

"What happened?" I asked.

"That's what we're trying to figure out." Gabe reached out a hand to Fanny. "I'm sorry, to have to tell you this," he began, but she stopped him.

"Travis is dead," she said quietly. "I heard."

Gabe stiffened. "Heard what?"

"I heard Janet, didn't I?" She closed her eyes and a tear rolled down her cheek. "And Ross." More tears. "I must go over there."

"Talk to me first?" Gabe said gently, and her head dropped even further.

"Did Travis have an overdose?" she asked.

A siren started up again so Gabe had to speak above the racket. "No," he shouted. "I confiscated all his drugs yesterday. I'm sorry, but Travis was murdered. He was stabbed."

Unfortunately, the siren stopped a second before Gabe, and the word stabbed probably echoed around the entire lake.

I got up to find some tissues, gave Fanny a handful, and kept an ample supply for myself. Meanwhile Gabe explained that an anonymous phone call had reported an accident at the La Barges.

"I didn't like the sound of that," he said. "So I called Janet and Ross, and Jason Sterling at the State Police. And then I got over here." He shook his head. "I feel terrible. I promised Janet I'd check in on Travis last night. He was fine. At least he was fine right after Ross's press conference."

"Was Travis alone?" I asked.

Gabe scowled at the La Barge house. "I assumed so." He looked at me. "You know something about this?"

I shook my head and kept what I knew, or didn't know, about Travis and Arlene to myself.

Gabe turned to Fanny and asked if she had heard anything unusual.

She sighed. "I usually go to the Hilleville Senior Center on Friday evenings for Senior Supper Club."

"Usually?" Gabe asked.

"I missed it for the first time in years." She stopped and tilted her head. "Make yourself comfortable, Captain," she called in Sterling's direction. "Have a seat anywhere."

None of us even bothered asking her how she knew it was Sterling. He paid his respects to her and spoke to Gabe. "They need you next door," he said. "They're about to remove the body."

Gabe seemed reluctant to leave, but duty called. He took his leave, and Sterling took the vacated chair.

He frowned at me. "What are you doing here?" he asked.

It's so nice to be appreciated.

***

What a shocker, he ignored whatever answer I was mumbling and spoke to Fanny. "I know you're upset, Mrs. Baumgarten," he said gently. "But I need any information you can give me about last night. Can you do that?"

She shook her head. "I wish I could."

"She wasn't here," I said.

Sterling shot me another impatient glance, and I shut up.

"Cassie's right," Fanny said. "I was in Woodstock with Lindsey." She perked up a little. "But you haven't met Lindsey, have you, Captain? Lindsey Luke's my assistant. She's such a love."

Sterling made the mistake of asking what Fanny and her assistant had been doing in Woodstock, and learned more than he ever wanted to know about Lindsey's pottery and the exciting art exhibit in Woodstock.

"And it's not just me who was excited," Fanny said. "I overheard many people saying such nice things about Love's work." She smiled in Sterling's direction. "No one paid the slightest attention to me. It's as if the whole wide world is blind to old ladies." She leaned toward me. "I confess I drank a little too much champagne," she whispered.

Sterling sighed audibly and asked Fanny what time she had gotten home, but by then she was talking to me. "Cross your fingers." She held up both hands, fingers crossed, to demonstrate. "The owner of a very exclusive gallery in Boston is interested in Love's work."

She must have noticed Sterling's second audible sigh. "I'm sorry, Captain," she said. "I've gotten off track, haven't I? You're more interested in what happened here, aren't you?"

"When did you get home, Mrs. Baumgarten?"

"It had to be close to midnight when Love and I said our good-byes and thank yous down in Woodstock," Fanny told me. "Love and I even debated going to a hotel for the night. But Woodstock can be quite expensive, and I like to wake up in my own bed. Don't you agree, Captain Sterling?"

"So you came home?"

"That's right. We got back in the wee hours of the morning, and Love put me straight to bed."

"But you didn't see—excuse me—hear anything unusual?" Sterling asked.

Fanny let out a sob. "You mean did I hear Travis? Did I hear someone kill Travis?"

I popped out of my chair and knelt in front of her. She held onto my hand and kept going. "I didn't hear anything," she told Sterling. "But you might ask Lindsey. She helped me to bed, and she insisted I put in my earplugs to help me sleep. She knows how any little noise tends to wake me."

We heard the ambulance leave, and Gabe Cleghorn returned to the patio. Our sheriff looked very tired. "Travis is gone," he said.

Fanny asked about Janet and Ross. "Are they still there?"

"For a few more minutes," Gabe told her. "Janet's brother is due here any minute. He'll take them home—to Montpelier, I mean."

Fanny stood up. "Well then, I don't like to be rude, but I should pay my respects. If you'll excuse me." I handed her the cane, but when she asked if I cared to join her, that bruise on my shin suddenly started throbbing again.

Call me a coward, but I begged off. "I'm the last person the La Barges want to see right now."

Fanny considered that. "You're probably right," she said.

Sterling jumped up and took her elbow. "Allow me."

"And I'll stay here with Cassie," Gabe said. "We'll chat." He shot me an ominous glance, and that bruise on my shin suddenly seemed the least of my problems.

Chapter 36

At least Gabe waited until Fanny was out of earshot. "Where were you last night?" he snapped at me, and I told him I had watched the Red Sox game.

"At home," I said. "And then we watched the press conference."

"We?"

"My father and Joe Wy—"

"After the press conference?"

I took a deep breath. "I went kayaking, and before you even ask, I was alone." I gestured toward the water. "So I don't actually have an alibi for when I was out there."

"Did you paddle down here?" Gabe asked a little too urgently. "Were you in Mallard Cove last night?"

"No. And no."

The sheriff waited for more.

"I'm a little spooked by Mallard Cove."

Gabe raised an eyebrow. "For someone who's spooked you're here often enough."

"Not in my kayak, I'm not." I reminded Gabe about the corpse in the cattails. "I may never kayak down here again. And I certainly wasn't about to paddle down here after dark and alone."

"How can I be sure of that, Cassie?"

"Because I'm telling you, Gabe. I wasn't down here last night."

He stared at me a long time. I held his gaze, and he finally backed off.

"I really wish you'd stayed home and watched the end of the Red Sox game like everyone else," he said.

"We Baxters are Yankees fans."

"Figures."

I glanced at Papa Bear house, and all those times I'd insisted Travis should be held accountable for Nancy Finch came flooding back to me. "Do I need an alibi?" I asked.

Gabe pulled a pen from his pocket and started clicking it on and off. "Anyone see you when you got back from kayaking?" he asked. "Anyone other than your father?"

"Why? Because I was a bloody mess when I got home from kayaking?" I shook my head. "Spare me."

"Were you a bloody mess?" he actually asked me.

"No!" I said. I remembered to lower my voice. "Look at me, Gabe. I weigh 98 pounds. I couldn't kill Travis even if I wanted to."

"Did you want to?"

"Nooo!"

"Okay, okay." Gabe held up a hand. "You don't need to get all testy about it, but I have to ask, okay? Everyone knows you've been dying—" He cringed. "—to have Travis pay for his sins."

I swore that I'd been satisfied with the outcome. "Until this morning, anyway," I said. "I was glad Travis was going to get help for his drug problem. And I was glad he was going to name his drug dealer." I again pointed to the lake. "I sat out there last night and decided we had gotten to a fairly happy ending."

"Okay, so back to my question. Did anyone other than your father see you when you got home?"

"Joe Wylie."

"Figures."

"Oh, come on! Joe was right there at the dock when I got back. He even sat with me a few minutes. We had a little chat." I emphasized the 'chat.' "You can verify it with him, but I promise you there was no blood on me."

"Did you talk about Travis?"

"Of course we did. I'm guessing lots of Vermonters were talking about the La Barges last night. And anyway, we talked about lots of things."

"Such as?"

I gave him a withering look. "I'm thinking of buying Joe a big red truck."

"Really?"

"He could use a truck," I said. "And he likes red."

***

"Who's Joe?" Sterling asked.

"Her boyfriend," Gabe answered.

Sterling looked to me for verification. I said nothing and hopped up to help Fanny find her chair.

"Is there anything else, gentlemen?" she asked as she sat down.

Gabe and Sterling glanced at each other, and my leg started throbbing again.

"Do you know where Evert is?" Gabe asked her.

"Well now, it's Saturday, isn't it? He must be sleeping in." Fanny faced Baby Bear. "But how he can rest today surely is a puzzle."

"He's not home, Mrs. Baumgarten," Sterling said.

"Then he must have gone to the Lake Store. Sometimes he treats us to some of Elsa Tucker's donuts on weekends."

"His truck's in the drive," Gabe said. "But no Evert."

Yep. My leg was definitely bothering me.

Fanny also seemed anxious. She kept shifting in her chair. "Is Miss Rusty home?" she asked.

"The dog?" Sterling said, and Fanny explained that Evert doesn't go anywhere without Miss Rusty.

Gabe spoke to Sterling. "Told you so."

"What's wrong with Evert?" The old lady had progressed from anxious to alarmed. "Oh, Cassie." She reached for my hand. "I'll never forgive myself if something's happened to Evert, too!"

"Tell her what's going on," I ordered the cops.

Sterling sat forward and took Fanny's free hand. "Sheriff Cleghorn thinks Mr. Osgood may be responsible for what's happened here."

Fanny snatched both her hands back, jumped up, and whacked Gabe's chair with her cane. "I beg your pardon, Gabriel Cleghorn!" she said. "What on God's green earth gave you that idea?"

Gabe moved his chair back an inch or two. "Now calm down," he said. "We all know you're great friends with Evert. But it's darn suspicious that he's gone without a trace."

Fanny looked about to hit him with her cane.

He moved his chair again. "And you got to admit his reputation isn't sparkly-shiny. You remember the rumors."

"Rumors?" I asked.

Both cops shot me a shut-up-Cassie look, but Fanny didn't see that. "Nothing!" she told me. "Don't worry about the rumors, Cassie."

"But Fanny," Gabe persisted. "You have to admit Evert hasn't always been such an upstanding citizen."

"I admit no such thing."

"Is there any basis to those rumors, Mrs. Baumgarten?" That was Captain Sterling. "We need to consider all the possibilities."

Fanny sat back down. "I'm sorry, Captain," she said. "But you will not hear those rumors from me."

And so, we heard it from Gabe. "Evert's wife Melissa left him a few years back," he began.

"About the same time Maxine's marriage fell apart," I said, and everyone told me to hush.

Gabe continued, "Evert started drinking." He looked at Fanny. "And maybe a few other things. Rumor has it he got caught up with the wrong crowd."

"No." Fanny was firm. "I wasn't blind back then. And I know my neighbors. Evert Osgood never took up with this supposed crowd."

"Come on, Fanny," Gabe said. "You have to admit not everything he did was on the up and up."

"Get to the point, Cleghorn." Captain Sterling again.

"Evert Osgood did drugs." Gabe got to the point. "This was back before I was sheriff, mind you. But rumor has it, Evert had himself a little side business selling the stuff."

"No, no, no, and no!" Fanny banged her cane on the floor. "He drank some, yes. But that is all."

"He was drunk or high all the time." Gabe said. "Are you denying it?"

"Evert did drink," Fanny admitted. "But he stayed home and off the roads. Land's sakes, if everyone was as well-behaved as Evert when he was drunk, we'd call it a blessing." She glanced around with her blind eyes. "He did not take drugs. And he never, ever, sold drugs."

Sterling stared at Gabe. "You're implying La Barge got his drug supply from Osgood?" he asked.

The sheriff shrugged. "All I'm saying is it's worth looking into."

"Nonsense!" Fanny, of course. "Evert has nothing to do with this tragedy, Captain Sterling. You can take my word for it."

In case you haven't quite caught on, I was being good and staying out of the argument. Not that I actually knew anything about anything anyway. I bit my lip watched Gabe watch Fanny.

"Maybe you can explain why your neighbor's all of the sudden missing," he said. "The same morning we find Travis La Barge dead as a doornail." He folded his arms and waited, but Fanny got distracted.

"Are those Oden's goats?" she asked. "Oh, and Evert."

We turned to look and sure enough, Rose, Ruby, and Evert rounded the corner of Mama Bear.

Gabe jumped up. "Evert Osgood, I want to talk to you!" he said, and Evert started to cry.

I'm not sure what anyone was expecting, but I think we were all a little puzzled. Perhaps Captain Sterling most of all.

"You realize you have two goats with you?" he asked.

Evert looked down. "I came across them at the old Nettles place while I was looking for Miss Rusty." He turned to Fanny and sobbed again. "She's gone, Miss Fanny. Miss Rusty's gone!"

Chapter 37

Rose and Ruby registered the crowd on Fanny's patio and decided to demolish a hydrangea bush a bit out of the way.

Evert registered the crowd when Gabe pulled up another chair and pointed. "Sit!" he ordered. Evert followed directions.

"I've been up since five," he told the gang. "Looking for Miss Rusty, high and low, up and down. I checked everywhere," he whined. "Where can she be, Miss Fanny?"

Fanny might have answered, but clearly Gabe wasn't interested. "Where were you last night, Mr. Osgood?" he asked.

"Mr. Osgood? It's just me, Evert." Evert scowled at me, and then at Sterling. "Is this about Travis?" he asked. "He's dead, you know. I'm awful sorry."

"You got a reason to be sorry?" Gabe asked.

"Of course I do. Travis was my neighbor."

Gabe gave Sterling an I-told-you-so nod, but the Captain was watching Evert.

"How do you know Travis is dead?" he asked.

"I saw him, didn't I? While I was out looking for Miss Rusty, if you know what I mean."

No one had a clue what Evert meant.

But Fanny gave it a try. "Listen to me, Evert," she said firmly. "I promise we'll find Miss Rusty. But right now Gabe and Captain Sterling need to know about Travis." She nodded at him. "Do you understand?"

"Okay." Evert wiped his nose on his pajama sleeve, and I reached over with that wad of tissues I was still clutching.

Not that I'm one to talk, but Evert's outfit that morning was mighty strange, even by Vermont standards. He wore the oldest, muddiest hiking boots I've ever seen, and a pair of plaid pajamas. He was proof positive that one should never leave home in pajamas.

Gabe frowned. "Where were you last night?" he asked, and Evert shrugged.

"Home watching the game, same as everyone else," he said. "Then me and Miss Rusty watched Ross the Boss, same as everyone else, and then the rest of the game. Then we went to bed."

"Did you notice anything unusual?" Sterling asked.

Evert gave it some thought. "The Sox lost."

Fanny cleared her throat and mentioned that Evert tends to have his TV volume on high.

He nodded and pointed. "Bum ear," he said.

Gabe asked what happened after he went to bed, and poor Evert looked a little puzzled.

"We went to sleep," he said. "We slept real well. I did, anyways. I did hear Miss Rusty get up, but that's not unusual." He nodded at Sterling. "She has her doggy door, and comes and goes as she pleases. She goes out to do her business, and I suppose she went over to Travis's for her midnight treat—"

"Can we stop worrying about Miss Rusty's treats schedule?" Gabe said.

Personally, I thought Miss Rusty's treats schedule was kind of crucial, and luckily Sterling thought the same. He told Evert he wanted all the details, and so we heard everything we ever wanted to know about his dog's eating habits.

"She goes to Travis for her midnight treat," Evert said. "Just like she visits over here most evenings for her evening treat. She knows where all the treats are, doesn't she, Miss Fanny?"

"Oh, yes," Fanny agreed.

Gabe groaned loudly. Sterling groaned quietly. "And she—your dog that is—never came back inside?" he asked.

"No, sir," Evert said. "I'm pretty sure she did not. Leastways, I never heard her come back in, and when I woke up a little after five to go to the bathroom myself, she was still gone. I looked all over the house. Then I panicked, if you know what I mean."

"We do," Fanny said.

Evert sat up. "After I finished looking for her inside, I went outside and started calling for her. You didn't hear me, Miss Fanny?"

She shook her head and apologized. "I must have been sound asleep."

"I figured as much," Evert said. "And besides, she don't go to you for her midnight treat. You're there for her suppertime treats."

"Travis is the midnight snack source," Fanny announced in case anyone still hadn't memorized the treats schedule.

"I checked at Travis's house first," Evert said. "And that's when I saw him. It made me real distraught."

Sterling had taken his face in his hands and was shaking his head. Gabe, however, watched Evert as if he might attempt an escape at any moment.

"I got to worrying that whoever hurt Travis, might have hurt Miss Rusty, too," Evert continued. "It's real distressing."

Sterling looked up. "What was La Barge's condition when you saw him, Mr. Osgood?"

"He was dead." Evert frowned at the cop. "Don't you already know that, sir?"

"How long were you over there, Mr. Osgood?"

"Not long. It was a bloody mess, if you know what I mean."

"Didn't you think you ought to report what you found?"

Evert threw up his hands. "Well, sir. Here I am! Reporting it!"

***

Sterling and Gabe groaned in unison, and Evert agreed that perhaps he should have reported it a little sooner. "It won't happened again," he promised. "But I was concentrating on Miss Rusty, and Travis didn't need no help. Other than turning off his TV."

Gabe and Sterling both jumped. "You mean you were in there?" Gabe snapped. "Moving things around?"

"It was wasting electricity."

"Mr. Osgood!" That was Sterling. "You should never touch things at a crime scene."

"But Travis wasn't watching TV no more." Evert started crying again, and the cops looked like they might join him.

Evert used one of those tissues I had given him and continued his story. After looking for his dog in Mallard Cove, he had headed to the Fox Cove. He looked at Captain Sterling. "Things were a little odd there."

"What was odd at the B and B?"

"The door to the Honeymoon Cottage was wide open." Evert spread his arms out to demonstrate. "So I walked straight in to look for Miss Rusty." He dropped his arms. "No Miss Rusty, but then I saw the pizza box on the coffee table. I was opening it up when Miss Pru ran in."

Evert glanced around. "Miss Pru was real puzzled to see me. She asked what I was doing, and I told her I was looking at leftover pizza from Santucci's." He slapped his knees. "That answered my question, if you know what I mean."

Sterling was rubbing his temples. "I have no idea what you mean, Mr. Osgood."

"I do!" Fanny raised her hand. "It means Miss Rusty must not have been by the Honeymoon Cottage. Not if there was any pizza left in that box. Pizza's her favorite."

Evert nodded. "Miss Rusty loves pizza."

For some reason Sterling frowned at me.

"No one leaves Santucci's pizza uneaten," I told him.

About then, Oden Poquette darted across the lawn. "Has anyone seen my goats?" he asked.

***

Rose and Ruby had long ago finished destroying Fanny's hydrangeas and had wandered down to the water's edge, where they were gazing across Mallard Cove. They looked like they were considering taking a swim, which could, of course, explain how they end up in such unlikely spots.

Oden didn't seem too concerned, however. Satisfied that his goats were safe, he turned his attention to the gathering on Fanny's patio. "Is this about Travis?" he asked. "He's dead."

Sterling blinked. "I know I'm going to regret this," he said, "but would you please join us, Mr.—"

"Poquette," the rest of us said, and Evert went inside Fanny's to find another chair.

"Let me guess," Gabe said once Oden sat down. "You saw Travis La Barge also?"

He nodded and pointed to Rose and Ruby. "I've been looking for the gals for hours."

Sterling glanced at me. "Can I assume these are the same goats as Tuesday?'

I nodded, and Oden told him the gals tend to wander a little.

"An understatement," I said.

Gabe and Sterling had to drag the story out of Oden also, but Oden did corroborate much of what Evert had said. He, too, had seen Travis—or Travis's body—earlier that morning.

He had milked the goats at four, as usual. And sometime after five Rose and Ruby had wandered off, as usual. So after Oden finished his usual morning farm chores, he did the Oden thing, and went out for his usual jog in search of goats. Like Evert, he had stopped at the B and B and peeked into the Honeymoon Cottage.

"The door was wide open." Oden held his arms out wide, and Evert asked him if the leftover pizza was still there.

"Yep. That's how I knew Rose and Ruby hadn't been there." He looked at Sterling. "The gals love pizza."

"No one leaves Santucci's pizza uneaten," Fanny said.

Sterling's eyebrow started to twitch.

Oden continued, "Soon after that I saw Travis and called 911."

"You're the 911 call?" Gabe cried. He looked at Sterling. "Whoever called hung up after a quick message to get out to the La Barge place. I haven't had time to trace it yet."

"You don't need to trace it," Oden said. "It was me. I reported there'd been an accident at the La Barge place."

"It was no accident," Gabe said. "Travis was stabbed to death."

Oden's face fell. "I'm sorry.'

"At least you reported it," I said. Gabe and Sterling gave me the shut-up-Cassie glare, and I went back to biting my lip.

Sterling sat forward. "I probably don't want to know this, but what phone did you use, Mr. Poquette?"

"The one at Travis's place."

Sterling took a very, very deep breath.

"I had to use the land line," Oden defended himself. "Cell phones never work around here."

"It's an interesting phenomenon, isn't it?" Fanny asked.

Sterling looked up. "What's that, Mrs. Baumgarten?"

"How with both Cassie's dead woman, and now with poor Travis, it's the animals who know all the secrets. Miss Rusty, Rose, and Ruby could tell you gentlemen everything you want to know about either tragedy."

"If they could talk," Oden said.

"If they were all here," Evert said and started crying again.

Chapter 38

Captain Sterling graciously offered me a ride home after I hopped into his car uninvited.

"I have some ideas about Travis," I told him.

"What a surprise."

"You remember Arlene Pearson?"

"The woman you insist is hiding something."

"You heard Evert and Oden," I said as he started the engine. "Something fishy was going on at the Honeymoon Cottage last night. No one leaves Santucci's pizza uneaten."

Sterling hit one of the many potholes on Elizabeth Circle. "What is it you think you know about the Fox Cove Inn?" he asked me.

"I think maybe Arlene was involved with Travis, I think maybe she has a history of violence, and I think maybe she has a history of poisoning dogs." I cringed. "Which might explain Miss Rusty's sudden disappearance."

"Arlene have a history of stabbing people to death?"

"Not that I know of. But there's a first time for everything."

He turned onto Leftside Lane. "What's gossip, and what's fact, Cassie? Let's get that straight."

I admitted I didn't know one from the other. I glanced at my neighbor's house as Sterling pulled into the drive. "Maxine claims Pru makes things up," I said. "But Fanny claims Maxy Tibbitts is the gossip."

Sterling parked his car but left the engine running. "I know I'm going to regret asking this, but who's Maxy Tibbitts?"

I pointed Maxine-ward. "Surely someone has shown you the latest *Hanahan Herald*? Lake Bess Lore to be specific?"

His mouth dropped open. "The town gossip is your next door neighbor? God help me."

I smirked. "Very funny. I'll have you know, Maxine and I hardly ever chat. But getting back to Arlene—"

"Oh yes. By all means, let's get back to Arlene."

I ignored the sarcasm and did so, and told him all the tales Pru had told me. "Evidently Arlene's the jealous type," I said. "And you yourself know the legends about the ghost-guys. All those Pearson men supposedly killed by Pearson women. Arlene's a Pearson woman."

"You think she killed Travis?"

"I don't know. But I do know you should talk to her again. I can go with you."

Sterling reached over and tapped my purse. "Got any pencils in there? I'll pay you top dollar."

"Very funny." I pointed to his keys and gestured to the Jolly Green Giant. "Cut the engine and come inside."

Sterling thought about his answer. "No," he said firmly.

"I've got pencils in there."

***

But Sterling refused to leave his car.

"Why are you so determined to pooh-pooh my theories?" I asked.

"I'm pooh-poohing the gossip," he said. "And I can't believe I just said pooh-pooh. Let's stick to the facts, please."

"Such as?"

"Such as there was a lot of physical evidence at the crime scene. I didn't mention it at Fanny Baumgarten's but someone threw up in the yard, and there was blood on the porch. The DNA's bound to turn up something."

"Speaking of DNA," I said. "You could have mentioned the twin sister to me. She scared the—" I sat back. "She scared the living daylights out of me yesterday."

"What!?" Sterling finally, finally, turned off his stupid car. "Nina Finch was here?"

"I thought I'd seen a ghost."

He apologized. "We kept it under wraps that they were twins to protect her. There was a chance that whoever killed Nancy really meant to kill Nina."

"Gosh, I didn't think of that."

"No reason you would have." He smiled a little. "You're not a cop, remember?"

I shrugged. "Anyway," I said. "Nina drove all the way up here to thank me for finding Nancy. But she ended up ranting and raving about Travis, and how he was getting away with murder."

"She was angry?"

"Oh, yeah. I had to talk her out of going over to Travis's right then and ther—" I gasped.

Sterling cleared his throat. "You think she listened to you?"

"Yes?" I shook my head. "Yes," I said loud and clear. "I'm sure she did."

"Look at me, Cassie."

I looked.

"What exactly did Nina Finch say about La Barge."

"She said she'd kill the bastard if she had the guts." I grimaced. "That's a direct quote."

"This is at least as feasible as Cleghorn's Evert Osgood theory," Sterling told me. "Or your Arlene Pearson theory. We'll look into it."

"Do you have a theory?" I asked.

"It could have been you."

"Oh, please."

"Cleghorn questioned you?"

"Lucky me. That theory is the most cockamamie of all, and you know it."

He frowned. "Unfortunately."

"What's that supposed to mean?"

"It means it would be kind of gratifying to arrest you. You're a pain in my—"

"Your theory?" I interrupted.

"It was La Barge's drug dealer." Sterling shook his head and reminded me what Ross had said during the press conference. "He announced to the whole state of Vermont that Travis was going to name names. Someone had powerful motivation to shut the kid up." He shook his head again. "I warned him not to say anything about it."

Unbelievable, but I stuck up for Ross. "He must have been flustered—facing the media like that." I asked Sterling if he knew where Travis got the drugs.

188

"If I did, I wouldn't be sitting here with you. Cleghorn won't admit it, but he's in the dark, too."

"It's not Evert," I said.

"Gee thanks. Cleghorn's checking some other, more likely, possibilities."

"Do you know about Mandy's?" My head snapped. Why did I say that?

Sterling raised an eyebrow. "I know it's one of the many places you've been snooping around in."

"Only because Travis hung out there."

"Anyone in particular I should talk to?"

I thought about Keith Wheeler but wasn't about to break the confidence of a former student. "You're the cop," I told the cop.

"I'll remember that, but will you?"

***

Sterling was in luck, since I had zero plans for further sleuthing. At least not at the moment.

After calling Bambi with the news, I worked on the Jolly Green Giant, avoided two phone calls from Larry the car guy, ate lunch with my father, and argued with my father.

What did we argue about? Oh, just about everything. Dad was sick of fielding phone calls from Larry, who, apparently, was very, very, anxious to talk to me.

"This is what you get for butting in and spying on people," Dad scolded. "There are repercussions for your actions."

I suggested he just hang up on Larry the next time. "I'm sure he's used to it."

"I'm not that rude."

"Well then, don't answer the phone at all. Concentrate on Chance Dooley's problems."

"How can I concentrate?" My father, in case you haven't quite caught on, was feeling a little testy. "Every time I look up and see you hanging out of that turret I worry you'll fall and hurt yourself."

"Well then, don't look up," I said. "And don't worry—I'm done for today." I pointed out the kitchen window where things had gotten dark and gloomy. "I'll clean up after lunch and run a few errands."

"Errands!" Dad didn't like that plan, either. "Where? What? Who?"

I rolled my eyes at Charlie and got up to load our sandwich plates into the dishwasher.

"You have some more snooping in mind, don't you?"

Okay, so maybe I had come up with a plan or two while I was hanging out of my turret trying not to think about Travis. I reminded my father to concentrate on Chance Dooley's problems, and headed for the stairs.

"Cassie, wait."

"For what?"

He blinked, clearly trying to think of a way to stall me. "Where are you going?"

"I'm going to take my second shower of the day, and then I'm going over to the Fox Cove."

"The leftover pizza?" he asked.

"It's got to be a clue."

Dad nodded, despite himself. "No one ever leaves Santucci's pizza uneaten."

Chapter 39

I may have had a plan in mind, but I'm not nuts. I called the B and B to make sure the coast was clear. "Is this a good time?" I asked Pru when she answered the phone.

"You mean is Arlene around? She's AWOL, as usual." Pru sighed. "Everyone's AWOL. What can I do for you, Cassie?"

"You can tell me what you know about Travis's murder."

"Travis is dead? No way."

"Pru! How could you live right there and not know?"

"I've been distracted, okay?" She started crying.

I felt like crying, too. I should have broken the news a little more gently. But shouldn't one of the cops have told her? Obviously, neither of them thought the pizza thing was worth checking into.

"Are you okay?" I asked.

"No! We had some problems last night."

"At the Honeymoon Cottage?"

Pru sniffled. "You know about that?"

"Not nearly enough." I asked if I could stop by, and she said why not.

"Arlene's not there?" I double-checked.

"It's just me and the ghosts."

                    ***

Pru really was all alone. Or at least her car was. I parked next to the lone vehicle in the parking lot, and she was at the lobby door waiting.

She held the door for me, and I explained the news about Travis as we found seats in the deserted drawing room.

"Thank goodness he was stabbed," she said.

"What?"

She held up a hand. "I didn't mean it like that, okay? I'm just glad my sister wasn't involved."

"Why, because stabbing isn't her style? I've got news for you, Pru. Miss Rusty is missing."

"Oh, no!"

"Oh, yes! Let's hope she turns up soon." I thought about it. "Alive, that is."

"It wasn't Arlene," Pru said, and I wondered if she were trying to convince herself, or me. "My sister was way too busy in the Honeymoon Cottage to kill anyone."

"She wasn't busy eating pizza," I mumbled.

Pru's mouth dropped open. "You know about the pizza?"

"Evert mentioned it. No one leaves Santucci's pizza uneaten."

"Not unless they're running away from Mrs. Chase."

"Who?" I asked impatiently. "Could you please just tell me what happened?"

Unbelievable, but Pru actually sat up straight and did so. It seems Arlene didn't suffer from insomnia after all. And she hadn't been pining away after Travis all those months, either. The real reason she'd been wandering the grounds and hallways at all hours was Buster Chase—the contractor who'd been staying in the Honeymoon Cottage.

"She's been sneaking out there for months," Pru said. "I had no idea, and I had no idea he's married."

"Oh, no."

"Oh, yes. Mrs. Chase showed up last night."

I groaned. "And walked in on her husband and Arlene?"

"I'm surprised they didn't hear the screaming down in Hilleville."

"What time was this?" I asked.

"I don't know. Midnight? What time was Travis killed?"

I scowled. No one had mentioned that.

"It was after Ross's press conference," I said. "Gabe saw him after the press conference. And." I thought some more. "It had to be before five this morning. That's when Evert found him dead."

Pru blinked, and I assumed she, too, was thinking about the timing.

"Anyway." She tried sounding casual. "The commotion in the Honeymoon Cottage woke up everyone. I ran out to see what was going on, as did all the guests." She grimaced. "It was quite a show."

"The Buster Chase and Arlene Pearson show," I said.

"Don't forget Mrs. Chase. The Chases left pretty quickly, though. With Buster trailing across the lawn behind his wife, apologizing and carrying loads of stuff. He was supposed to stay all summer."

"What about Arlene?" I asked. "Did she go back to her own bed?"

Pru didn't answer.

"Where is she, Pru?"

"I don't know. She left in a huge huff, right after the Chases."

"Please don't tell me she hasn't been home."

"She hasn't been home."

While I thought of all the implications of that— whatever they were—Pru informed me everyone else had left also.

"The Chases and Arlene last night, and all the guests checked out early today." She waved at the deserted drawing room. "It really is just me and the ghosts."

***

"You will report this to Captain Sterling, or Gabe, or both," I told her in my sternest teacher-voice. "No more pussy-footing around, Pru. Two people and maybe a dog are dead."

She swore to me she'd call Gabe and frowned at the front door. "I wonder why he hasn't come by already."

"Because he's busy checking out some other possibilities." I told her that neither of the cops had taken Miss Rusty's pizza preferences very seriously. "Hopefully they're right." I stood up. "Even if Arlene is AWOL, what would her motive be for killing Travis? It doesn't make any sense."

"My sister never makes any sense."

"Terrific," I muttered. I asked to borrow a phone and a phone book, and Pru led me to the front desk.

"Are there other suspects?" she asked as she handed me the teeny-tiny Hanahan County phone directory. She tried to peek at who I was looking up.

I closed the book. "Don't the ghost-guys need you upstairs or something?"

She sighed. "I can go shut the windows." She pointed to the bay window overlooking the water, and sure enough a storm was brewing. The wind was howling and there were actual white caps out on Fox Cove. I watched until she disappeared up the staircase and punched in the number.

***

"Me?" Lindsey said. "Why do you want to talk to me?"

"Did you hear about Travis?" I asked. "Did Fanny call you?"

"Of course she did. But I don't know anything. Fanny and I were gone all day yesterday."

I glanced at the ceiling and spoke quietly. "But I'm still curious about a few things. And I'd like to talk to you without Fanny around."

"No," she said, but then she thought a second. "Why?" she asked.

I sighed. "Never mind, I guess. I'll just talk to you the next time you're at Fanny's."

"Is that a threat?"

I scowled. "I don't think so."

"Yeah, right." Lindsey gave me some cursory directions to the farm in Stone City where she rented her trailer. "Don't fall off Stone Mountain," she said and hung up.

Chapter 40

"She was serious," I told the windshield wipers as I drove up the dirt road. I was learning the hard way that Lindsey Luke lived on the most remote farm, off the most remote road, in Stone City. And don't let the word "city" fool you. Stone City is a boondocks even by Vermont standards.

"Road" is also a relative term. The path my poor little car was struggling with made Elizabeth Circle look like the New Jersey Turnpike. The incline was steep, and the mud was deep. But not quite as deep as the ravines lying in wait over either edge.

I was thinking a set of propulsion pistons would be mighty handy when I spotted Lindsey's van. I parked in a nearby puddle and slogged my way over to her door, skirting three piles of defunct farm equipment along the way.

I knocked, but was left standing outside long enough to appreciate that Lindsey's trailer actually improved the landscape. At least it and what must have been her pottery studio next door were clean and in good repair, unlike the other buildings on the property. The roof of the barn sagged, and the farmhouse was in worse shape than Papa Bear back in Mallard Cove.

Papa Bear. I sighed into the fog and rain and thought about Travis La Barge until Lindsey finally opened her door. She didn't smile, but at least she let me inside. She pointed me to a minuscule kitchen table and sat down, folding her arms across her sweatshirt.

I sat down, and acting way more cheerful than I felt, promised I wouldn't take much of her time.

"Good."

"You seem kind of defensive," I said quietly.

"And you wouldn't be? You think I killed him."

"Nooo. What gave you that idea?"

"Travis is dead, you're here, and you know I was in Mallard Cove last night. And you know I hated the guy."

I swore I didn't think she killed anyone. "But I am curious about you and Travis." I took a deep breath. "And you and Dean Taylor."

Trust me, a withering look from those incredible blue eyes would make anyone squirm.

"What is it you think you know about me?" she demanded while I squirmed.

I asked her not to hold it against the messenger and told her what I thought I knew—about Dean Taylor the drug dealer, about her having lots of boyfriends in high school, and about one of them being Travis La Barge.

"I am so sick of this garbage," she said. "Who told you this? Maxine?" Luckily she held up her hands and stopped me before I had to answer. "It doesn't matter."

"But the truth matters, Lindsey. Obviously I've heard some false rumors." I tilted my head. "Would you tell me the truth?"

She frowned. "Fanny likes you a lot."

"I like Fanny a lot," I said. "She's pretty special."

"She's the most special person I know." Lindsey took a deep breath. "If Fanny thinks you're okay, I guess I do. You want some ginger ale?"

I said that sounded nice, and while she got up to pour the drinks, I relaxed enough to look around. Lindsey had drastically improved what could have been a pretty depressing place with some bright paint and very cool pottery. "This is nice," I told her.

She looked up from pouring. "You picking on me?"

"No, I like it." I waved a hand at the orange and yellow checkerboard cabinets. "The Baxters like bright colors."

"Then why are you painting your house gray?"

I blinked. "I like bright colors sometimes," I corrected myself.

"How's living with your father?" Lindsey directed me toward the small couch a few feet away, and as we took seats, I told her Bobby drives me nuts.

"He seems like a sweet old guy anytime I see him at the Lake Store."

"He is sweet," I had to admit. "But I'd like a lot more privacy."

"I hear you." Lindsey told me she had an open invitation to move in with Fanny, but as much as she loved Fanny, she loved having her own space. "This will sound bad," she said. "But now that Travis is gone, maybe I'll change my mind."

"Tell me about Travis?" I asked.

She sighed. "Maybe we should start with Dean. As you obviously already know, he was the drug dealer of Hilleville High when we were in school." But according to Lindsey, Dean was also a straight A student. "He seemed so goody-two-shoes no one ever suspected him."

She twisted her glass in her hands. "By the way, Fanny knows most of this, but could you still not mention it?"

"Believe it or not, I'm not much of a gossip."

"Yeah, right." She sipped her drink and continued. "Dean was smart, but I was really dumb. The only subject I passed with flying colors was art. So I dropped out after my junior year when he graduated."

"You don't seem dumb to me, Lindsey."

"Yeah well, Fanny helped me get my equivalency. I didn't drop out because of my grades. I was just so unpopular."

"But you're so beautiful!" I pointed to a tray on the coffee table. "And talented."

She stared at the blue and orange platter. "I know it sounds stuck up, but it's hard to look like I do. The girls hated me, and the boys told lies about me."

"Travis?' I asked.

"Of course. You want to know what they called me?"

"Probably not."

"Get Lucky Luke. You want to know what else? Dean's the only boyfriend I ever had. He's the only guy I've ever been with." She shook her head. "What's it called? Irony?"

I asked her why she picked the school drug dealer of all people.

"I don't know." She sounded exasperated. "Maybe because I had low self-esteem or something. But the truth is, we liked each other." She shrugged. "What can I say?"

"You can say you didn't do drugs."

"Pretty close—I guess that's more irony. I maybe smoked pot once or twice. Whoop-dee-doo." She put her glass down on a royal blue ceramic coaster. "Anyways, my parents couldn't care less, so I quit school and moved in with Dean. We rented a house in East Round Hill. Out in the sticks where he thought he'd never get busted. We had lots of parties. People were over all the time."

I told her she didn't seem like the partying type, and Lindsey agreed.

"Most nights I ended up working on my wheel out in the garage while everyone else got wasted. It's what saved me."

"Was Dean Travis's pusher?"

"Until he got busted."

"By Gabe?"

She nodded. "I was out back with my hands full of clay when he showed up. I guess he decided I wasn't involved, and let me be. Who knows? Strange stuff happens around here."

I asked what happened to Dean, and learned he had gone to prison for a while, but the last Lindsey heard he was enrolled in a college somewhere in Albany.

"And you?" I asked.

"I got a lot smarter, too." She looked out the window at the rain. "I got a lot more serious about my pottery business. I don't make much money, but the rent is real cheap and no one bothers me up here."

"No kidding," I mumbled.

"I have privacy," she said. "But I was getting pretty lonely until I saw Fanny's ad in the *Herald*. I can't believe she hired me over everyone else she interviewed."

"I can." I asked how long she'd working for Fanny, and Lindsey told me four years.

"It's not even work anymore. Fanny's my best friend."

"Which bring us to my main question, actually."

She cringed. "You want to know about the ear plugs last night."

I nodded.

"I never make Fanny do anything, okay? But she was so wound up, Cassie. My art show went really well. A gallery in Boston wants to carry my stuff. Boston!"

"It's very exciting," I agreed.

"Yeah, but it was too exciting for Fanny. She was all wound up, even by the time we got back to Mallard Cove. It's like the champagne had the opposite effect on her than you'd think." Lindsey shrugged and mentioned that Fanny could have taken a sleeping pill. "But I didn't think that was a good idea because of the champagne."

I agreed that seemed reasonable.

"So I gave her the ear plugs instead. At least then once she got to sleep, she'd stay asleep. Fanny can hear a pin drop in case you haven't noticed."

"What time was it?" I asked.

"Way late. About two."

"You didn't see anything unusual over at Travis's?"

"No."

"Did you see Miss Rusty?"

"No again. I was concentrating on getting Fanny settled."

I thanked her for the drink, and got up to leave, but thought of one more thing on my way out. "Any ideas where Travis was getting his drugs lately?" I asked.

"None," she said. "Dean got busted years ago."

Chapter 41

"Meet me at Mandy's?" I asked Bambi when we spoke a little later.

"You're kidding, right?"

"Nooo. I'm serious."

"Cassie! You just told me your suspicions. And Mandy's is a rough place on Saturday night. Call me a coward, but I refuse to go in there looking for knife-wielding drug dealers with my ninety-pound friend for backup. I don't have a death wish."

"But I've run out of people to bug." I listed all those I had recently bugged. "Pru Pearson and Lindsey Luke, and then I stopped by the Lake Store and talked to Oliver again. And by default, Hollis and Chester. I even had another chat with Maxine when she got home from work. No one knows anything."

"They know you're nuts. And you told me earlier you planned on leaving the cop-work to the cops."

"I changed my mind," I said. "It's either Mandy's or try to track down Arlene Pearson. What do you say?"

"Nuts, Looney Tunes, and wacko."

"So you refuse to help me? Some sidekick you are."

Bambi reminded me she'd already done Mandy's duty with me. "I'm watching the Red Sox game with Pete tonight."

"Pete can come with us," I said. "The game will be on at Mandy's, and he can protect us. He's twice my size."

"Everyone's twice your size," Bambi said and reminded me her husband is a mild-mannered accountant. "What about the state trooper guy?" she asked. "Didn't you just tell me he's checking into Mandy's?"

I frowned and got up to look down at the lake. A loon was out there, but it was still pouring. "Mandy's was probably a bad idea, anyway," I grumbled. "The weather stinks, and if Sterling learned anything, he would have called me."

"Has he put you on the payroll yet?"

"No. I'm totally useless." I plopped back into my rocking chair. Charlie came over to sit with me, and Bambi gave me a pep talk.

She insisted I wasn't such a bad sleuth. "You don't know who the killer is, but you have ruled out a few people." She listed the Elizabethans she'd been hearing about all week while I petted Charlie. "We can't rule out this Arlene woman completely, but surely Pru, and Fanny, and Maxine are off the list of suspects?"

"Lindsey, too," I said. I thought about the men. "Let's also rule out Evert and the gang at the Lake Store."

"What about the goat guy?" Bambi asked. "He seems to pop up everywhere."

"That's because the goats pop up everywhere, but I doubt it was Oden Poquette." I tilted my head and listened to the FN451z. "I'm also fairly certain it wasn't Joe Wylie," I said. "But I haven't ruled out the FN."

***

Maybe Bambi had a point. Maybe I really am nuts. Because after I got off the phone with her, I thought of someone I hadn't bugged for days. Someone who actually wanted to talk to me. Someone who would have a different perspective on things. I called Larry Suggs.

And don't worry—I immediately realized the error of my ways. He was so excited that I had actually called him, he dropped the phone. Then he dropped the price of the Jolly Red Monster a whopping thousand dollars and threw in a pre-owned scooter and reconditioned coffee pot. I'm pretty sure he was about to offer me his first born child when I interrupted, and as firmly as humanly possible, said I was still thinking about it.

"Thinking," I emphasized.

"Seriously?"

I shot a glance Wylie-ward. Oh, what the heck. "Seriously," I said.

"Excellent!" Larry shouted for joy. "We're about to close for the evening. But let's meet at the showroom at opening tomorrow. What do you say, Dr. Jones—I mean Dr. Baxter?"

Clearly Janet had enlightened Larry on my true identity at some point.

I interrupted something about a full season ski-lift pass in Thornley to ask about the Sunday hours at Cars! Cars! Cars!

"Excellent question!" Larry said. "We're open from noon to six! Let's make an appointment! We'll take that big, beautiful truck for another test spin!"

Wow! He really was desperate for a sale.

I desperately tried to think of how to re-direct our conversation while Larry reminded me of all the excellent "special features" on the Jolly Red Monster. Evidently it would come ready to roll off the lot, with tires and everything, if we closed the deal within twenty-four hours.

He must have looked at a clock. "Excellent!" he shouted. "That would make it five o'clock tomorrow afternoon. Right before closing!"

"It's interesting to me," I said firmly, "that you're even open this weekend."

"Why? It's Saturday. And we've been open on Sundays for years."

"Yes, but Ross the Boss's son just died—" I stopped and waited for Larry to respond.

"We're flying the flag at half mast," he said.

"I'm surprised Ross didn't close up shop for a few days."

"He wanted to. But word is Mrs. La Barge wouldn't go for it. She says Travis loved the pre-owned car business too much for us to stay closed for even one day. She says Travis's dream was to manage Cars! Cars! Cars! on his own. You know, once Ross the Boss was busy being governor."

"So she considers it a tribute to Travis?" I asked. "To stay open?"

"She says Travis would have wanted it that way."

***

"Son of a bitch," I said as I walked into the kitchen.

Dad stood up from the oven. "But you like mac and cheese."

"Not the dinner. Janet La Barge." While I set the table I told my father about my conversation with Larry the car guy. "I might feel worse about Travis than his own mother does. Although grief hits people in odd ways, right?"

"You would know." Dad set the casserole on a hot plate and glanced at Charlie. "Should we even ask how she spent her nervous energy this afternoon?"

We sat down to eat, and I explained how I'd spent my nervous energy that afternoon. I even admitted I was glad there was a ball game that night. "Maybe it will take my mind off feeling so guilty. "

Dad finished his dinner and put his fork down. "You're not to blame for Travis's death, girl. No more than Evadeen Deyo is to blame for the terrible accident in the Echo Space Crater.

About then, Joe Wylie walked in carrying a way nicer bottle of wine than Dad and I had been working on. "Who's Evadeen?" he asked.

I got up to load the dishwasher and handed him the corkscrew. "Have you eaten?" I asked and indicated Dad's casserole.

He assured us he had and started working on the wine while Dad identified Evadeen as the best mechanic in the whole Hollow Galaxy.

Joe looked up from pouring. "What about Zach Cooter, the Whooter-scooter guy?"

"Poof," I told him. "Zach's zip."

"But back to Evadeen," Dad said. He gave us a lengthy explanation of why she had switched careers from spaceship repair to bartending at the Whoozit Loozit. Just as I had predicted, there'd been a terrible accident a few years earlier. Due to some odd mechanical glitch, two spaceships collided in the Echo Space Crater.

"Poof," Dad said. "Two spaceships and five crew members gone. And poor Evadeen had recently worked on one of the ships. Luckily, they recovered the black boxes from both spaceships."

Evidently Joe had the same question as I. "They still use black boxes in the fifty-first century?" he asked.

"Unbelievable, but true." Dad sipped his wine thoughtfully and explained how investigators from the Interspace Transport Protection Agency concluded a faulty vacuum gravity reactor in the other ship—the one Evadeen had not worked on—was to blame for the accident.

"But Evadeen still felt guilty," Dad continued. "And from that day forward, she vowed never to lay her hands on any spaceship, ever again." He raised an eyebrow. "Or on any spaceship pilot ever again."

"But then she met Chance Dooley." I gave Joe a meaningful look. "And the sparks—no pun intended—went flying."

Dad agreed. "I think LuLu will be quite pleased with the sexual tension between Chance and Evadeen."

"Excuse me?" Joe asked, and I informed him my father was actually going to write a sex scene.

"Maybe several," Dad said.

Joe scowled. "Really, Bobby? You seem kind of—" he hesitated "—mild-mannered for that kind of thing."

Dad rolled his eyes. "I do know what a sex scene is, Wylie." He pointed to me. "You've been admiring the results of my knowledge for months now."

"Yeah, but outer-space sex?" Joe was still skeptical.

"I will write a sex scene, and it will be darn good." Dad was positively indignant. "LuLu has faith in me."

"LuLu?" Joe asked, and Charlie and I burst out laughing.

Dad gave me a withering look. I straightened my smile and told Charlie to behave himself, and my father told Joe who LuLu is.

"Sounds like she has a crush on you, Bobby."

"Ohhh, yeah," I said, and Dad gave me another withering look.

"What's LuLu like?" Joe asked. "Is she cute?"

"As a button," I said.

Dad sighed. "Can we please concentrate on Chance and Evadeen? Poor Chance is in quite a pickle trying to lure an exceedingly reluctant Evadeen Deyo out of the Whoozit Loozit and into the inner workings of the Destiny. He desperately needs her to take a good solid look at his Turbo Thrust Propulsion Pistons!"

Joe bit his lip.

"Chance will persuade her," I said with confidence. "He's a hunky-boo. All the girls in the galaxy say so."

"I'm sure he's very charismatic," Joe agreed.

I nodded. "And once Chance gets Evadeen into his spaceship—"

"It's only a matter of time before he gets her in his bed," Joe said, and we couldn't hold it in any longer. We laughed hysterically, and generally har-harred.

Bobby put his hands on his hips and told us to grow up. "You're acting like two sex-starved adolescents."

Joe and I wiped our eyes and blinked at each other.

Chapter 42

I tried to concentrate on Chance Dooley's sex life. Then I tried to concentrate on the baseball game. I tried to not think about Travis La Barge. I wasn't having much luck, and the Red Sox weren't either, when the phone rang.

"We've made an arrest," Captain Sterling told me, and I jumped ten feet in the air.

Dad and Joe looked up from the TV, where the Yankees were busy scoring another run. "They've arrested somebody," I told them, and Dad put the TV on mute.

"Who?" I spoke into the phone. "Who, who, who?"

"First of all I want to apologize for the lateness of the hour," Sterling said.

"Who?" I said. "Who, who, who?"

"I would have called you earlier. But I just got back to the office."

"Who!?"

"Has anyone ever told you patience is a virtue?"

"What do you think?" I said and waited for Sterling to spit it out already.

"You were right," he said.

"About what? About who?"

"The dog greeted the officers at her door. She claims she found it wandering her neighborhood and took it in. Not going to fly—the dog isn't wearing a name tag, but it knows its name."

"Arlene Pearson has Miss Rusty?" I was incredulous.

"Huh? What are you talking about?"

"Miss Rusty, Travis La Barge, the killer." I waved my free hand. "Who are you talking about?"

"I'm talking about Nina Finch," Sterling said calmly.

"Nina Finch has Miss Rusty?" I stepped around Charlie and started pacing back and forth in front of the TV. No one told me to move. "Does Evert know?" I asked Sterling.

"No, but you have my permission to tell him. I'm a little surprised you're not more interested in why she has the dog."

I shut up, and Sterling continued, "It looks like she killed La Barge, and for some strange reason, she then took the dog."

I looked at my father, but spoke to Sterling. "Nina Finch killed Travis?" I said, and mouths dropped open while Sterling told me the DNA collected at the La Barges' matched Nancy Finch.

"Nancy?" I scowled. "Oh, but that makes sense. Since she died there."

"No, Cassie," Sterling said. "The DNA is Nina's. Remember that evidence I told you about this morning?"

"Identical twins," I whispered as it occurred to me.

"Identical twins have identical DNA," Sterling said. "The DNA we collected at the murder scene was Nina's. Nina's," he repeated. He told me she'd been brought to Montpelier for questioning late that afternoon. "I arrested her about an hour ago."

"That poor girl." I paced over to a rocking chair and plopped down. "Are you sure?"

"DNA doesn't lie. And what other explanation would she have for the dog? Why did we find that basset hound from Mallard Cove in her apartment in Burlington?"

"What's going to happen to her?"

Sterling wouldn't say for sure. But he did assume Nina's lawyer would advise her to plead guilty. "It's pretty clear what happened."

Thinking about Nina was too awful, so I concentrated on something I could help with. "Can I come get Miss Rusty?" I asked. "I don't mind. I can be there in a half hour."

My father and Joe were gesturing that they'd go with me. But Sterling refused to release the dog from custody, claiming she was evidence.

"So the dog really is a witness?" I asked.

"She's evidence," Sterling corrected me.

"She's a living creature, Captain. She's much loved. You'll treat her well?"

"I won't be feeding her Santucci's pizza, but give me some credit."

I apologized and asked what else I could do to help. "I can't sit here doing nothing. I'm not good at sitting still."

"An understatement," Dad mumbled.

"Tell you what," Sterling said. "Why don't you let Mr. Osgood know his dog is safe. Right now I have a million other things to do, and that would be a big help."

"Absolutely." At least something to make a few people smile. But then I frowned. "Should I tell people about Nina, or is that top secret?"

"Not secret. It will be on the news by tomorrow morning."

Good thing it wasn't secret, because my father and Joe had lots of questions when I got off the phone. But Evert and Miss Rusty took precedence.

Or maybe not. I couldn't find a phone number for Evert in the Hanahan County phone book. I tried Fanny, who was overjoyed by the happy news, and insisted I not worry at all about the lateness of the hour.

"Evert's here with me," she said. "We've had a very long day."

"I hope he didn't have you traipsing through the woods?" I asked.

"No, but we did take quite a long drive. Goodness, we must have visited every animal shelter this side of the Canadian border."

Evert got on the phone. "Oh, Miss Cassie! You found her?"

I explained Miss Rusty's whereabouts, and needless to say, Evert was hugely disappointed he couldn't get his dog back right away.

"Captain Sterling promised he'd take very good care of her," I assured him.

"But how will he know what to feed her? Miss Rusty's real particular, especially in a strange environmen—"

Luckily Fanny saved me any further discussion of Miss Rusty's dietary needs. I could almost picture her wrestling Evert for her phone, but Fanny won that battle. She asked me to explain the news about Nina, and everyone, on the phone and listening in from the sidelines, agreed it was really, really, tragic.

I told Fanny to get some rest, and she agreed she'd try. "But you will call me when you know more?" she asked.

I promised I would and hung up.

My father and Joe were still staring at me.

"Nina's actually in jail?" Dad asked, and the gruesome reality of it hit me full force.

"This is all my fault!" I slammed the phone down. "I'm going kayaking," I said and walked out.

"Cassie, wait," Dad said.

"No!"

"Cassie, wait," Joe said.

"Nooo!"

***

"How long have you been waiting for me?"

"A while."

I pulled my kayak up and climbed out. Joe knew better than to try to help. "Who won?" I asked.

"The Red Sox. Bobby called out to tell me they scored three runs in the last inning."

"And you missed it?"

"I wanted to be out here when you got back." He dragged my kayak onto the yard. "There's something I want to tell you."

"Oh, no."

"Oh, yes. But first, there's something I want to ask you."

"Well then, ask," I said. We plopped down cross-legged on the dock, and Charlie practically sat in my lap.

"Why are you so upset with yourself?" Joe asked me. "This wasn't your fault."

I shrugged. "Why didn't I go along with Gabe and say the redhead wasn't dead?"

"Because she was dead."

"But I still feel guilty. About Nancy, about Travis, and now about Nina." I shook my head. "I even feel guilty about Larry, for Pete's sake."

"Who's Larry?"

"The Cars! Cars! Cars! guy. You spoke to him on the phone."

Joe almost smiled. "You feel guilty about Larry the car guy?"

"He thinks I'm actually going to buy that stupid truck tomorrow."

"I really don't want that truck, Cassie."

"Try telling Larry that."

Joe got serious. "Other than the very intriguing truck story, none of this was your fault."

"Said Chance Dooley to Evadeen Deyo."

"Chance is right, and so am I. You and Evadeen should listen to us."

I guess my silence implied I was listening.

"Let's start with Nancy," Joe said. He insisted someone would have found her body floating around the lake on Tuesday, even if I hadn't. "And Travis would have been implicated since Gabe Cleghorn was bound to figure it out sooner or later."

"So then Nina would have been informed?" I asked.

"Sooner or later, yes. The truth has a way of coming out."

"Well, the truth stinks," I said. "Two young people have died here this week. And another one's in jail tonight."

We stared at each other a long time.

I took a deep breath. "What is it you were waiting out here, missing the Red Sox, to tell me?"

"Lake Bess is a good place to die, Cassie."

I stared again. "Is this about your parents?"

"Them and my wife. If Nancy Finch had to go, at least she got to do it here." He waved at the water, lapping around the dock. "And whatever we think about Travis, we know he loved Lake Bess. He died at home."

I turned around and looked at Joe's house. "Your wife died in there?"

He nodded. "And that's what Helen told me. Several times she told me Lake Bess is a good place to die." He reached over and squeezed my hand. "And that's what I wanted to tell you."

Chapter 43

Three's a charm, but I had to be dreaming to think my father would let me sleep in three days in a row. He woke me up at 5:30 and asked about Joe. "What did you two kids talk about last night?" He winked at Charlie, but the dog was too busy getting comfortable on my bed to notice.

Dad was not discouraged. "Did you discuss Chance and Evadeen?" he asked. "Did you come up with some sex scene scenarios for me?"

"Da-aad! For Pete's sake. Get LuLu to help you with that."

"I am. We've been e-mailing each other."

I rolled my eyes and told Charlie I really, really, needed to get more sleep.

"Well then, you shouldn't stay up till all hours with Joe," Dad said. "What were you talking about?"

"Death."

Bobby's rocking chair ceased rocking. "When he walked out at the bottom of the seventh, he promised he'd make you feel better. Not worse."

"He did actually. He convinced me Lake Bess is a good place to die."

Dad started rocking again. "It would be, wouldn't it?"

"I guess so." I petted Charlie. "But I'm still worried about Nina Finch, who's alive and kicking, and in serious trouble."

"You can't change what happened, Cassie. If she killed Travis, there's nothing you can do about it."

I agreed I couldn't help Nina with her legal issues. "But how about her medical problems?" I told my father Nina was going to need medical care. "There's a good chance she has the same heart condition her sister did. I'm guessing prison won't make it any easier."

My father asked me what I had in mind, and I admitted I wasn't quite sure.

"But she's going to need good doctors, surgeons, medicines," I said. "And think of the insurance hassles."

"Her parents didn't sound like they'd be much support."

"Exactly," I said. "But maybe we can help her. Are you in?"

Dad smiled, and we agreed Nina Finch wouldn't die like her sister did. Not if we Baxters could prevent it.

***

I started priming the house that day, and Dad continued sexting (!) with Lucille Saxby.

I have no idea how far my father got, but I had to give up on my project pretty quickly since rain was threatening. And Dad abandoned LuLu by early afternoon when Joe came over to watch the third game between the Sox and the Yankees.

Charlie and I watched an entire inning before getting restless. We left the guys arguing over the umpire's latest call and went upstairs to make a few calls ourselves.

"We have to be brave," I told the dog. We sat down in the turret, and I punched in the number for Cars! Cars! Cars!

I'll spare you the gory details, the pleading, the begging, and the bargaining. To finally, finally, convince Larry I wasn't going to buy the Jolly Red Monster, I told him Joe and I had broken up.

Whatever.

Larry made one last desperate attempt. "I'm missing the Rex Sox game to be here for you."

"Well then, go home and watch the game. It's only the second inning."

"Excellent idea!" he said and invited me to join him at Mandy's to watch the rest of the game.

Say what?

I said no thanks and called Bambi.

"What, what, what?" she snapped. "The Sox have the bases loaded."

"I think Larry the car guy just asked me for a date."

"You're kidding me, right?"

"Nooo. I told him Joe and I broke up."

"That's a neat trick. Since you and Joe haven't started dating."

I frowned at Charlie. "I'm planning ahead for the inevitable."

"It's always you who does the breaking up, Cassie. Not the guy."

I frowned again. "Never mind about Joe. I'm calling about Nina Finch."

Bambi asked Pete to turn down the volume. "We saw the news this morning," she said. "I'm so sorry it was her."

"No kidding," I said. "I'm sad for Travis, but I'm also sad for Nina. Does that make any sense?"

Bambi reminded me there's a reason I love teaching college. "You like young adults, Cassie. And clearly you feel a bond with this woman, who looks exactly like her sister, who you worried about for days."

"Which is why I'm calling. I want Nina to be healthy." I explained my plans to help the remaining Finch sister, and Bambi agreed.

"Count me in," she said. "Whatever Pete and I can do."

I gave Charlie a thumbs up. "Joe's in also," I said. "I talked to him during the first inning. And I'll have a chat with Maxine."

"You're kidding me? I thought you were done chatting with her."

"But she's great at research, and we want to learn all we can about this disease. The best treatment options, the best doctors—"

Call-waiting beeped, and I told Bambi we'd talk later. "It's Captain Sterling."

***

"What, what, what?" I asked.

"Hello to you, too."

"Hello," I said. "What's the news about Nina? Something good, I hope."

"No. Something bad," Sterling said. "She wants to see you."

"Terrific. I need to talk to her."

He skipped a beat. "You realize she's angry with you."

I cringed at Charlie. "She knows I'm the one who turned her in, doesn't she?"

"She's not dumb. She knows someone told me about her little jaunt to Lake Elizabeth yesterday." Sterling insisted I wasn't under any obligation to talk to Nina. "Especially in the middle of a Red Sox game."

"Why aren't you home watching the game?" I asked.

"Because I'm having way too much fun dealing with Nina Finch and the dog."

Chapter 44

Charlie had questions, Dad had questions, Joe had questions. Heck, Mr. Hooper's cows probably had questions. I handled each delay with my usual impatience and finally, finally, made it to the State Troopers office.

The trooper assigned to babysit me led me down the beige hallway to a glass room just large enough for two folding chairs. "Prisoners meet with their attorneys in here," she said. "Make yourself at home."

She walked off, and I glanced around. At home?

She came back with Nina, and when we sat down, our knees practically touched. "Fifteen minutes," the trooper said. And then she shut, and locked, the door.

Nina folded her arms and glared at me.

"This isn't what I expected," I said as pleasantly as humanly possible. "I thought we'd have a sheet of Plexiglas separating us."

"Why? Are you afraid I'm gonna kill you?"

***

Actually, I was glad Nina Finch didn't pussy-foot around. Because two seconds later she told me she wasn't about to kill me, and that she did not kill Travis. "Not, not, not," she said and stamped her foot.

I pulled my own feet further under my chair and quietly suggested I wasn't the one she needed to convince.

"Who else am I gonna convince? Santa Claus?" She threw her hands up, and I flinched. "My stupid lawyer keeps telling me there's all this evidence against me. And I keep saying, like, I don't care, because I didn't do it. Why did you tell them I'm some kind of axe murderer?"

"I did no such thing!" I protested. "But I had to tell Captain Sterling you were at Lake Bess. And I had to tell him what you said."

"Why? Why, why, why?"

"How about because you threatened to kill him?"

"But I wasn't serious! I was just talking is all. Did you really think I was serious?"

I took a deep breath and watched the state trooper watch us. "No. I didn't. But Travis is dead." I took another deep breath. "Tell me what happened," I said. "And start with your sister. I'm guessing she wasn't the perfect angel you claim she was."

Nina agreed, reluctantly, and told me the Finch twins had always been kind of wild. "Nancy especially," she said. "Mom kicked her out before we even finished high school."

"I'm sorry."

Nina shrugged and fast-forwarded a few years. The twins both ended up waitressing in downtown Burlington and had remained very close. She started crying. "But then Nancy got sick."

"She knew she was sick?"

"Like, duh. She started fainting all the time and got fired from her job. It got so bad she went to a doctor. They did all these tests."

Nina sobbed some more.

"Do you have this heart condition, too?" I whispered, and she nodded at her lap.

"Mine's not as bad."

I reached out and touched her hand. "I understand there's a surgery." I looked her in the eye. "There's got to be some treatments, Nina. You don't have to die."

"I'd rather die than go to prison," she mumbled.

I squeezed her hand and asked what happened once Nancy understood about her illness.

"She never understood. That was the problem. She went nuts, okay?" Nina cringed. "She took that awful job."

"Where she met Travis."

Ms. Trooper tapped her watch, and Nina cried.

"Cry later," I said firmly. "Right now you need to tell me about Friday night."

She wiped her nose on her shirt sleeve and continued, "Me and my roommates watched Ross the Boss's press conference. We talked a long while afterwards. Everyone was real nice to me."

"But then for some reason you went back to the lake."

"I couldn't sleep." She shook her head. "Ross said something about Travis going into rehab. I don't know," she whined. "I decided I had to see him first."

"So you got to Travis's house," I prompted.

"And the lights were on."

"What time was this?"

"About one. I stood in the yard, trying to get up the nerve to knock. Then I heard the dog whining."

"Miss Rusty," I said.

"I didn't know her name. But yeah. The front door wasn't all the way shut. I knocked a little and sort of let myself in." She held her head in her hands, and I caught a glimpse of the gruesome cut she had gotten running away from the scene.

"You got flustered and ran away," I said.

"It was awful," she said into her hands. "I got sick, and then I heard the dog again."

I groaned. "And so you took her."

"She looked so sad."

I thought about Miss Rusty's perfectly basset hound, perfectly melancholy, face.

"I felt sorry for her with her master dead and all."

"But she's not even Travis's dog, Nina."

"I didn't know that, okay? How was I supposed to know that? She came right to me the second I called her, and she jumped in my car without me even trying."

"Was there food in there?"

Nina thought a second. "I stopped for a burger earlier that day. I don't know—maybe a few French fries?"

***

The door wasn't all the way shut. I knocked a little and sort of let myself in. "I need to talk to you," I said.

"Same here." Captain Sterling looked up from his desk and waved me to a chair. "Do me a favor and take that dog back where she came from."

"I thought she was a witness."

"She's evidence," he corrected me. "I've changed my mind. The dog's a menace."

"Miss Rusty?"

"Little Miss Rusty devoured the entire mattress in her cell last night. And now she's working on the metal bed frame. When the dog isn't eating, pooping, or farting— pardon me, but that's the report—she's howling, drooling, and peeing." Sterling broke a pencil. "I thought you'd like to take her back to Mr. Osgood?"

"Absolutely."

He thanked me and got up to see me out, but I remained seated. "Aren't you curious about my conversation with Nina?" I asked.

"I don't want to know."

"Yes, you do." I pointed him back to his desk. "Sit down and take out some more pencils."

He sat down and watched me—warily would be the word—while he pulled a brand new package out of his desk. He fiddled to open the cellophane, but kept his eyes on me.

"Do taxpayers pay for those?" I asked. I was joking, but Sterling took me seriously and told me he supplies his own.

"Some cops drink. Some do donuts. I do pencils." He snapped one in half. "Okay, I'm ready. What's up?"

"Nina Finch is innocent," I said, and the pencil parts went flying.

"You're kidding me, right?" he said. "The woman talks to you for ten minutes and convinces you she's innocent? Has anyone ever told you you're nuts?"

"Take a number," I said. "But Nina Finch is innocent."

"Cassie! We have DNA, we have the dog, we have motive. Heck!" Another pencil lost its life. "We even have you. Remember she said she'd kill the bastard? Remember you—" he pointed a pencil part at me "—telling me that?"

"She does admit she was there," I said.

"No kidding!"

"Okay, okay," I said. "There's no need to get all testy about it. Nina admits she had some vague notion of confronting Travis. But he was already dead when she got there."

"What's her proof?"

"Miss Rusty, of course."

"What!?" Sterling argued that the dog was evidence against Nina. "Against," he repeated. "Against, against."

I very calmly argued the opposite. If Nina had killed Travis, she wouldn't turn around and steal the dog. "Why would she purposely keep a key witness safe?" I asked.

"The dog is not a witness. She's evidence."

"Exactly," I said. "Miss Rusty is evidence that Nina's not guilty. She has a big heart, Captain. She thought Miss Rusty belonged to Travis and felt sorry for her."

While I watched Sterling murder a few more pencils another thought occurred to me

"What about the timing?" I asked. "Nina got to Lake Bess about one o'clock, and Travis was already dead. And we know he was alive when Gabe saw him after the press conference. Sooo." I was thinking. "That means Travis was killed between ten and one, right? Probably before midnight, right?"

Sterling stared at me, aghast.

"Don't tell me I'm right?"

"The coroner puts the time of death between ten and twelve."

I sprang forward. "This is good!" I said. "Not that Travis is dead, but the timing. Now all you have to do is have Nina's roommates verify her story. Find out what time she left Burlington, and that will prove she didn't kill him. It takes well over an hour to get from Burlington to Lake Bess. Period! End of subject!"

"Not quite," Sterling said. "But we are tracking down the roommates. There's three of them, and they all work at restaurants and bars. They're in and out at odd hours."

He stood up to see me out. I stayed put. "Maybe you should look at that pusher theory of yours again," I said.

"I've already talked to the people at Mandy's." He pointed at his office door.

I stayed put. "There is one other possibility."

He gave up and sat back down. "Go ahead," he said. "Get it out of your system."

"Arlene Pearson," I said, and he started groaning. "All kinds of hanky panky was happening at the Fox Cove that night, Captain. And then Arlene went AWOL."

"Cleghorn's been over there. No mention of anyone being AWOL."

I grabbed a pencil and snapped it in two. "Someone is lying," I said. "Period. End of subject." I stood up and dropped my pencil halves onto his. "You should check into it."

He muttered something incoherent, and I reminded him I was taking Miss Rusty home. "You owe me one," I said.

Little did I know.

Chapter 45

By the look of things in her cell, Miss Rusty's untidiness had not been exaggerated. Now that I think about it, they had her in solitary confinement. She was whining in protest, but perked up when she saw me. She shook her head and let the drool fly—new goo joining the puddles on the floor and the slime already dripping down the walls.

Sterling hadn't exaggerated about the mattress, either. Or the smell. Let's just say Miss Rusty's fiber-filled diet wasn't agreeing with her.

"You're one brave woman to take this beast," the trooper who was guarding her told me. "But hey, don't let me discourage you." He handed me a leash. "The sooner the Hound From Hell disappears, the better."

I knelt down to pet Miss Rusty and distract her from the insults.

"We wanted to shoot her," the cop continued. "But the Captain wouldn't go for it."

***

I settled Miss Rusty in the back seat of my car, but she climbed over and onto the passenger seat before we left the parking lot.

Still not quite comfortable, she stretched out. Luckily, her front third ended up on my lap, but there was a lot left over, and her other two thirds stretched across the console and passenger seat. And way over yonder at the passenger door, her tail thumped steadily, keeping perfect time with the windshield wipers. Either my Accord was smaller than I realized, or basset hounds are bigger.

At some point on the drive I got sick of wondering who weighed more—Miss Rusty or I—and went back wondering about the murder. If Nina wasn't to blame, who was?

Sterling's drug-pusher theory seemed plausible. But he'd have to pursue that on his own, since I had no clue, other than some vague suspicion of Mandy's.

"How about the Arlene Pearson possibility?" I asked Miss Rusty. She looked up, and I caught a whiff of dog-breath. "You're right," I said. "It's fishy. Maybe I'll stop by there after I drop you off."

Her tail stopped wagging.

"You're right again." I decided to let Sterling and Gabe handle the Pearson sisters also. They were paid to deal with people like Arlene.

Have I mentioned the drool? Miss Rusty's, not Arlene's.

I was discovering the gross way that her jowls aren't just for good looks. They are, in fact, a set of very efficient drool collection and distribution devices. Whenever the mood struck, she shook her head and let it fly. Miss Rusty needed no propulsion pistons.

After a particularly slimy glob of goo found its way to my cleavage and trickled southward, I pulled over to deal with the dog.

I heaved, hoed, and shoved until she was more or less on the passenger seat. Then I explained the concept of personal space. "Elbow room," I said and jabbed my elbows to demonstrate.

She licked my right elbow, I started the engine, and she instantly went back to her preferred position of driver torture.

Have I mentioned the weight?

But whenever I was about to lose my patience, she looked up at me with those soulful eyes. I don't know if she's worth her weight in gold. I don't know if anyone is worth Miss Rusty's weight in gold. But her sweet expression inspired me onward.

***

Evert was on his porch when we pulled up. The look on his face when he saw his dog? Now that was worth Miss Rusty's weight in gold. I let her out and she ran to Evert. Evert screamed, Miss Rusty barked, and they rolled around together, one big happy glob of man, mutt, and mud.

Eventually he remembered me and stood up. "Oh, Miss Cassie!" Overcome with joy, he picked me up and spun me around.

It happens. People realize how little I am when they hug me, and can't resist sweeping me off my feet and spinning. While Evert and I hugged and spun, Miss Rusty leaned back, lifted her snout to the sky, and howled.

At some point we managed to collect ourselves. Evert led us onto the porch and settled Miss Rusty down with a treat.

"How'd you manage it?" he asked as he served me a can of ginger ale. "Captain Sterling said it would be days before I got her back. Got me so distraught, I couldn't watch the Red Sox."

I made up some excuse for her early release, and Evert agreed Miss Rusty belongs in Mallard Cove.

"Lake Bess is a good place for dogs," he said. "But the people at the shelters yesterday scolded me for letting her roam around like I do. They said bassets are known for wandering off and getting lost."

I asked if she had a chip. She does, but of course the RFID chip only works if the person who finds your pet realizes the animal is lost.

"Why did that girl take Miss Rusty?" Evert asked, and I explained Nina's reasoning.

"I talked to her, Evert. She asked me to apologize to you."

"Did she really kill Travis?"

"No." I watched Miss Rusty eat. "Nina swears she didn't do it. I don't know why, but I believe her."

He patted my knee. "Always trust your gut, Miss Cassie."

I asked him what his gut said about the murder, but Evert insisted his wasn't talking. "Sheriff Gabe will sort it out, though," he said. "He's impressive, if you know what I mean."

"Not really. To be honest, I'm not that impressed with Gabe."

"But he nabs the bad guys every time," Evert argued. "Don't you read the *Hanahan Herald*?"

I shrugged, and Evert had to admit Gabe isn't perfect. "He never did figure out where Travis got all his dope, for example."

"It's interesting," I agreed.

"It's surprising. Especially since he was here most every Friday."

I choked on my ginger ale and pounded on my chest.

"Shocking, ain't it?" Evert said. "Sheriff Gabe was always trying to ward off trouble for the boy."

"Every Friday," I squeaked. "Gabe was here every Friday?"

Evert pointed at Papa Bear. "He came over about when I got home from work. Too bad Travis never listened to him."

"Did you?" Maybe I asked that question a little too urgently. I sat back and tried for nonchalant. "I mean, did you happen to hear their conversations?"

Evert shook his head and reminded me about his bum ear.

I stared at Miss Rusty. "What about the car?" I asked. "What did Gabe drive on these Friday nights?"

"Why's that matter?"

"I'm just wondering, is all." I shrugged in a nonchalant way. "I wonder if Gabe came by officially. You know, in his patrol car. Or more friendly-like, in his own car."

Evert nodded. "More friendly-like."

Chapter 46

I meant to drive straight home. Really I did.

And I tried hard to forget what Evert had said. Really I did.

"People think I'm crazy enough," I told myself. But somehow I missed the turn for Leftside Lane and kept on driving around Elizabeth Circle.

I passed Rose and Ruby, the public beach, and the Lake Store. And still, I kept on driving. Unfortunately, I had a clear destination in mind. And unfortunately, two cars were parked at the Fox Cove Inn.

"No. Fortunately," I scolded myself. I parked smack dab between Arlene and Pru, and marched straight into the lobby. And stopped short.

Arlene Pearson looked up from the front desk and spat out a selection of colorful words.

"I'm surprised to see you, too," I said.

"I bet you are." She gave me a withering look. "I'm AWOL no longer."

I cleared my throat. "I thought Pru manned the front desk."

"You thought wrong. She's upstairs nursing a migraine."

"Oh."

"Well?" Arlene shook her head at me. "Don't just stand there like an idiot. What do you want?"

I wanted to know if she killed Travis, but was wondering exactly how to phrase that.

Arlene helped me out. "You want to know if I killed him."

I let out a breath. "Yes."

"Sorry to disappoint you, but no." She looked up. "No!" she screamed at the ceiling. "I did not. Kill. Travis!"

I heard a door slam above us and decided I really, really, needed to sit down. Again, Arlene helped me out.

"Sit!" she ordered. She came out from behind the front desk and pushed me into the drawing room, and we both plopped onto an overstuffed couch.

Who knows why, or from where, but I mustered up a little courage and point blank asked where she was when Travis was killed.

"You want my alibi." She again directed her answer to the ceiling. "I was with Buster Chase in the Honeymoon Cottage," she yelled. "As everyone in this whole stupid town now knows!"

"How about after Mr. Chase left?" I asked.

She turned back to me. "I got in my car and drove over to Travis's."

I was kind of glad I was sitting down.

"He was dead." Arlene's volume had changed so much I could barely hear her.

"I'm sorry," I said.

"Me, too."

"I'm sorry," I said again. "But—"

"You don't believe me."

"No, I do. But the timing is important, Arlene. What time was it?"

"Midnight. Five after to be exact. I checked my watch."

I thought about Nina's visit. "Was Miss Rusty there?"

Arlene scowled. "Yes." She scowled again. "I didn't even remember that until now. Is Miss Rusty important?"

I nodded. "I think so."

She took a deep breath. "Travis and I were friends."

"I know."

"Nooo. You don't." She raised an eyebrow. "Whatever you've been told, Travis and I were friends. Who talked." She emphasized the talked. "We talked about our screwed up families." She closed her eyes. "But not that night."

"What did you do?" I asked. "When you saw him."

"I got out of there." She let out a sigh. "I know I should have called Gabe. I know I should have done something. But I was—" she hesitated.

"Flustered?"

"An understatement, but yes. I got back in my car and drove to Boston."

"Why?"

"I have no idea," she said. "But I had to do something. I had to be moving."

"I understand."

"Then maybe you can explain it to our stupid sheriff." Arlene shook her head. "This is the reward I get for finally cooperating with him. He's right now verifying with my credit card company that I stopped for gas in Woodstock."

I blinked. "Speaking of timing. When was Gabe last here?"

"About ten minutes ago. You just missed him."

Chapter 47

Joe Wylie grimaced, but my father wasn't quite so polite. "What the hell happened to you?" he asked me.

I glanced down and truly wondered why Arlene had let me sit on her couch. "I brought Miss Rusty home," I said. "Sterling released her."

"What about Nina?" Joe asked.

"He's about to release her, too." I walked onto the porch. "She didn't do it."

"Arlene?" Dad asked.

"Nope. I talked to her, too. I asked her point blank if she killed Travis."

"To her face?" Joe said. "Are you nuts?"

"Wacko and Looney Tunes."

Bobby turned to Joe. "Why do I know she has a new cockamamie theory?" he asked.

"She has that cockamamie-theory look in her eye," Joe answered.

They turned to me and waited. But I insisted I needed to take a shower and make a phone call before I said anything to anyone. "Because you're both right. It's totally cockamamie."

About then it hit me that the guys were on the porch, which meant the game had ended. And Joe was obviously not in his kitchen. "I take it the Yankees lost?" I asked.

He grinned. "Bobby's grilling steaks tonight."

I looked at my father.

"I don't want to talk about it," Dad said, but he did want to start dinner. And Joe wanted to pour some wine. And both of them wanted to hear my latest theory.

I reminded them patience is a virtue and went upstairs to make that phone call.

***

"Let's hope my voice doesn't have a cockamamie-theory sound to it," I told Charlie as we sat down in the turret.

By that point I had Fanny Baumgarten on speed-dial, and she immediately thanked me for rescuing Miss Rusty.

"You've spoken to Evert?" I gave Charlie a thumbs up. "We had quite a talk. Did he mention it?"

"He did. I'm so glad you think Nina Finch is innocent, Cassie. That poor girl has suffered enough—losing her sister like that. Has Captain Sterling released her?"

"Soon," I said, and Fanny told me she'd like to call Lindsey with the latest.

"Can Lindsey wait a few minutes?" I asked.

"Oh, dear. What's wrong?"

So much for my acting skills. I tried to convince Fanny nothing was wrong and again aimed for nonchalant. "Evert told me something about Gabe Cleghorn that I'm curious about," I said. "He told me Gabe used to visit Travis a lot. Most every Friday evening, as a matter of fact."

"Is that so?"

"It is," I said, oh so casually. "Evert says Gabe was trying to help Travis stay out of trouble."

"That didn't work very well, did it?'

My father hollered that he and Joe were getting hungry. I ignored him.

"But is it true?" I asked Fanny. "Did Gabe check in on Travis like that?"

"If Evert says he did, he did."

I started rocking a little faster. "So you've seen—I'm sorry—you've heard Gabe over there on Fridays?"

"No, that's Supper Club night at the Hilleville Senior Center. I never miss it. Oh, but that's not quite true, is it?" she asked. "I missed it the other night."

"Lindsey's art show."

"That's right. Is something wrong, Cassie?"

"Ohhh, no," I said and feigned great interest in the Senior Super Club. But actually, I was interested—the timing was key.

And good old Fanny explained every detail, in detail. Lindsey drops her off at the Senior Center at six o'clock in time for supper. And after dinner the senior citizens enjoy "activities."

"We make a real evening of it," Fanny said. "Board games, cribbage, dominoes, dancing. I'm not much for board games, but Howard Bapp is such a dear. He insists I'm still the best dancer this side of Lake Champlain." She giggled. "That may be true, unless I'm dancing with Cornelius Souter. I don't like to be unkind, but Cornelius always did have two left feet."

"What time does the dance end?" I asked.

"Betty Fitkin gives me a lift home afterwards," Fanny said. "Eighty-four and she still drives."

"About what time is that, Fanny?"

"We always stay until the very last minute. The center closes at ten o'clock sharp."

"Girl!" Dad called up, and I told Fanny I had to go.

"My father's grilling steaks tonight," I said.

"Doesn't that sound good." She gasped as she thought of something else. "Maybe Bobby would like to join us some Friday," she said. "Is your father a good dancer, Cassie? I'm sure he'd be quite popular with the ladies. More popular than Howard Bapp, even."

***

"Girl!"

Guess who.

I walked over to the stairwell and told my father he drives me nuts. "I still have one more phone call to make," I yelled down.

"We're waiting on you to start the steaks," he yelled back.

"Keep waiting."

"Joe's coming up there to get you."

"Not if he values his life, he isn't."

I looked down at the dog. "Am I really going to make this next phone call?"

Charlie wagged his tail, but I stalled anyway. I took a shower and thought about it under the hot water and while I got dressed. And then I did it.

"Courage," I told Charlie and punched in another number I had recently added to speed dial.

***

Captain Sterling wasn't all that happy to learn I had him on speed dial.

"But I have news that should make you happy," he said. "We've verified the timing on Nina Finch."

"And she couldn't have done it," I said impatiently. "I'm way past the Nina Finch theory, Captain. Way, way, past."

"But you'll forgive us poor slobs who have to connect the dots with something like actual facts?"

I apologized and gave him a big, sincere thank you for connecting the dots. I made sure Nina had been released and told Sterling I'd been connecting the dots with actual facts also.

"Oh, no," he said.

"Oh, yes. And I have a new theory."

"Oh, no."

"Oh, yes. You might want to have a few pencils handy." I thought a second. "But maybe you won't find this new theory so pencil-breaking worthy, after all. Since it's all about Travis's drug dealer, which has been your pet theory all along. But of course, you wouldn't, in your wildest dreams, suspect this guy. I mean, it's truly cockama—"

"Cassie?"

"Yes?"

"Don't worry about the drug dealers, okay? Cleghorn's working on that."

"Say what?"

"He's rounding up every pusher and addict Hanahan County's ever known for questioning," Sterling said. "Anyone he hasn't already put behind bars, that is."

"That's not such a good idea."

"Why?" he asked, and I heard a few pencils snapping in the background.

"Because I know who Travis's dealer was."

I could practically hear Sterling sit up straight. "Who?" he asked. "And how do you know him?"

"Gabe Cleghorn," I said. "And I know him because he's the sheriff."

Chapter 48

Dead silence.

"It will need some investigating," I said.

Let's just skip over Sterling's response to that.

"So you'll look into it, Captain?"

"Nooo, I will not look into it, Captain. What is it with you? Wacko theories with goats as witnesses, wacko theories with dogs as witnesses, wacko theories with ghost-guys. And now this? Who's your witness this time? A cow?"

I told him I didn't know any cows personally. "Which is kind of unbelievable, considering I live in Vermont."

"You are unbelievable," Sterling said. "And I have work to do."

"Captain, wait," I said before he hung up.

"For what?"

I blinked at Charlie. "You owe me," I said. "I took Miss Rusty off your hands."

Pencils broke, but he remained on the line.

I took a deep breath and explained my new theory. Gabe Cleghorn was Travis's drug dealer, and he killed Travis when it became clear Travis was going to name names.

"Cleghorn is a good sheriff," Sterling insisted. "One of our best."

"People aren't always what they seem," I said. "For instance, I thought Travis was a bad guy. But he was just misguided, and then a victim. And I thought Nina was so scary, but she's a big softie. She loves Miss Rusty. Oh, and the Pearson sisters." I frowned. "I wouldn't exactly call Arlene a softie, but Pru's opinion has been very mislead—"

A loud groan at the other end of the phone shut me up.

"Tell you what," Sterling said. "Let's have Cleghorn narrow down the focus with whoever he rounds up tonight. But I'll be busy, too. I'll take a look at La Barge's phone records. Cleghorn's already done that, but maybe he missed something."

"Maybe his own phone number," I said.

Another groan. "In the meantime, I need you to do me a favor."

"Anything."

"Sit still and stop thinking up new theories."

I told him I wasn't very good at sitting still. "But I promise I won't come up with any new theories. Because this time. I'm right."

***

"There's the wine." Joe pointed to the glass on the counter and continued chopping a cucumber.

I glanced into the salad bowl. "I thought we were making you dinner?"

"But you're shirking your responsibilities." My father came in from the porch carrying a bowl of freshly-husked ears of corn.

I told him he should join the Friday Night Supper Club at the Hilleville Senior Center. "Fanny needs a new dance partner. Evidently there's not enough of Howard Bapp to go around."

"Who?"

"Howard and his daughter own Hilleville Hardware," Joe said. "Maggie runs the store, and Howard mans the help desk and flirts with the female customers."

"That's Howard?" I stole a cucumber slice. "Gosh, he really is a hunky-boo. For an octogenarian."

Dad rolled his eyes. "This is what we've been waiting dinner on?"

"It is," I said. "The timing is crucial, and I needed to verify Fanny's whereabouts on Friday nights. She usually goes to the Senior Center, but this past Friday she was in Woodstock with Lindsey."

"Girl! Surely Fanny doesn't need an alibi. Exactly how cockamamie is this new theory of yours?"

I took a gulp of wine. "It's Gabe Cleghorn."

"Gabe has a new theory, too?" Dad asked as he took the tray of steaks from the fridge.

"Nooo. Gabe Cleghorn is the new theory. Gabe killed Travis."

Bobby put down the tray before he dropped it, and Joe put down his paring knife.

"Think about it," I said. "If Gabe was supplying Travis his drugs, everything else fits together. The timing is perfect."

"Unbelievable," Joe said.

"Cockamamie." Dad grabbed the steaks and walked outside.

Joe caught my eye. "At the risk of making you angry, Gabe Cleghorn is a fantastic sheriff."

"I'm not angry." I stole a slice of mushroom. "But people aren't always what they seem. And our sheriff is a drug dealer. I'm guessing he has a limited, but lucrative, clientele.

Dad came back in. "Did Captain Sterling go along with this cockamamie theory?"

"Sort of," I said. "Almost." I frowned. "Let's just say he's happy my new theory doesn't involve livestock."

"Excuse me?"

"I said, Sterling is looking into the possibility." Okay, so maybe I stretched the truth a little. Sue me.

Joe set the salad aside and asked me to spell it out in more detail.

"The facts," Dad said.

"All scientific," I agreed, and while the FN beeped her approval to that sentiment, I guided my father to the kitchen table and told him to sit. Charlie and Joe did so also.

"Fact," I began. "Gabe Cleghorn visited Travis every Friday night." Everyone's mouth dropped open, and I nodded. "Evert told me that when I returned Miss Rusty, and it got me thinking—Travis would find it mighty convenient to have his party supplies delivered just as the weekends began, right?"

No one agreed, but I continued anyway, "Evert never heard the transaction since he's half deaf."

"Neither did you," Dad told me. "You have no idea what they discussed."

"Yep. And neither does Fanny since she's gone every Friday." I raised an eyebrow. "No one knows what they discussed. That's my point."

"Gabe knows Evert's hard of hearing," Joe said. "And I'm sure he knows the schedule at the Senior Center."

"And it wouldn't take much to figure out Fanny attends Supper Club," I said. "Gabe knew the woman who can hear a pin drop from across the lake was never home on Friday night." I got up to pour more wine. "And Gabe would have whatever drugs Travis wanted, right?"

"Not right," Dad said. "How do you know that?"

"Because of all those drug busts we read about in the *Hanahan Herald*. He must confiscate lots of dope."

"But there must be rules about reporting that sort of thing," Dad said. "Gabe must have to hand it over to some agency or something?"

"Yes." Joe was thinking. "But he often works alone. Who would check up on the details?"

"Not his deputies," I said. "They come and go pretty quickly, and if they're all as bright as P.T. Dent, Gabe could get away with anything."

Dad frowned. "The Hilleville police probably would never catch on either."

"Because they're too busy untangling their cars from their latest fender bender," I added. "And the people he arrested would never tell the truth. Can you see any criminal arguing that Gabe actually seized more drugs than he officially reported?"

"And he's underpaid," Joe said. "I'm not making excuses, but."

"Exactly." I nodded. "The *Hanahan Herald* is always going on about how poor Gabe deserves a raise. I'm guessing this side business was a tidy little supplement to his income."

Dad grimaced and got up to flip the steaks. When he came back inside, I moved on to what had happened on Tuesday.

"We know I woke Travis up when I was banging around Nancy's canoe."

"And then he hustled to get the body out of the lake," Dad said.

"But who wasn't hustling at all?" I asked. "Who was really, really, late getting here that morning?"

"Gabe," the guys said. They stared at each other, then they stared at me.

"Yep." I nodded. "I got really impatient."

"An understatement," Dad mumbled.

"But I had a reason to be so testy. The stupid sheriff took forever to show up."

Dad admitted I had a good point and spoke to Joe. "He told Philip Hart not to start the search without him."

"If you think about it, that was positively criminal," I said. "I knew she was dead, but supposedly no one else did. If Nancy had actually been alive and in distress, the rescue squads waiting around would have been the absolute wrong thing to do."

"And when Gabe finally did show up, he moved slower than molasses." Dad got up and put the corn in the pot of boiling water.

"So Travis and Gabe were in cahoots that morning," Joe said.

"Exactly," I said. "If Nancy had died of a drug overdose, which is what Travis assumed, who would be in trouble?"

"Travis and his supplier," Dad sat back down.

"So Gabe stalled the rescue efforts while Travis got rid of the body." I nodded at Joe. "Cahoots is a good word for it."

He shrugged. "At the risk of making you angry—"

"I know, I know." I waved a hand. "We've abandoned the facts and are now in pure conjecture territory. But how about Gabe's ridiculous sleeping beauty theory? Why was he so insistent there was no dead body?"

"Wishful thinking," Joe said. "He must have loved the Miss Looney Tunes label."

"But he was nervous about the truth." I got up to dress the salad. "He's been popping up at Mallard Cove all week—checking for Travis, checking on Travis."

I looked up and both guys were staring at me.

I shrugged. "Not that I'm one to talk."

Dad went out to fetch the steaks. He set them on the counter, and Charlie lost all interest in my theory.

"Gabe must have been really nervous when the body was found." I got out the salad forks and started tossing.

"Especially when they connected Nancy Finch to Mallard Cove and Travis," Joe said.

"That's thanks to you, girl," Dad added.

"Gabe had to get rid of Travis—Travis was about to name names." I turned to the stove to get the corn. "Which brings us to Gabe's most recent Friday night visit to Papa Bear."

The three of us started bringing things out to the picnic table.

"Perfect timing again," I said as we got settled. "Ross's press conference was Friday, so he and Janet were definitely preoccupied. As was Fanny. She wasn't at Supper Club, but she was away from home."

"And Evert was probably watching the baseball game," Joe said. "Like us, Bobby, but at full volume," Dad added.

"Ga—" I stopped myself and glanced at Maxine's house. "You-Know-Who knew he needed to act that night. He was pretty clever the next morning, too. He flat out admitted he had visited Travis. I heard him myself."

"Because you were over there snooping again." Dad put the largest steak on my plate. I handed that plate to Joe, took the smallest steak, and reminded everyone Fanny had invited me.

"You-Know-Who told us loud and clear he stopped by to check on Travis that night. Something about easing Janet's worries." I looked back and forth between the guys. "What a perfect alibi."

Chapter 49

Patience is a virtue, but come on. Sterling kept us waiting all through dinner and dessert. I had loaded the dishwasher, and we were watching the lake get dark when he finally, finally, called.

"Are you sitting down?" he asked me.

"Of course not, I'm pacing. What is it?"

"It's La Barge's phone records. Right in front of me. I think this is it, Cassie. La Barge made a call to Cleghorn's home at 5:12 a.m. Tuesday morning. They talked for six minutes."

I stopped short and blinked at the guys. "The timing is crucial."

"It sure is," Sterling said.

I resumed pacing and picked up some speed while he told me Travis had made quite a few other calls to Gabe over the past two years.

"It's fishy," he said. "But that Tuesday morning call is key. That is, if I have your story right—your timing."

"You do," I said loud and clear. "Oliver Earle didn't make his call to Gabe until after 5:30."

"So that means—"

I finished for him. "It means Gabe knew about Nancy before we ever called him."

Dad mumbled a colorful word. Joe mumbled a different colorful word. I asked Sterling when he planned on arresting Gabe. And Sterling told me to hold my horses.

"I'm not very good at that."

"I've noticed," he said. "But I have to get a search warrant, which will take a little time on a Sunday night. Especially since we're talking about searching your sheriff's house. And you know what you need to do on your end."

I snarled. "Sit still?"

"Very good."

I muttered a few colorful words.

"I mean it, Cassie. You have got to be patient. You don't want to do anything that could tip him off, right?"

"Right."

***

Dad and Joe sat still on the porch. I did my level best.

What a shocker, their discussion of the stupid baseball game didn't distract me much. I watched another storm brew, listened to the loons and the FN451z, and continued thinking about Travis, and Nancy, and Nina. And Gabe.

Joe actually interrupted something Dad was saying about a call on the Yankees. He held his hand up to shush Bobby and looked at me.

"What?" I asked.

"I don't want to spook you, but could anyone else be in danger?"

"You mean while we sit here twiddling our thumbs? How about anyone else who knows about You-Know-Who's extracurricular activities."

"His other clientele," Dad said, but we agreed there was nothing we could do about that.

"What about Evert?" Joe asked. "He's the one who gave you this idea."

"And Fanny's proven over and over you can't put anything past her," I said. "You-Know-Who should be worried about her, too."

"Give them a call," Dad suggested, but I refused.

"Sterling will kill me if I don't sit here sitting still. And Evert doesn't even have a phone."

Joe asked about Fanny, but I shook my head.

"It's kind of late to be bothering her," I said. "And she's safe. She wasn't even home when Travis got killed. You-Know-Who knows tha—"

I sat up straight. "Holy moly! Shit, shit, shit!"

"What?" the guys asked. "What, what, what?"

"He might not realize Fanny wasn't home." I jumped up, waved everyone inside, and shut the door.

"Yesterday morning!" I leaned back on the door as if Gabe might try to storm it. "Yesterday morning he asked Fanny if she heard anything Friday night. But she never actually answered him." I thought back. "Not completely anyway. Sterling interrupted us and sent Gabe away to do something about the body." I started pacing between rocking chairs. "Gabe heard Fanny say she didn't go to her usual Senior Citizen shin-dig. But he wasn't there when she talked about the art show." I stopped in front of my father. "He might not know Fanny was in Woodstock."

"He might think she was home," Dad said.

"He might think she heard something," Joe said.

"Of course he does!" I said. "She hears everything! And now that Nina's been cleared—"

"—and he's already killed once," Joe added.

"Da-aad!" I flapped my arms. "What should we do?"

"Call her." he said and went for the phone.

"But Captain Sterling," I said.

Joe took the phone from my father and thrust it into my hands. "Tell her you're checking on Miss Rusty. You don't need to mention Gabe at all."

I called her. She answered immediately, and I apologized for the late hour. She assured me she wasn't in bed yet.

"I'm sorry to bother you," I said. "But gosh, I'm still worried about Miss Rusty." I scowled at the guys. "How's she feeling? Is everything in Mallard Cove, umm, peaceful?"

"Oh, yes," she said. "Evert and Miss Rusty must be sound asleep by now. Miss Rusty needs her rest, doesn't she? What with being away from home, the poor girl's digest—"

She stopped suddenly.

"Fanny?" I asked.

"I'm sorry, Cassie, I have to go. I appreciate your calling."

"Fanny?"

"Gabe Cleghorn just pulled up. What on earth could he want at this hour? Goodbye, dear."

"Fanny, wait—"

She hung up.

Chapter 50

I slammed down the phone. "He's there!" I screeched.

My father took me by the shoulders and shook me. "Call Sterling," he ordered me.

"Sterling!" I wiggled away. "He can't help her, he's in Montpelier. She's in danger now!"

"We're not sure of that." Joe said.

"Yeah, right!" I pointed to the kitchen clock. "What's he doing over there at nine freaking forty-five? He's supposed to be tracking down every pusher this side of Lake Champlain, and he's got time to visit Fanny Baumgarten?"

Dad grabbed his car keys. "Let's go," he said, and we all headed to the door.

"No, wait!" I stopped short, and Joe bumped into me. "The three of us showing up is way too obvious. Sterling will kill me if we screw this up."

"Only one of us should go," Joe said. "To stall Gabe until we can get Sterling there."

"Exactly." I held out my hands for the keys, but my father held them behind his back.

"No, girl."

"Okay, fine! I'll take my own car." I headed to the closet for my purse, but Joe stepped in front of me.

"Two against one," he said and pointed to Bobby.

"Spare me!" I looked back and forth between them. "You guys know I'm the most likely candidate. Fanny's used to me stopping by and snooping around." I lunged for Dad's keys, and he tossed them over my head to Joe, who held them up where I couldn't reach them.

"This is ridiculous!" I jumped up and down and slapped at his chest.

"I'll go," he said.

"Yeah, right!" I stepped back. "And what reason will you have for dropping in on her? On Sunday night? At ten o'clock?"

That stumped him.

"I'm waiting."

"I've got it!" He smiled at us. "Fanny was my first teacher. She's the one who got me interested in science."

"What are you talking about?" No, that wasn't me. It was my father.

"The FN451z," Joe said as if this made any sense at all. "I'll tell her about the trouble it's been having lately and ask her opinion."

"Spare me!" both Baxters said, and Dad snatched the keys back from Joe. "I'm going."

"Dad, wait!" I jumped between him and the door.

"Think," he told me. "I really do have a legitimate excuse to see Fanny tonight."

"Like what?"

"I'll say I'm interested in the Senior Citizen Supper Club. I'll say I haven't danced in a while. I'll say I'd like to practice with her before we do it in public."

"That's your legitimate excuse?" I cried.

"It might work," Joe agreed, and I twirled around to slap his chest a few thousand more times.

He ignored me and spoke to my father. "She'll talk your ear off. Keep stalling until we can get the State Trooper there."

I twirled around and stomped my size-five foot. "I forbid you to go alone, old man."

"Okay, I'll bring Charlie." He moved me aside and headed to the coat closet. "And I'll bring my gun."

"What!?" I screeched and Joe screeched. The FN screeched, and Charlie let out one of his rare barks. But Dad still came out of the closet toting his rifle.

"This will make Gabe stop and think," he said.

"Stop and think!" I screamed. "What excuse will you have for bringing your stupid rifle to dance practice?"

Dad looked at Charlie. "We'll think of something."

"You'll hurt someone," I said.

"With this thing?" Dad held it up. "Impossible. It's not loaded."

"You should check that, Bobby," Joe said.

"I know it's not loaded, because I don't know how. And besides, I never bought bullets."

I stopped jumping around. "Say what?"

He shrugged. "I knew I wasn't ever going to actually use the thing." He called to his dog, and they ran out the door.

"Until now," I said and stared into the empty space where my father had been.

***

"If he gets hurt."

Joe stepped up from behind me. "We're calling 911."

"No!" I snapped out of it and twirled around. "The sheriff is already there, remember? And Deputy Dent wouldn't know what to do. Gabe's his boss."

"The Hilleville PD?" Joe suggested, and we both shook our heads.

I called Sterling, got no answer, and was about to pop an artery, when Joe started for the door. "Bring your cell phone," he called over his shoulder. "I've got an idea."

"What idea?" I grabbed my purse and raced after him.

"Oliver Earle," he said as we made it to his driveway and his car. "He's our high bailiff."

High bailiff?

I jumped. "Our high bailiff!" I jumped some more. "Oliver!"

"Get in."

I got in and tried Sterling again, and of course my stupid, stupid, cell phone didn't work. I banged the stupid thing on the dashboard.

"Text him," Joe said.

Yeah, right. But as we careened over every pot hole on Elizabeth Circle, I made an attempt. I typed in "lake bess," I think. I typed in "fanny," but didn't even try "baumgarten." I typed in "asap" and hit send as Joe slammed into park.

The Lake Store closes at nine, so we ran up the back stairs to Oliver's apartment. He was in his pajamas, and didn't look all that happy to see us.

We barged in anyway and started explaining, and Oliver looked less happy by the second. When we got to the part about him arresting the sheriff he re-opened his front door to wave us out.

I closed the door. "This is exactly the kind of situation the high bailiff is made for," I told him.

"Yeah, right."

"Yes, right. You're supposed to help the sheriff in case of emergency."

"Help," Oliver said. "Not arrest. I'll get in all kinds of trouble."

"And I won't?" I jabbed a finger at my chest "Think how I'll look if we're wrong. Looney Tunes doesn't begin to cover it."

"We're talking about Fanny," Joe said quietly, and Oliver stopped wrestling me for control of the door.

"You're absolutely sure about this?" he asked.

"Pretty sure," Joe said.

"Pretty sure!? I'll end up in jail, and you're pretty sure?"

"Oh, for Pete's sake!" I flapped my arms. "Will you help us if I get someone with authority to say it's okay?"

"Who would that be?"

I took a deep breath. "Sarah Bliss. She must know the rules, right?"

"What if she's in cahoots with Gabe?" Joe asked.

"She's not," I said, and hoped I knew what I was talking about. "She's rude, but she's not a criminal."

Oliver rummaged around for his phone book and handed me his phone. "Call her," he said and read me the number.

***

"This is Cassie Baxter," I said when Sarah answered. "Don't hang up."

She didn't.

"I have a cockamamie story to tell you. Don't hang up."

She didn't.

"I think Gabe killed Travis La Barge. Don't hang up."

She didn't.

I blinked at Joe. Sarah did not hang up.

"Do you know about this?" I asked her.

"I'm listening."

I told her the Gabe Cleghorn theory as quickly as humanly possible. "He's at Fanny Baumgarten's, Captain Sterling's unavailable, so we want Oliver Earle to go arrest Gabe. He can do that, right?"

"What are you talking about?"

"Our high bailiff!" I think I was shouting. "Oliver is our high bailiff!"

A very long pause.

"Let me talk to him," she said, and I jammed the phone into his hands.

He did a lot of 'Mm-hmming' and 'Okaying,' and with one final 'Mm-hmm' he hung up.

He clapped his hands. "Let's go."

"Really?" Joe and I said in unison.

"Let me get my rifle."

"Rifle?" we said and watched him rummage through his coat closet.

"I don't suppose either of you brought a weapon?" he asked from beneath a few jackets. He stood up and scowled at his volunteer posse.

Let's face it—I was totally useless. And Joe? He might be good back up in a barroom brawl at Mandy's, but everyone in town knew Josiah Wylie does not do guns.

"My father's over there with his rifle," I said.

Oliver blinked. "He ever use it?"

"Umm," I answered, but Joe said it didn't matter anyway.

"Bobby's gun isn't loaded."

"Oh, that reminds me." Oliver started rummaging through his kitchen drawers. "Where are my bullets?"

"Bullets?" Joe asked.

"You're actually loading it?" I asked.

Oliver looked up from actually loading it. "Sarah said to." He focused on me. "I'm depending on you two to do exactly what I say." He focused on me again. "You understand?"

"We'll be very helpful," I promised.

"That's what I'm afraid of."

He hurried out the door, and as Joe and I raced after him, I wondered if there were any rules against high bailiffs making arrests in their pajamas.

Chapter 51

Joe drove, Oliver rode shot-gun—no pun intended—and I gladly hopped in the back seat.

We hit a pot hole about the size of the Echo Space Crater at the exact same moment Sterling called.

Through heavy static I think I caught on that he had the search warrants and was wondering why I kept calling him.

"What's this text message about my fanny?"

"Not your fanny. Our Fanny!" I shouted through the terrible reception. "It's an emergency. Meet us at Fanny Baumgarten's."

"What?" Static, static, static. "Emerg—"

Joe rounded a curve and headed toward Mallard Cove.

"Meet us at Fanny Baumgarten's," I shouted into the phone.

"What?"

"Fanny Baumgarten! Fanny Baumgarten!"

"You found a bomb in your garden?"

I hung up and told the guys Sterling was on his way.

***

I was thinking we might actually make it to Mallard Cove sometime before the next millennium when Joe slammed on the brakes. "You really have to wonder," he said, and Oliver asked if that would help.

I poked my head between the front seats and peered out the windshield. Rose and Ruby peered back.

"Oh, for Pete's sake!" I screamed.

I hopped out, and coaxed, cajoled, and prodded the stupid beasts. But ended up cursing the stupid beasts. I swear they laughed at me. The stupid beasts in the car were also enjoying themselves.

Oliver poked his head out the window. "You want I should I shoot them, Cassie?"

I made a gesture I don't use very often, and had gone back to tugging and pushing, when lightning struck nearby. A downpour began, and I was immediately drenched. But the thunderclap startled Ruby, and she ran off with her sidekick in tow, and we finally, finally, made it to Fanny's.

Oliver ordered me to wait in the car. "You follow me," he told Joe, and they hopped out.

Yeah, right. I waited a whole split second before running to catch up, and our high bailiff informed me I was under arrest.

"Would you get in there, already!" I pushed him forward, and the three of us stumbled through the doorway.

***

"What's going on here?" Oliver asked.

A very good question.

I'll get to all the guns in a minute, but let's start with Fanny. She sat on her couch between Evert Osgood and Oden Poquette. They were holding hands and all three were in their nightclothes. For Fanny that meant a royal blue bathrobe with matching slippers. Oden's pajamas sported a maple leaf print, and Evert wore those same plaid pajamas I'd already seen him in.

"I'm glad he doesn't sleep in the nude," I whispered, and Joe shot me a confused glance. I pointed to the dog sitting at Evert's bare feet. "Miss Rusty's here, too," I said.

Of course my father and Charlie were also present. I expected them. But Maxine Tibbitts was kind of a shocker. She wore polka dot pajamas and was toting a shotgun. Like I said—kind of a shocker.

Maxine, my father, and Charlie stood in a corner opposite the couch, and Dad and Maxine had their rifles aimed at Gabe.

Which brings me to the most important point. Gabe Cleghorn stood in another corner. And yes, he had a gun. His was much smaller than everyone else's, but it looked a lot more lethal. It was aimed at Fanny.

Oliver pointed his gun at Gabe, and the sheriff looked at Fanny. "You expecting anyone else?" he asked.

Evert nudged her to respond, and her blind eyes scanned the room. "May I take attendance, please?"

***

Let's face it, Mrs. Baumgarten had taught half the room about attendance. Her former students called out their names, and the rest of us quickly caught on. Miss Rusty barked when it was her turn, and my father spoke up for Charlie.

"We must be very crowded," Fanny concluded, and Oliver asked how her living room had gotten quite so crowded.

"It's interesting," she said. "I was all alone until Cassie called a while ago." She turned in my direction. "I'm sorry I hung up on you, dear. But that's when Gabe arrived. He seemed quite upset."

Gabe shifted slightly.

"He started badgering me about what I heard the night Travis was killed."

"I wasn't badgering," he said. "I was interviewing."

"With a gun?" the rest of us asked.

"She didn't hear anything." That was me. "She wasn't even here."

Gabe's mouth dropped open.

"That's right," Fanny said. "I was in Woodstock. Lindsey had her big art show that night. It went so well! Love met a very exclusive dealer from Boston and sold seven of her vases right then and there. And Mr. Prather put in orders for tea sets, and serving trays, and fruit bowl—"

"Fanny," Oliver interrupted. "What about tonight? What about Gabe?"

"Oh, yes. As I was saying, he was quite belligerent." She spoke to me again. "That's when I remembered our earlier conversation. Remember? About Sheriff Gabe?"

"Yep," I said.

"Yep, indeed. I figured it out right then and there. 'Fanny, you old fool,' I said to myself. 'It's Gabe. That's what Cassie was getting at.'"

"They're both nuts," Gabe said. "Fanny's got it all wrong."

Oliver ignored him. "Go on, Fanny, we're listening."

"Well now, I asked Gabe, didn't I?" she said. "I asked him if he killed Travis, and he told me I should be grateful.

'The kid was scum,' he told me." She stopped and closed her eyes.

Evert patted her knee. "That's when Miss Rusty and me came in." He looked up and explained his little piece of the puzzle to the rest of us. I'll spare you the details of Evert and Miss Rusty's nightly routine, but evidently they were getting ready for bed when Evert noticed Gabe's car at Fanny's.

"Something in my gut told me to get over here." He waved his free hand at me. "Me and Miss Cassie talked about that. Always trust your gut. That's what we say."

Gabe snarled at me. "Do you ever shut up?"

Oden raised his free hand to point to Gabe. "Sheriff Gabe was snarling just like that when I got here."

Gabe snarled at Oden. "Your stupid goats aren't here."

"But I didn't know that." Oden glanced around the room. "I was looking for the gals when I heard some commotion in here." He nodded at Evert. "Something in my gut told me to see if I could help."

"About then, I got here." That was Maxine. "Gabe was showing off his gun to the three of them." She indicated the trio on the couch and then glared at Gabe. "You want a gun? I'll show you a gun." She nodded at hers.

"But Maxy," Fanny said. "How did you know we were in trouble?"

"Yes, Maxy," I said. "I'm a little curious about that myself."

Maxine cleared her throat. "I might have overheard some tiny little bits of your conversation this evening."

"You spied on us," Dad said.

"Somebody had to!" Maxine's tone changed considerably. "None of you seemed in any hurry whatsoever. Pussy-footing around while Mrs. Baumgarten was in trouble!" She shook her head in disgust. "I grabbed my i-Tablet, but then something in my gut told me to take this instead." She held up her shotgun, and everyone but Fanny jumped ten feet in the air.

Maxine looked a little miffed. "I do know how to use it. Daddy taught me to shoot when I turned sixteen." She frowned at her weapon. "I'm sure I haven't forgotten."

My father chimed in. "And this," he said, "is how Charlie and I found them."

"I wonder why Rose and Ruby aren't here," Oden said. "The gals love a party."

***

I nudged Oliver, and he stepped forward. "Gabe Cleghorn, you are under arrest for the murder of Travis La Bar—"

"What!?" Gabe swung around and aimed his gun at Oliver. "What?" he repeated, and several others had the same question.

Joe reminded them Oliver is our high bailiff. "He has the authority."

"Yeah, right," Gabe said. "Got a set of handcuffs in those pajamas, Mr. High Bailiff?"

About then, Sarah Bliss barged in, with P.T. Dent close behind. "Deputy Dent brought handcuffs," she said. "Didn't you, P. T.?"

Gabe re-aimed his gun. "You're both fired."

"Just try to fire me," Sarah hissed. "I promise you, I won't go quietly." She raised her purse and shook it at him. "I've been keeping records."

Gabe blinked at the purse.

"Oh yeah, babe. Of all those drugs you've been confiscating—confiscating, but not reporting." She glanced around the room and assured us her records were accurate.

No one argued.

She tossed me her purse. "The print-outs are in there, Cassie. You want to get them?"

I pulled out the Excel spreadsheets, and Joe and I glanced at the charts while Sarah summarized the details.

"Your ass is nailed," she told Gabe. "I've been too worried about my job to do anything until I had solid proof." She grinned at me. "I think tonight should do it."

About then, Lindsey Luke walked in carrying a small suitcase.

She had gotten wet in the rain, and her Tee-shirt clung to her. And for a minute there, it was pure pandemonium as every man reacted. Evert turned bright red and whispered a

'If you know what I mean,' to no one in particular, Oden stood up and sat back down a few dozen times, Joe stuttered a few dozen 'Why-why- whys,' Deputy Dent dropped his handcuffs, and my father dropped his rifle. Gabe stuck out his beer belly and strutted around in a circle like some kind of deranged rooster. But unfortunately, he didn't drop his gun. Fortunately, Oliver didn't drop his either. His hands were a little shaky, but our high bailiff held on tight.

What a shocker, Fanny caught on. "Is that you, Love?" she asked.

Lindsey offered a small 'Hello' and told the crowd she'd had trouble sleeping. "I was worried about Fanny being alone with Travis's killer still on the loose. I'm here to keep her—" she gazed around the room, "—company."

She located Gabe amongst the crowd. "If the twin sister didn't kill him, who did?"

Gabe's mouth fell open, but no words emerged.

"He did," I said loud and clear. "Gabe killed Travis."

Lindsey's head snapped in my direction, but Gabe's actions were more critical. He shouted something obscene and took aim at me. I remember seeing a mass of people and dogs leap toward the gun as my knees buckled.

Chapter 52

Sarah Bliss lifted me up. I guess I didn't get shot. Neither did Sarah, my father, Charlie, Evert, Miss Rusty, Oden, Fanny, Lindsey, Maxine, Deputy Dent, or Oliver.

Have I forgotten anyone? Oh, yes. Gabe. Gabe didn't get shot, either.

Joe, however.

I leapt across the room and landed beside him.

"I hate guns," he told me as I knelt down.

"You can still talk!"

Sarah knelt down with me, and we took a look at Joe's shoulder.

"It looks pretty minor," she said.

"I think it's called a superficial flesh wound," I agreed.

"Perfect," Joe told Sarah. "I take a bullet for her, and she calls it superficial."

***

But back to Gabe.

My father, Evert, Oden, Charlie, and Miss Rusty had him pinned against the wall. His hands were down at his side, but he still held onto his gun. Meanwhile the barrel of Oliver's rifle was poised a mere inch away from his forehead.

I was glad I was down there on the floor with Joe, but Maxine seemed sturdy enough. Remarkably, if you ask me, she still stood in the corner, her rifle aimed in the right direction. "Where is my i-Tablet when I need it most?" she asked.

About then, Sterling arrived.

"Jason Sterling, Vermont State Police," he announced as he entered. "Everyone freez—" He caught sight of Joe. "Are you okay?"

Joe gave me a withering look. "I'm told it's superficial," he said, but Sterling had already changed his focus.

He stepped over us, and slipped past Lindsey without batting an eyelash. "What is it with this town and goats?" he asked the crowd.

The gang parted, and he faced Gabe. He held out a small plastic bag, and Gabe dropped the gun. "I took Route 19 at about ninety miles an hour to get here. Ms. Baxter made it sound kind of urgent."

"She's nuts," Gabe said.

"Wacko and Looney Tunes," Sterling agreed. "The whole time I'm praying I don't meet a moose. I make it to Elizabeth Circle and almost hit a goat instead. You guys have a wild herd of them?"

Oden excused himself and ran out, but the room was still chock full of people, and Sterling glanced around. Some of us were in pajamas, but only one of us was in uniform, and just so happened to be holding a set of handcuffs.

"May I borrow those?" he asked Deputy Dent, and they traded. Sterling got the handcuffs, and P.T. got the bag with Gabe's gun. "Tag it, please," Sterling said, and then he addressed Gabe. "Gabriel Cleghorn, you are under arrest—"

Sarah stood up and interrupted, "Mr. Earle was already in the middle of that, sir."

"Excuse me?"

I stood up. "Oliver Earle is our high bailiff."

"He has the authority." Joe was also struggling to his feet.

"We Elizabethans think he should arrest Gabe," my father added, and everyone but Gabe agreed.

Sterling was muttering something about the quirkiest of quirky Vermont towns when Fanny sat up straight and gasped.

"Oh, no!" she said, and about then the rest of us heard the crash.

Make that several crashes.

Actually, make that a lot of crashes. The sounds of many fenders bending in domino-effect fashion.

"It's my fault." Sarah raised her hand. "I called them before I left the house. I thought we might need help."

About then, two of Hilleville's finest appeared in the doorway.

"We're here to help," the cop carrying the hubcap announced.

Epilogue

I learned a lot that summer.

First of all, it's best to leave some things, such as the Pearson sisters, alone. I hear life at the Fox Cove Inn is still pretty volatile, but I'm steering clear and letting the ghost-guys help Arlene and Pru sort out their differences.

My father has gotten a little better at minding his own business, too. He lets me sleep until almost six, almost every morning, and only asks me how things are going with Joe once or twice a day.

Maybe Dad lost interest in my love life when Chance Dooley's heated up. Good old Chance finally figured out how to coax Evadeen Deyo out of the Whoozit Loozit.

Turns out she had never seen the other side of the Crystal Void, and in fact, had never even left the confines of the Hollow Galaxy. Chance promised to taxi her anywhere she wanted to go, anytime she wanted to go, in exchange for her mechanical expertise. With several intergalactic itineraries in mind, Evadeen went straight to work on Chance's propulsion pistons and got the turbo thrust thing working just so.

This, of course, brings us to Chance and Evadeen's sex scenes. What a shocker, Lucille Saxby continues to help Bobby with that particular facet of his stories.

Help—giving it and getting it—I learned a lot about that, too.

As far as giving help, Dad and I and a few friends have stayed in touch with Nina Finch. We helped her navigate through some medical decisions, and she has major surgery scheduled for next month. The heart specialist is in Los Angeles, and you'll never guess who stepped forward to pay her travel expenses. Ross the Boss! If the guy ever runs for governor again, I might have to vote for him.

Well. Let's just say I'll think about voting for him. At least for a minute.

But back to Lake Elizabeth. I'm the new caller at Lake Bess Bingo. I volunteered the night Celia Stump quit, and Maurice Gallipeau was so excited he did a back flip-somersault combination off the stage at Town Hall. My Bingo-calling skills probably aren't worth that much enthusiasm, but the Bingo crowd seems happy so far. They keep telling me I'm a local hero. That is, when they're not reminding me I'm Looney Tunes.

Accepting help from others was a tougher lesson for me, but I made huge progress on that front when I asked some friends and neighbors to help me paint the Jolly Green Giant.

First up was Howard Bapp at Hilleville Hardware. Howard helped me match the Kelly green of the Jolly Green Giant just so. And yes, of course the old Tumbleton place— make that the new Baxter place—stayed green.

Dad and I supplied pizza from Santucci's, Hollis Klotz loaned us an extension ladder that would reach to Whoozit if need be, and a bunch of us Elizabethans painted the giant in one weekend. Turns out Oliver and Joe like heights. While they worked on the turret and third floor, the rest of us managed the lower two-thirds. Evert and I took charge of the second floor, and Dad and Maxine the first. Lindsey Luke painted most of the yellow trim, the Gallipeaus helped out wherever needed, and Oden Poquette picked up a paint brush and a slice of pizza anytime he ran by.

This was often, since Rose and Ruby were fascinated by the proceedings. As were Charlie and Miss Rusty. The animals supervised the painters, and Fanny Baumgarten kept an eye on the animals. Well, maybe not an eye. But she managed to keep them out of the pizza.

Have I forgotten anyone?

Oh, yes. The FN451z serenaded us the entire weekend.

***

The last lesson hit me as the final coat of paint was drying.

After the brushes had been cleaned, the ladders taken down, and everyone else left, Joe suggested we take a spin on the pontoon boat to see how the giant looked from the water.

Dad begged off, but Charlie, Joe, and I convinced him he should see the Jolly Green Giant in all its brilliant and

258

bright splendor with the sun setting behind it. And so the four of us climbed aboard.

We watched the paint dry and the sun set, we floated around with the ducks and Canada Geese, we listened to the loons, and eventually we watched the moon rise over the mountains.

I sat back and smiled. "Let's face it," I told the guys. "Lake Bess is a good place to live."

The End

Sad to say goodbye to Cassie and company? Never fear! A new Cassie Baxter mystery is coming your way once Cassie figures out the culprit in **Unexpected**. Available through Amazon in late 2015.

Also coming up in 2015, a brand new Cue Ball Mystery, **Five Spot**. Be on the lookout!

In the meantime, why not read the other Cue Ball Mysteries by Cindy Blackburn?

Murder meets menopause. Take a guess which wins.

The Cue Ball Mysteries

Book One: Playing With Poison

Pool shark Jessie Hewitt usually knows where the balls will fall and how the game will end. But when a body lands on her couch, and the cute cop in her kitchen accuses her of murder, even Jessie isn't sure what will happen next. Playing With Poison is a cozy mystery with a lot of humor, a little romance, and far too much champagne.

Book Two: Double Shot

Jessie Hewitt thought her pool-hustling days were long gone. But when über-hunky cop Wilson Rye asks her to go undercover to catch a killer, she jumps at the chance to return to a sleazy poolroom. Jessie is confident she can handle a double homicide, but the doubly-annoying Wilson Rye is another matter altogether. What's he doing flirting with a woman half his age? Will Jessie have what it takes to deal with Tiffany La-Dee-Doo-Da Sass and solve the murders? Take a guess.

260

Book Three: Three Odd Balls

A romantic vacation for . . . five? This wasn't exactly what Jessie and Wilson had in mind when they planned their trip to the tropics. But when Jessie's delightfully spry mother, Wilson's surfer dude son, and Jessie's rabidly hyperactive New York agent decide to tag along the fun begins. What kind of trouble can these three oddest of odd balls possibly get into? Take a guess.

Book Four: Four Play

Bad news comes in . . . fours? For romance author and former pool shark Jessie Hewitt it does. She hasn't written a decent sex scene in months, she hasn't shot a decent game of eight ball all year, and don't even ask about her supposed love life. Just when Jessie thinks things can't get any worse, a body lands on her car. Altogether infuriating cop Wilson Rye suggests she concentrate on solving her other problems and leave the murder investigation to the experts. Does Jessie agree? Take a guess.

Book Five: Five Spot

At long last! Jessie Hewitt, a.k.a. Adele Nightingale, is about to be take her rightful spot in the Romance Writers Hall of Fame. Wilson Rye, much to his chagrin, has his own role to play at the meeting where Jessie will finally be inducted. But things don't go exactly as planned. How can a conference named Happily Ever After take such a wrong turn? Take a guess.

Five Spot: Available from Amazon, summer 2015.

Ready to play with poison? Keep reading for a sneak peek at the first Cue Ball Mystery.

Playing With Poison

Chapter 1

"Going bra shopping at age fifty-two gives new meaning to the phrase fallen woman," I announced as I gazed at my reflection.

"Oh, Jessie, you always say that." Candy poked her head around the dressing room door and took a peek at the royal blue contraption she was trying to sell me. "Gosh, that looks great. It's very flattering."

I lifted an unconvinced eyebrow. "Oh, Candy, you always say that."

"No really. I hope my figure looks that nice when I'm old."

Okay, so I took that as a compliment and agreed to buy the silly bra. And before she even mentioned them, I also asked for the matching panties. To know my neighbor Candy Poppe is to have a drawer full of completely inappropriate, and often alarming, lace, silk, and satin undergarments.

I got dressed and went out to the floor.

"*Temptation at Twilight* giving you trouble?" she asked as she rang me up. Candy hasn't known me long, but she does know me well. And she's figured out I show up at Tate's whenever writer's block strikes.

I sighed dramatically. "Plot plight."

"But you know you never have issues for very long, Jessie." She wrapped my purchases in pink tissue paper and placed them in a pink Tate's shopping bag. "Even after your divorce, remember? You came in, bought a few nice things, and went on home to finish *Windswept Whispers*." She offered an encouraging nod. "So go home, put on this bra, and start writing."

I did as I was told, but wearing the ridiculous blue bra didn't help after all. The page on my computer screen remained stubbornly blank no matter how hard I stared at it. I was deciding there must be better ways to spend a

Saturday night when a knock on the door pulled me out of my funk.

"Maybe it's Prince Charming," I said to my cat. Snowflake seemed skeptical, but I got up to answer anyway.

Funny thing? It really was Prince Charming. I opened my door to find Candy Poppe's handsome to a fault fiancé standing in the hallway. But Stanley wasn't looking all that handsome. Without bothering to say hello, he pushed me aside, stumbled toward the couch, and collapsed. Prince Charming was sick.

I rushed over to where he had invited himself to lie down and knelt beside him. "Stanley?" I asked. "What's wrong?"

"Candy," he whispered, and then he died.

He died?

I blinked twice and told myself I was not seeing what I was seeing. "He's just drunk," I reassured Snowflake. "He passed out."

But then, why were his eyes open like that?

I reached for his wrist. No pulse. I checked for breathing. Nope. I shook him and called his name a few times. Nothing.

Nothing.

The gravity of the situation finally dawned on me, and I jumped up. "CPR!" I shouted at the cat.

But Snowflake doesn't know CPR. And I remembered that I don't either.

I screamed a four-letter word and lunged for the phone.

***

Twenty minutes later a Clarence police officer was standing in my living room, hovering over me, my couch, and Candy's dead fiancé. I stared down at Stanley, willing him to start breathing again, while Captain Wilson Rye kept repeating the same questions about how I knew Candy, how I knew her boyfriend, and—here was the tricky part—what he was doing lying dead on my couch. I imagined Candy would wonder about that, too.

"Ms. Hewitt? Look at me." I glanced up at a pair of blue eyes that might have been pleasant under other circumstances. "You have anywhere else we can talk?"

Hope drained from his face as he scanned my condominium, an expansive loft with an open floor plan and very few doors. At the moment the place was swarming with people wearing plastic sheeting, talking into doohickeys, and either dusting or taking samples of who knows what from every corner and crevice. Unless Officer Rye and I decided to talk in the bathroom, we were doomed to be in the midst of the action.

"I'll make some tea," I said. At least then we could sit at the kitchen counter and stare at the stove. I glanced down. A far better option than staring at poor Stanley.

"Ms. Hewitt?"

"Tea," I repeated and pointed Officer Rye toward a barstool. I turned on the kettle and sat down beside him while the plastic people bustled about behind us, continuing their search for dust bunnies.

"Let's try this again," he said. "What was your relationship with Mr. Sweetzer?"

"We had no relationship."

"Mm-hmm."

"No, really. He was Candy's boyfriend. She lives downstairs in 2B."

The kettle whistled and I got up to pour the tea. Conscious that this cop was watching my every move, I spilled more water on the counter than into the cups. But eventually I succeeded in my task and even managed to hand him a cup.

"How do you take it?" I asked.

"Excuse me?"

"Your tea. Lemon, cream, sugar?"

"Nothing, thank you." He frowned at the tea. "So you knew Sweetzer through Ms. Poppe?"

"Correct." I carried my own cup around the counter and sat down again. "She and I met a few months ago."

"Where? Here?"

I sipped my tea and thought back. I had met Candy in the bra department at Tate's of course. It was the day after my divorce was finalized, and she had sold me a dozen bras spanning every color in the rainbow. Candy had even mentioned it that afternoon.

"Ms. Hewitt?"

"We met in the foundations department at Tate's."

"The what department?"

So much for discretion. "The bra department," I said bluntly. "Candy sold me some bras."

Rye's gaze moved southward for the briefest of seconds, and I remembered the brand new, bright blue specimen lurking beneath my white shirt.

My white shirt.

If there had been a wall handy, I would have banged my head against it. Instead, I mumbled something about not expecting company.

Rye cleared his throat and suggested we move on.

"Candy and I got to talking, and I told her I was in the market for a condo, and she told me about this place." I pointed up. "I took one look at these fifteen-foot ceilings and huge windows and signed a mortgage a week later. We've been good friends ever since."

"And Stanley Sweetzer?"

"Was Candy's boyfriend. He had some hotshot job in finance, and he was madly in love with Candy."

"So what was he doing up here?"

Okay, good question. I was trying to think of a good answer when one of the plastic people interrupted. "Will someone please get this cat out of here?" she called from behind us.

I turned to see Snowflake scurrying across the floor, gleefully unraveling a roll of yellow police tape. I quick hopped down to retrieve her while the plastic people sputtered this and that about contaminating the crime scene.

"She does live here," I said. They stopped scolding and watched as I picked her up and returned to my seat.

Snowflake had other ideas, however. She switched from my lap to Rye's and immediately commenced purring.

Rye resumed the interrogation. "Did you invite Mr. Sweetzer up here?"

"Nooo, I did not. I was working. I was sitting at my desk, minding my own business, when Stanley showed up out of the blue."

"You always work Saturday nights?"

I raised an eyebrow. "Do you?"

Rye took a deep breath. "You were alone then? Before Sweetzer showed up?"

"Snowflake was here."

More deep breathing. "Did he say anything, Ms. Hewitt?"

"He looked up when he hit the couch and whispered 'Candy.'" I shook my head. "It was awful."

"Could he have mistaken you for Candy?"

I shook my head again. "She's at least twenty years younger than me, a lot shorter, and has long dark hair." I pointed to my short blond cut. "No."

"Well then, maybe he had come from Candy's." Rye twirled around and called over to a young black guy—the only person other than himself in a business suit—and introduced me to Lieutenant Russell Densmore.

The Lieutenant shook my hand, but seemed far more interested in the teacups and the cat, who continued to occupy his boss's lap. His gaze landed back on me while he listened to instructions.

"Go downstairs to 2B and get them up here," Captain Rye told him. "Someone named Candy Poppe in particular."

"She's still at work," I said, but Lieutenant Densmore left anyway.

I looked at Rye. "I really don't think Stanley came here from Candy's," I insisted. "She's at work. I saw her there myself."

"Excuse me?"

"I was in Tate's this afternoon."

Rye took another gander at my chest. "That outfit for Sweetzer's benefit?"

"My outfi—What? No!"

Despite the stupid bra, only a madman would find my typical writing attire even remotely seductive. That evening I was wearing a pair of jeans, cut off above the knee, and a discarded men's dress shirt from way back when, courtesy of my ex-husband. As usual when I'm at home, I was barefoot. Stick a corncob pipe in my mouth and point me toward the Mississippi, and I might have borne a vague resemblance to Huck Finn—a tall, thin, menopausal Huck Finn.

I folded my arms and glared. "As I keep telling you, Captain, I was not expecting company."

"Is the door downstairs always unlocked?"

"Umm, yes?"

"You are kidding, right? You live smack in the middle of downtown Clarence and leave your front door unlocked? Anyone and his brother had access to this building tonight. You realize that?"

I gritted my teeth, mustered what was left of my patience, and suggested he talk to my neighbors about it. "For all I know, they've been here for years without a lock on that door."

Rye might have enjoyed lecturing me further, but luckily Lieutenant Densmore came back and distracted him. He reported that, indeed, Candy Poppe was not at home.

"What a shocker," I mumbled.

One of the plastic people also joined us. "You were right, Captain," she said. "This definitely looks unnatural."

"Yet another shocker." My voice had gained some volume, and all three of them frowned at me. I frowned back. "This whole evening has been extremely unnatural."

Rye turned and gave directions to the plastic person— something about getting the body to the medical examiner. He told Lieutenant Densmore to go downstairs and wait for Candy. Then he scooted Snowflake onto the floor and stood up to issue orders to the rest of the crowd.

I stood up also. Everyone appeared to have finished with their dusting, and I was happy to see that Stanley had been taken away. But it was a bit disconcerting to watch my couch being hauled off.

"You wouldn't want it here anyway, would you?" the Captain asked me. We stood together and waited while everyone else gathered their equipment and departed.

Rye was the last go. "I'll be downstairs if you think of anything else, Ms. Hewitt. Or call me." He handed me his card and headed toward the door. "I can't wait to hear what Ms. Poppe has to say for herself."

"She'll have nothing to say for herself," I called after him. "She's been at work all day."

He turned at the doorway. "Stay put," he said. "That's an order."

"Shut the door behind you, Captain. That's an order."

***

I headed for the fridge, desperately in search of champagne. Given the situation, this may seem odd. But champagne became my drink of choice after my divorce, when I decided every day without my ex is a day worth celebrating. Even days with dead bodies in them. I popped the cork. Make that, especially days with dead bodies.

I opened my door to better hear what was happening below and sank down in an easy chair. Candy got home at 9:30, but Rye and Densmore quickly shuffled her into her condo, and someone closed the door.

"Most unhandy," I told Snowflake. She jumped onto my lap, and together we stared at the empty spot where my couch had been.

The Korbel bottle was nearly half empty by the time Candy's door opened again. I hopped up to eavesdrop at my own doorway and heard Rye say something about calling him if she thought of anything else. Lieutenant Densmore asked if she had any family close by.

"My parents," she answered. "But I think I'll go see Jessie now, okay?"

I didn't catch Rye's reply, but the cops finally left, and within seconds Candy was at my doorstep.

"Oh, Jessie," she cried as I pulled her inside. She stopped short. "Umm, what happened to your sofa?"

"We need to talk," I told her. I guided her toward my bed and had her lie down.

The poor woman cried for a solid ten minutes. I held her hand and waited, and eventually she asked for some champagne. Like I told Rye—Candy and I are good friends.

I went to fetch a tray, and she was sitting up when I returned to the bedroom.

"Do you feel like talking, Sweetie?" I asked as I handed her a glass.

She took a sip, and then pulled a tissue from the box on my nightstand and made a sloppy attempt to wipe the mascara from under her eyes. "Those policemen told me what happened, but I could barely listen."

"They wanted to know why Stanley was here tonight. Do you know?"

She shook her head. "They kept asking me where I was. I was at work, right?"

"At least you have a solid alibi." I frowned. "Which makes one of us."

"Captain Rye was real interested in you, Jessie. I think he likes you."

I rolled my eyes. "Would you get a grip, Candy? Rye's real interested because he thinks I killed your boyfriend."

Her face dropped and she blinked her big brown eyes. "Did someone kill Stanley?"

Okay, so Candy Poppe isn't exactly the fizziest champagne in the fridge. Even on days without dead bodies.

"It looks like Stanley was murdered," I said quietly and handed her another tissue. "Did he have any enemies?"

"That's what Captain Rye kept asking me," she whined. "But everyone loved Stanley, didn't they?"

I had my doubts but thought it best to agree. I asked about his family, and over the remains of the Korbel, we discussed his parents. Apparently Margaret and Roger Sweetzer did not approve of Candy.

"They think I was after his money," she said. She put down her empty glass. "They don't like my job either. I swear to God, his mother comes into the store twice a week to embarrass me in front of the customers. And every time Mr. Sweetzer sees me, he asks how business is and stares at my chest."

While Candy blew her nose, I stared at her chest. The woman is my friend and all, but I could see how people might get the wrong impression. On this particular occasion she was wearing her red mini dress—and I do mean mini—and had accessorized with a truckload of red baubles and beads that would have fit better on a Christmas tree than on

Candy's petite frame. An unlikely pair of red patent leather stilettos completed the ensemble.

I stifled a frown. Hopefully, Captain Rye understood she had not known her fiancé was about to die when she wiggled her curvaceous little body into that outfit.

I mumbled something about trying to get some rest. If I still had my couch, I would have slept on it and let Candy drift off on the bed. I lamented such as she got up to leave, but she assured me she would be fine and teetered out the door in those ridiculous red shoes.

About the Author

Cindy Blackburn is living the dream! She spends her days sitting around in her pajamas, thinking up unlikely plot twists and ironing out the quirks and kinks of lovable characters. In other words, Cindy's a writer.

When she's not typing on her laptop or feeding her fat cat Betty, Cindy enjoys taking long walks with her cute hubby John. A native Vermonter who hates snow, Cindy divides her time between the south and the north. Most of the year you'll find her in South Carolina. But come summer she'll be on the porch of her lakeside shack in Vermont. Yep, it's a place very similar to Lake Elizabeth.

Cindy's favorite travel destinations are all in Europe, her favorite TV show is The Big Bang Theory, her favorite movie is Moonstruck, and her favorite color is orange. Cindy dislikes vacuuming, traffic, and lima beans.

www.cbmysteries.com

www.cbmysteries.com/blog

@cbmysteries